CHR
HIN   Hines, T. L.
      The falling away

DATE DUE			
AG 28 73			
OC 31 73			

Other Books by T.L. Hines

Waking Lazarus
The Dead Whisper On
The Unseen
Faces in the Fire

THE
FALLING
AWAY

T.L. HINES

THOMAS NELSON
Since 1798

NASHVILLE DALLAS MEXICO CITY RIO DE JANEIRO

Published in Nashville, Tennessee by Thomas Nelson. Thomas Nelson is a registered trademark of Thomas Nelson, Inc.

Published in association with the literary agency of Alive Communications, Inc., 7680 Goddard Street, Suite 200, Colorado Springs, CO 80920. www.alivecommunications.com.

Thomas Nelson, Inc., titles may be purchased in bulk for educational, business, fund-raising, or sales promotional use. For information, please e-mail SpecialMarkets@ThomasNelson.com.

Publisher's Note: This novel is a work of fiction. Names, characters, places, and incidents are either products of the author's imagination or used fictitiously. All characters are fictional, and any similarity to people living or dead is purely coincidental.

Scripture references are taken from the New King James Version. © 1982 by Thomas Nelson, Inc. Used by permission. All rights reserved.

Library of Congress Cataloging-in-Publication Data
Hines, T. L.
　The falling away / T.L. Hines.
　　p. cm.
　ISBN 978-1-59554-454-4 (pbk.)
　1. Indians of North America—Fiction. 2. Supernatural—Fiction. I. Title.
PS3608.I5726F35 2010
813'.6—dc22

                    2010021109

Printed in the United States of America

10 11 12 13 14 15 RRD 6 5 4 3 2 1

For Iraq and Afghanistan veterans

While we were People of the Earth, when the birds and animals could talk, some of us wanted to fight each other. They wanted warfare. They approached our Creator and asked if they could fight each other. Our Creator said, "First you must prove to me that you are men enough to fight." He placed a man with a bow and arrow at the bottom of a sheer cliff in the water and told the men to dive off the cliff, but they soon changed their minds once they saw the man with his bow and arrow cocked and ready to shoot anyone who dove off the cliff.

Finally one man walked up to the cliff and dove off into the water. He lay dead in the water with an arrow protruding from his collarbone and blood streaming from his nostrils. Our Creator said, "I won't make too many of him, [and] from this day forward, [I will] try to wipe him out." From that time we have been called Biiluke. Even unto this day we still refer to ourselves as Biiluke.

HISTORY OF THE APSÁALOOKE (CROW PEOPLE),
CROWTRIBE.COM

Let no one deceive you by any means; for that Day will not come unless the falling away comes first, and the man of sin is revealed, the son of perdition.

2 THESSALONIANS 2:3

It is a fearful thing to fall into the hands of the living God.

HEBREWS 10:31

1.

Having your leg almost blown off was much easier than having it reassembled, regrafted, and rehabilitated.

The blowing-your-leg-off thing, well, that was quick. Easy. Automatic. You just join the army, deploy to Baghdad with the 710th Explosive Ordnance Disposal Company, and start taking daily missions to seek and destroy improvised explosive devices. IEDs.

Better known as roadside bombs.

After 237 days in Iraq, after some three hundred successful missions fueled by radio jammers and armor-plated robots, you find out that your high-tech gadgets can't stop all the low-tech explosives when a farmer and a donkey find a hidden pressure plate behind you.

Dylan should have considered himself lucky. Claussen, the second man in his three-person squad, shielded him from most of the blast. Claussen was the one who insisted they scavenge for extra iron and steel around Baghdad, haul it back to their workshop at Camp Victory, and weld it to their Humvee for extra protection. In a cruel, ironic twist, it hadn't been the hillbilly armor on their Humvee that had taken the blast. It had been Claussen himself.

Lucky, of course, wasn't the word Claussen would have used. He would have said *chosen*. Did say chosen, in fact—he told Dylan they were *chosen* many times in their months together.

Claussen always said that like it was a Good Thing. Dylan knew better now.

And once again, the whole blowing-up bit, that was the easy part. How long had the explosion lasted? Couple of seconds, followed by the hollow echo of the blast reverberating, something Dylan hadn't heard because his ears had only picked up a steady whine, as if one long, looping broadcast of the Emergency Broadcast System were playing inside his head.

Then it was over. Not even painful, really, even as one of the 68-Whiskeys, the combat medics, screamed inside the chaos while hovering over him. Not that he'd heard the medic screaming—that high-pitched whine drowned out everything for Dylan—but he could tell the medic was screaming because even when you watch a silent movie, you get a sense of what's happening on the screen.

The pain didn't sink its jaws into him until he awoke the next morning. Which suggested he had drifted to sleep, or something like it, during that night. Maybe that afternoon. He didn't remember much of that, didn't remember much of anything following the boom-of-the-Humvee/whine-of-the-ears/scream-of-the-medic sequence.

Which was just as well, perhaps, because it saved him from the first part of the reassemble-the-muscle/regraft-the-skin/rehabilitate-the-leg sequence.

That part was most definitely filled with screams as well. Screams he heard quite well, because they were his own.

That bothered him, the inability to remember, because Dylan was precise. Part of what had drawn him to enlisting; he found comfort in the delineations and absolute order of military life. Waking at the same time each day, eating at the same time, following exact orders, reporting detailed observations. It was all about order, compartmentalization, numbers. Comfort.

"I said, you want some more coffee?"

Dylan blinked his eyes, feeling their dryness for the millionth time, resisted the urge to rub them. Rubbing them only made it worse. He focused on Webb, sitting in the passenger seat of the pickup. Granular snow, buffeted by the wind of the eastern Montana plains, sprayed against the window that framed Webb's scruffy face. Old, gritty snow, punished by the ever-present winds. It reminded him of the gritty sand of Iraq in some ways. Even sitting here in the opposite temperature extreme.

You're not in Iraq, a voice said inside his head.

Thanks for pointing that out, Joni, he answered mentally.

Just saying.

Well, just don't. Not right now.

Dylan let out a long breath, looked at Webb, shook his head. "Nah, I'm good. I'm golden." He glanced at his watch; they had been parked here exactly seventeen minutes and thirty-two seconds.

"Yeah, you're the golden boy." Webb unscrewed the cap of the metal thermos, poured some dark, lukewarm liquid into a mug that said *I won a pullet surprise!* on the chipped exterior.

"Why don't you get a travel mug?" Dylan asked. "Actually keep your coffee warm."

Webb took a drink from his stained mug, smacked his lips extravagantly. "Give up my lucky pullet surprise cup? Not until you pull it from my cold, dead hands."

"Yeah, well, your hands are cold because your coffee's always cold."

Webb shrugged. "Least my cup's always half full. You're the guy who looks at everything half empty."

3

He's got a point there, Joni's voice said inside his head.

Dylan looked out his own window, watched the winds whipping snow into fresh images of ghosts and monsters. "Nah. It's usually totally empty." He was answering both of them, Joni and Webb.

"Touché. How 'bout a bump?"

Dylan turned to look again at Webb, who had pulled out a prescription bottle. He shook it, rattling the tablets inside. There would be sixty-two tablets inside, Dylan knew. A full month's prescription of Percocet, with instructions to TAKE TWICE DAILY FOR PAIN.

"Little bon voyage gift from Krunk," Webb continued. "He gave them to me so you wouldn't gobble them."

"I'm good." Mostly because he'd already popped three Perks that morning. Had a secret stash neither Webb nor Krunk knew about.

Webb shrugged, slipped the pills back into his pocket. "Got 'em when you need 'em."

Webb's coat was a powder blue, down-filled monstrosity that made him look like a large blue marshmallow. Dylan had counted seventeen horizontal lines of stitching from the neck of the coat to the elastic band at the bottom.

Webb had a little bit of padding beneath that coat as well; he was the kind of guy the old Sears catalogs would have called "husky" on their pages devoted to flannel shirts and work boots. The dark, short-cropped beard only added to the rustic lumberjack look.

"You need to relax, man," Webb said, smiling. "Hogeland's the closest town—and that barely shows up on the map. Not exactly a hot spot for the border patrol."

They were just south of the Canadian border, an endless expanse of white enveloping the plains. Across the dappled haze in front of them lay the Great White North of Canada. Soon someone would appear at the end of this road, that was really little more than a set of tracks in the thin snow, and meet them for a drop. At least that's what Dylan had been told. He'd feel better about the whole thing when it was done.

Told you not to come, Joni's voice whispered. *I knew it was a mistake. You knew it was a mistake.*

I told you: Not now, Joni.

Just saying.

Just don't.

"You think the Feds are worried about us," Webb continued, evidently feeling the need to lecture, "when Mexicans are sneaking hash and Mary Jane into Arizona and Texas? We're in the middle of Nowhere, Montana, picking up some Perks and Vikes. Not even illegal."

"Unless you're smuggling a couple thousand caps across the Canadian border," Dylan said, staring out the windshield now, hoping to see some sign of a vehicle.

Webb shrugged, took another sip of his kinda coffee. "You say tomato, I say tomahto. Governor of Montana brought drugs across the Canadian border when he was running his campaign."

"Those were legal prescriptions." The current governor of Montana had made a big splash by arranging bus trips for seniors to Canada, where they could fill prescriptions for a fraction of their U.S. price. That had been during his first major campaign for office, when he was running to be a senator.

He'd lost that race.

Webb drained his mug, tilted it toward Dylan. "Hey, look. Pullet surprise cup is totally empty. You should be happy now."

Dylan ignored him and kept his eyes forward. This, too, was a lot like his time in Iraq. Always looking. Always patrolling. Always hoping to find . . . something. Something that would alert you to danger.

Trouble was, you never spotted any such thing. You knew it was there, some ever-present monster lurking just beyond your view, but you never really saw it. You only felt it. Even spinning numbers and geometric patterns inside your head—counting lighted windows and subtracting them from the number of unlit windows, then changing your equations whenever another light flickered on during night watch—didn't settle you. The monster was always there. Always waiting.

In the distance, lights flashed in the white haze. Once. Twice. Like the lights in the shattered brick buildings on the streets of Baghdad.

"You see that?" Dylan asked.

Webb turned, looked out the windshield. The lights flashed twice again. "Yeah."

Dylan pulled a lever on the dash, flashing his own headlights twice in return.

"Seriously? They're in a white pickup?" Dylan said, not really expecting an answer.

"Harder to spot," Webb responded. "Aren't you at least happy about that? Keep the big bad DEA and border patrol on their toes. Bet the thousands of secret cameras they got here in eastern Montana won't even pick it up. Those Canucks are crafty."

Dylan ignored Webb, shifted in his seat, zipped his parka, pulled on his nylon gloves.

"Those the warmest gloves you could find?" Webb asked, displaying his own padded mittens. They fit the rest of Webb's marshmallow getup.

"I'm good," Dylan said. He put his hands in his pockets, not bothering to explain that he wore thin gloves so he could move his fingers easily. So he could use the .357 Mag revolver tucked into the right pocket of his parka if he had to. Loaded with 158-grain soft points. No need for Webb to know about such a thing; he'd just laugh, chalking it up to paranoid delusions on Dylan's part.

Dylan wasn't paranoid, didn't hear voices out to get him or anything like that.

There was Joni's voice, of course.

And the numbers and patterns thing.

And the kill box inside his mind, where he sent unwanted thoughts.

And . . .

Okay. Maybe he was paranoid. Or schizophrenic. Or mentally unbalanced. A bit of that posttraumatic stress disorder, as the therapist at the VA hospital was fond of telling him.

After all, Joni wasn't out to get him. And the mental kill box and the strange manipulation of numbers and shapes were just . . . mental exercises. Ways of controlling his environment. Perfectly healthy ways of coping with stress—another nugget of wisdom imparted by the VA therapist.

You didn't tell your therapist about me. Joni's voice.

No. If I did, we'd probably still be in the hospital.

Dylan and Webb sat in silence for a few moments, studying the area ahead of them.

Dylan cleared his throat, waiting patiently. His eyes still itched, almost as much as his leg. It was always worse in the cold like this, his leg. He knew it would start to roar with pain even more when he stepped into the frosty air outside.

"There they are," Webb said.

"Yeah." Dylan watched as two figures slowly materialized, moving slowly. Like mules on a long, hard trail.

And that's what they were. Drug mules. What he himself was about to become. A limping mule.

I can think of another word for mule that might be more fitting, Joni's voice said in his mind.

Hilarious, that Joni.

"Let's go," Webb said, popping open his door. The lights in the cab of the old Ford Ranger sputtered to life.

Dylan, shaking his head, opened his own door and struggled into the biting cold. He closed it behind him, leaned on the pickup's fender as he made his way to the front. At the front of the pickup he returned his right hand to his coat pocket, loosely cradled the revolver's grip.

Outside, even though he stood on the vast, flat plains of northeast Montana, it felt as if he were in a tunnel. The wind was part of that; it lapped at any exposed skin, whispered hollow echoes in his eardrums, swirled dirty snow around him in a cloud. He could even taste the wind on his tongue as he breathed: it should taste fresh and clear, he thought, but instead it was loamy, like soil.

Yeah, he was in a tunnel. A long, dark tunnel to nowhere, and coming down that tunnel were two guys carrying drugs.

Webb stepped away from the front of the pickup, clutching a dusty blue rucksack of his own in his left hand as he raised his right hand in a greeting. Webb was what you'd call a people person; he loved bull sessions, loved telling and hearing jokes, loved slapping shoulders and shaking hands and exchanging high fives. It energized him.

Dylan wasn't a people person.

Webb hailed the two men, a greeting of some sort Dylan didn't quite catch; Webb was turned away from him, and the wind was carrying his voice to points unknown. But Dylan knew Webb was grinning expansively as he spoke. He always did.

The two Canadians stopped a few feet away from Webb, their breath misting as the wind carried it away from their mouths, as if they were exhaling smoke. The two exchanged a quick glance, and the taller man spoke. "Nah, let's just get this over with."

Dylan could at least make out what he was saying, since he was shouting to be heard over the wind. Even though they'd only walked a short distance from their pickup, crossing the U.S. border in the process, ice crystals had formed on the taller man's beard, longer and fuller than Webb's. He wasn't a good beard guy, though, not like Webb. Webb looked like the guy on the Brawny paper towels packaging. This guy's beard made him look more like a wannabe biker.

The other Canadian was thin, almost anorexic. Oily hair pooled over his shoulders from beneath a knitted cap as he shuffled in place. What'd the Canadians call those stocking caps?

Tuques, Joni's voice answered helpfully.

Dylan didn't like this at all. These guys seemed too edgy, even if they were the type to partake of the cargo they were carrying (and he had no doubt they'd done a little skimming from their backpack).

Oh, so now you don't like it.

Never wanted in this deep, Joni. You know that.

Webb said something else, turned and flashed a grin at Dylan. Dylan decided he should move closer so he could catch whatever Webb was saying.

Both the Canadians looked at Dylan as he stepped forward, evidently taking this movement as a signal he had something to say. Instead he kept his head down, hunching his shoulders and keeping his hands in his parka pockets, avoiding eye contact. His finger found the trigger guard on the revolver.

Just in case.

2.

Quinn pushed away her cup of coffee, convinced it had been brewed roughly around the time she was born twenty-seven years ago. She glanced at the scowling face of Greg, who was sitting by himself at a booth in the corner, and waited. Greg wasn't talking to anyone else, which was good. If he were, that might mean Quinn would have to do something drastic, figure out a way to shoot him in a crowd.

But Greg was eating his breakfast alone, lost in his own world. Probably still getting his bearings after leaving the safety of the HIVE.

HIVE was well known to just about everyone in Montana. It was something like a cross between an Amish community and an old hippie commune. The letters stood for Hope Is Via Earth, but most people just called HIVE members drones.

Drones like Greg here, finishing his breakfast, his eyes dark and cloudy for reasons he probably didn't even understand. Understanding wasn't the job of the drones; the drones existed to spread their disease, while Li, the leader of HIVE, built his power and influence.

Li, an enigmatic, bald figure, had started the community in the early nineties; together with a band of a few dozen followers he purchased several hundred acres of central Montana farmland and established the New-Agey commune. He had attracted a growing base of followers since then, adding mobile homes in a crude phalanx while the HIVE population expanded, and eventually building permanent accommodations to create his self-sustaining community in the proverbial Middle of Nowhere.

As it grew, HIVE branched into different sections of agriculture: dairy, eggs, wheat. Soon stores across Montana and adjoining states began stocking their wares; people drawn to the whole Earth-is-our-loving-mother spiel bought their organic products.

In the early twenty-first century, Li had obviously seen ahead of the curve and tapped into the growing green movement by signing a contract with an energy company to build dozens of giant wind turbines on HIVE property. That was what identified HIVE to the rest of Montana: more than a hundred giant turbines stood as silent sentinels over the mysterious compound.

Many people in Montana had a vague uneasiness about the community. HIVE members had a good story to tell, and various media ate it up; after all, HIVE members always wore impossibly wide smiles, always talked about sustainable living and saving the earth. Great sound bites. But most Montanans who came into contact with HIVE members would tell you the smiles and the chatter felt too . . . rehearsed. Maybe too robotic. Which was another reason why the "drone" moniker fit so well.

These drones, the ones who ventured from the HIVE into the surrounding communities, were the only members most people saw. What Quinn thought of as the light drones.

The dark drones were another matter. Most people never saw them. No, that wasn't right; most people who saw dark drones never realized they had any connection with HIVE at all, because dark drones didn't have bright smiles and canned stories about loving the earth. They said nothing about their connection to HIVE.

Dark drones weren't sent out to recruit; they were sent out to infect.

Released from the HIVE, dark drones such as Greg invariably found their way either here to Great Falls or south to Billings and then on to points unknown. If they weren't stopped before they boarded a plane or a bus, well, there really was no way you'd catch them except by chance. It was a big country, a big world, and they could hide underground almost anywhere. Infecting people all around them. Spreading the disease.

But for right now, at least, Greg seemed more interested in his burned toast than in casual conversation with anyone around him. Which meant he wasn't actively trying to infect anyone. Yet.

Quinn found herself thinking of Dylan Runs Ahead, wishing she'd been able to follow him instead. Her overall goal was keeping him out of the HIVE, of course, and she knew HIVE would be quite interested in welcoming him into their fold.

He was, after all, a chosen.

But Dylan was hundreds of miles away from the HIVE right now, far away from their influence, so her priority had been Greg. Dark drones, when released from the HIVE, always took priority; if they made it to their destinations they could go underground, infect hundreds, even thousands. Dylan, though important, was just one person.

Quinn sighed, traced the faint outline of her new staple with a light finger, then pressed it, reassured by the pain.

She was an embedder. Self-embedding disorder was the precise diagnostic term, describing the compulsion to embed objects—usually metal items such as needles, staples, and nails—into various parts of the body. Quinn had read all about it on the Internet; it even had its own Wikipedia entry. SED, the entry said, was a form of self-mutilation (otherwise known as self-injury or SI), related to cutting and trichotillomania, the odd name for the compulsion to pull out your own hair.

Self-mutilation. Well, who didn't mutilate themselves in some form or another?

Her mother had done it, when Quinn was a young girl. After her father left without explanation, her mother had self-mutilated by sinking into the depths of her depression and dementia. They'd spent two years together on the streets of Portland, a wandering, aimless existence; then, after her mother had mysteriously disappeared, Quinn spent another two years on her own. Before Paul. Before the Falling Away.

She understood that her need for cutting, and her subsequent need for embedding, were tied to issues with her mother. And her father, she supposed. But mostly her mother. She had seen the pressure building inside her mother, and wanted so much to be able to relieve that pressure. After her mother's disappearance, when she felt her own pressure building inside her, she'd discovered the perfect way to release it.

She didn't resent the embedding, didn't wallow in self-hatred for her self-injury. She understood it was a necessary part of what she did, really; those who didn't have a release valve for the poison they pulled out of others felt the pressure build inside until it forced them to explode. So in an odd way, the compulsion was what had led Quinn to become part of the Falling Away.

God worked in mysterious ways, indeed.

Stop.

This was no time to think about the embedding; right now, she needed to concentrate on Greg, concentrate on removing him before he could escape and infect others. Quinn uttered a silent prayer, asking for strength, asking for focus, and felt better.

An informant had called the previous afternoon, told Quinn someone from the HIVE was scheduled to check in at the O'Haire Motor Inn. Quinn had driven over from Judith Gap, had watched through field glasses as Greg checked in late that evening before slipping into the attached Sip-N-Dip Lounge.

In hindsight, Quinn should have followed him back to his room, done the job while he was sleeping. It would have been easier. But HIVE usually sent two or three dark drones out together, and Quinn had been sure others would meet Greg at the bar. That's part of why neutralizing dark drones always took precedence over other activities.

When the bar shut down, Greg had finished his beer and retreated to his room. Alone. So Quinn had waited, hoping other dark drones would meet him this morning.

None had, and Quinn was now sure Greg was a loner. Which meant he could have been neutralized hours before.

Quinn felt the pressure building inside, pressed the staple again, felt the pressure subside. Be still. Be quiet. Be patient.

Greg left money on the table, slid out of the booth, and headed for the glass door. Quinn slid off the stool at the counter and followed.

He had likely been dropped off the day before with a plane ticket or a bus ticket, so he'd either be walking to the Greyhound depot just a few blocks away or calling for a cab to the airport.

When he began walking down the alley toward Central Avenue, Quinn knew he was destined for the bus depot. Good. That would be easier.

She followed, increasing her pace to catch up with him, knowing it would be best to catch him before he reached the end of this alley. This was a nice, secluded spot, especially in the morning. No traffic or activity, as there would be on Central. Or at the bus station.

"Greg?" Quinn's fingers closed over her pistol as Greg turned, the question forming in his eyes before it crossed his lips.

"Who are you?" Greg snarled, pain and hatred in his eyes.

In answer, Quinn flashed the pistol and pulled the trigger, continuing to approach as Greg slumped to the ground. She put away the gun, dropped to a knee beside Greg's body, watched as his eyes rolled to white a few times and closed.

Then Quinn put her hands on Greg's body and began to pray.

3.

Dylan watched as Webb thrust the rucksack toward the two Canadians, looking like some kid on the playground in his puffy blue jacket and matching bag. "Fifty large," he said. At least Dylan could hear him, now that he'd stepped forward. "Just like Krunk promised."

Krunk was their contact back home in Billings, the guy who had sent them here to the Canadian border for a drug swap. Dylan didn't know Krunk's real name. Didn't really want to know Krunk's name. For that matter, he often wished he didn't know his own name; more than once he'd fantasized about forgetting everything known as the life of Dylan Runs Ahead.

But when you were addicted to painkillers, you were deprived of life's luxuries, and one of those luxuries was the ability to forget. True, when you drifted into that warm, comforting haze, you left behind the pain, left behind any real, rational thought. But you never truly *forgot*; popping the drugs just let you hit the Pause button for a time. And so, even though painkillers introduced you to guys like Webb (a Good Thing), it also introduced you to guys like Krunk (not a Good Thing), and after so many days and months of hitting that Pause button repeatedly, you found yourself in the middle of the gritty Montana prairie, swapping bags with greasy-haired Canadians, wondering when exactly this whole ride had started and why you hadn't gotten off it before.

The anorexic Canadian pulled Dylan from his thoughts as he stepped forward and took the bag from Webb before retreating again. As if he were standing on the very border itself and uncomfortable with the thought of crossing into the United States for long.

After an awkward pause, Webb was the first to speak again. Of course. "The way it works is, now you take off your backpack and give it to us." He was speaking to the thinner one, the anorexic one, who had the kind of backpack you might see a school kid carrying looped over his shoulder. It only added to Dylan's sense that they were standing on a playground, the four of them, about to fight over a kicked ball or a lost bag of marbles.

Anorexic Guy exchanged another glance with Biker Beard, then unshouldered his pack slowly and set it on the ground. While he did this, the taller one, the bearded one, produced something Dylan was afraid he might see.

A pistol.

Not a revolver, but a semiautomatic, nickel-plated. Condensation formed on its surface as he pointed the gun at Webb.

"Whoa, whoa," Webb said as his arms went into the air, instantly entering negotiation mode. "Let's just take it easy here."

"That's what we're doing," Biker Beard said, glancing at Dylan as he spoke. "We're taking it. And it's easy."

"Krunk—"

"Is your problem," Biker Beard said. "You just turn around right now, get into that truck, and drive away, Krunk's the only problem you're gonna have. Otherwise, your biggest problem might be how to stop yourself from bleeding to death out here."

On cue, a fresh gust kicked up more dirty snow. Very spaghetti western, but Dylan didn't like playing the part of the gunslinger. Didn't have the stomach for it, after Iraq. Or the leg.

The anorexic heaved Webb's rucksack over a shoulder, then stooped to pick up his own backpack on the ground in front of him.

Dylan picked that moment to act, pointing the .357 and firing at Biker Beard without pulling the revolver from his pocket. A crack lapped at the air, carried away instantly by the wind. White down exploded from Dylan's jacket, and Biker Beard staggered.

As he stepped backward, Dylan saw the muzzle of Biker Beard's pistol emit a bright flash, followed by a hollow *thunk*; he tripped the hammer on his revolver again, punching another round into Bearded Guy and knocking him to his knees. Quickly he spun and aimed at Anorexic Guy, who was trying to dig into his backpack for something, and squeezed the trigger again. Anorexic Guy fell and went still.

Biker Beard was still on his knees, running his hands over his chest as he crouched in the snow, an unformed question on his lips, a look on his face that said the preceding events hadn't happened as he'd planned.

Dylan knew how that went.

"You hit?" Dylan called to Webb, watching as Biker Beard finally slumped to his side in the snow.

"I . . . yeah. I think so."

Dylan glanced at Webb, who was cradling his right arm. A bright bloom of blood appeared at the shoulder, turning a spot of Webb's blue coat a wet purple.

"Okay. Just kick that guy's gun away—don't pick it up, but kick it away."

Webb did as instructed, holding his injured arm against his chest, then looked at Dylan again, waiting for new instructions. Evidently Webb wasn't much into talking after being shot.

"Go back to the truck," Dylan instructed.

"What about the money?"

Surprise, surprise, Joni's voice said. *Guy gets shot, he's still worried about the money.*

But the question was still there: what about the money? There really wasn't a right answer; he knew this scenario was going to be bad news for him and Webb—even if Webb didn't bleed to death—whatever he did. He could leave the money, walk away, and pretend this never happened. Trouble was, border patrol or drug runners or Indians from the Fort Belknap Reservation would likely stumble on the money and drugs . . . and none of them would just leave it sitting there. Krunk wouldn't likely buy the story if he said they left everything, because Krunk would always be convinced that Dylan himself had hinked the deal. What was that old line?

There's no honor among thieves, Joni's voice said.

Or among drug mules, he answered.

No, the better option was to take the cash and drugs.

"You just get in the truck," he finally said. "I'll take care of it." He took two steps forward, struggling as his left leg threatened to give, and pushed Anorexic Guy's motionless body off the backpack.

Told you this was a stupid idea.

"Well, Joni," he said aloud, "I'm a magnet for stupid ideas."

4.

After the IED in Iraq, after the months of rehab and pain, after dozens of therapy sessions talking about PTSD and feelings of helplessness, Dylan discovered the old saying was true: you can't go home again.

They cut him loose from the VA hospital in Sheridan, even booked him a flight home to Billings. He'd expected a car ride, maybe even a bus ticket, since he was only a few hours away from Billings, so the flight was something of a surprise. Just one of the many benefits of having your leg mangled in Iraq.

He hadn't spoken to his parents, hadn't spoken to anyone on the Crow rez, really, since . . . since Joni. Hadn't even spoken to the therapist about Joni, even though she'd asked him several times. Joni was off-limits to the outside world; the only place he could discuss her was inside his own mind. That was the one place, at least, he could still control. The outside world was filled with too many people wanting to help and diagnose and absolve you of your regret and guilt.

But he needed to carry his regret and guilt; no one else could carry it for him.

The VA hospital had wanted to inform his family of his discharges: his honorable discharge from the army as a wounded vet, and then, months later, his unceremonious discharge from VA care at the hospital. But he wouldn't allow it. How could he? Your family and your heritage were vital components of your very essence as an Apsáalooke; by forsaking Joni, he'd forsaken a part of who he was. How could he expect his parents, his friends, his fellow members of the proud Greasy Grass Clan, to accept his failures when he himself could not?

The army had given him a sense of belonging he'd lost on the rez. It had even connected him, in some ways, with his heritage. As part of the army, he'd become a proud Apsáalooke warrior, one of many dating back generations among the Crow people. On the rez, people still told the stories of Apsáalooke conquests, of Apsáalooke traditions and creation stories and honors. Most people on the Crow rez could even speak the Crow language, keeping the ancient and honored ways alive. Dylan had heard these stories so many times they'd become an ingrained part of who he was.

At the same time, explosive ordnance disposal had been the perfect spot in the army for him. Finding and neutralizing IEDs, ammo stockpiles, and suspicious packages demanded precision and detail, traits that were also an ingrained part of who he was. His mind thrived on patterns, something he had been comfortable discussing with his therapist. She told him his mild compulsions—counting, grouping objects, even splitting anything in his field of vision into equal sections and shapes—were healthy ways of dealing with stress and disorder. Provided they didn't take over his every waking thought.

Of course, he hadn't told her about Joni. Or the kill box. He was pretty sure those didn't fit under the "healthy way of dealing with stress" label.

EOD was also perfect because it demanded secrecy and separation. In Iraq there were too few EODs to go around, which was why his company was much smaller than most at thirty soldiers, and why his squad was only three. Insurgent groups in Iraq had promised a $50,000 bounty for any EOD tech killed, and so entire EOD companies had been forced to live apart from other troops in their own workshops, interacting only among themselves and cutting off all contact with the outside world.

In a way that mirrored what Dylan had done since losing Joni. He'd cut himself off from his family, from the clan to which he belonged, from friends and all he knew. Enlisting in the army, becoming an EOD, embarking on a tour of Iraq . . . those were all efforts at a personal penance, and nothing anyone outside could hope to understand.

All of those feelings had coursed through his body as his flight landed at Billings Logan airport. Even today, the Apsáalooke people welcomed back their sons and daughters from the battlefield with smudging ceremonies in the airport itself, an honoring of their warrior tradition. For that to happen, though, they had to know a son or daughter was coming home. And the son or daughter returning had to be worth honoring.

Dylan had done a fair job of making sure neither of those applied to him.

He waited for all the other passengers to clear the plane before he ventured into the narrow aisle himself, propping his still-healing leg on a cane and making his way first to the Jetway, then to the interior of the airport itself. He moved slowly up the ramps toward the baggage claim area and paused at the top of the escalator that would take him to the main floor. Below him, dozens of people were welcoming friends and family, returning home from business trips or vacations or adventures.

But no one had been there to welcome Dylan Runs Ahead. Just as it should be.

5.

Twenty minutes after shooting two Canadian drug runners, Dylan pulled off the rutted tracks that looked like scars in the frozen earth and back onto State Route 338. He headed south toward Harlem and the Fort Belknap Reservation. From this exact point, he knew, they were 47.6 miles from the town of Harlem; he'd checked the odometer earlier.

Dylan looked at Webb, who hadn't spoken since they got back in the truck. The scent of blood filled the cab. "Can you move your arm?"

Webb turned his face toward Dylan. It looked as if he were having a hard time focusing his eyes. "Huh?"

"Your shoulder. Can you move your arm?"

"No. I mean . . . it hurts."

"'Course it hurts. You just got shot."

He really needed to get them out of there, put as many miles as he could between the two dead Canucks and themselves. But he also needed to see Webb's injury. Dylan pulled the truck to the side of the road, unbuckled, walked to the passenger side, and opened Webb's door. "Pull your good arm out of your coat," he said.

Webb did as he was told, wincing in pain as Dylan helped him.

"Okay," Dylan said. "I'm gonna pull your right arm out of the jacket now. It's gonna hurt like a mother, but we're gonna see if it's just a meat wound or something worse."

"Something worse?"

"Like a broken bone."

"How will you know?"

"If you scream, it's a meat wound. If you scream and pass out from the pain, it's worse."

Webb took a few deep breaths, exhaled forcefully, skipped the effort to come up with a good comeback. "Okay," he said.

Dylan pulled on the sleeve, working it away from Webb's arm as he went down. Webb's screams filled the cab.

Dylan pushed Webb's shirt out of the way and examined the wound. Blood oozed from the small hole. Oozing was good; it meant the bullet hadn't hit any major blood vessels. Dylan knew what that looked like.

"I think it's broken," Webb said.

"Did you pass out?"

"No," Webb admitted.

"Then it's not broken. You still got those Perks in your pocket?"

"Yeah."

Dylan dug into the left pocket of Webb's coat, retrieved the bottle. "Lucky for you, we got plenty of Percocets." He thought briefly of popping one himself, but resisted; he needed to stay clear right now.

Dylan glanced at the packs he'd thrown into the back of the

pickup. One of them contained several thousand tabs of Vicodin and Percocet painkillers. The other contained several thousand dollars in U.S. currency. On an ordinary day, a load he'd be happy to carry. But this wasn't an ordinary day anymore.

Webb took the pills and dry-swallowed them. "Yeah," he said. "Lucky me."

Dylan hobbled back to the driver's side, slid in, and wheeled back onto the road again.

"What now?" Webb asked.

"Now you just keep that coat pressed against the wound, keep the blood from flowing. Looks like you're starting to clot, which is good."

Webb draped the coat over his shoulder and hunched forward in the seat, putting his head against the truck's dash. He closed his eyes and spoke, almost as if he were about to start praying.

Like Claussen, Joni's voice said inside.

Yeah, he answered. *Webb's the real praying kind. Let's not start comparing him to dead guys just yet.*

Gotcha.

Webb spoke softly. "Where we going?"

"Harlem. We gotta get that arm looked at."

"There's a hospital in Harlem, Montana?"

"Indian Health Services."

"But I'm not an Indian."

"Which is why we aren't going there."

"And don't they have to report gunshot wounds?"

"Another reason we're not going there."

Webb rolled his head on the dash so he could look at Dylan. "Which brings me back to my original question: where we going?"

"It's the rez," Dylan said. "I'll find someone."

"Someone? Like a medicine man or something?" Webb's words were starting to slur now, soft and mushy. Maybe it was a weak attempt at a joke, but more likely it was the Perks kicking in, mixing with the adrenaline and shock.

"Yeah," Dylan said. "A medicine man. He'll smudge some ash on your forehead and you'll be just fine."

Webb went quiet and Dylan drove, listening to the rumble of the engine as the pickup's tires spun on the highway.

6.

Dylan watched egg yolk drip down Scott's chin and tried to ignore the runny yellow stain.

Not much luck in that department. When he was amped up on Vikes or Perks, odd inconsistencies—items that would normally be simple throwaways—became objects of intense interest and scrutiny. Consciously, he wanted to ignore such things; subconsciously, his mind was fascinated.

Which, really, was part of the appeal of the drugs. Much better to concentrate on runny egg yolks, because the conscious alternative (the undrugged conscious alternative) was to concentrate on images of Claussen blowing up in the Iraqi desert. Which brought out thoughts of Joni, thoughts of the rez, thoughts of abandonment, thoughts of so many things that really needed to go into the kill box right away.

Vikes and Perks took away the need for the kill box. At least for a time.

Dimly, Dylan realized Scott's mouth and egg-splattered chin had stopped moving, which meant he'd stopped talking. He chanced a quick glance at Scott's eyes, which were staring at him expectantly.

Dylan tried a smile. "Sorry," he said. "I didn't catch that."

Scott was Dylan's VA counselor, his lifeline to services and support and follow-up in the few months since he'd been discharged from the hospital in Sheridan. Every week Dylan was seeing a therapist here in Billings, working through such things as POSTTRAUMATIC STRESS DISORDER and PSYCHOLOGICAL TRAUMA and DIMINISHED CAPACITY and other textbook terms that were always spoken in all cap letters by the therapist.

Good thing he never told her about the deepest, darkest things. Joni's internal voice, for instance. Or the odd compulsion to subtract items from his field of vision, put them away in the kill box, and let the item fade from view. Think of the textbook names those things would have.

Funny, he couldn't even remember the therapist's name right now, only that she had this odd crescent-shaped scar on her forehead he always wanted to ask her about.

Even more interesting than the egg yolk on Scott's chin. Scott, who met with him monthly and wrote reports that probably got filed away on some government server, never to be looked at again.

"I said," Scott repeated, his voice rising a bit, "what are you doing to keep busy?"

Dylan pursed his lips, thought. "Bought the house, you know."

Scott nodded, encouraging him to continue.

"Needs some work. Painting, remodeling, that kind of thing."

It was a lie, of course. Dylan had done nothing to the small house he'd purchased on the south side of Billings with part of his disability settlement. For the most part, it was a large hotel room; he'd never even unpacked his clothing and belongings, limited as they were. Sometimes he watched television. Sometimes he took Vicodins or Percocets, both of which had been prescribed for him during his stay at the VA hospital. When he wasn't taking Vicodins or Percocets, he wished he were.

That's how he was keeping busy.

Scott returned his attention to the Cattle Queen Platter in front of him, dabbed a big hunk of steak in the runny yolk that remained on his plate. "Building, repairing—those kinds of things can be very therapeutic." He stuffed the bit of steak in his mouth, then pointed his fork at Dylan while he talked around a mouth full of meat. "Good for you. So maybe next month you could show me."

Dylan shrugged. "Sure."

Strictly playing by the book, Scott was supposed to be monitoring Dylan's home and living conditions each month. Just as he was supposed to keep in regular contact with Dylan's therapist and Dylan's doctor at the local clinic. But Scott had never been to Dylan's home; Dylan had discovered at their first meeting that Scott had a certain affinity for the Cattle Queen Platter at the Sharpshooter Café, and so he always managed to get his meetings with Scott pushed here—even if they were scheduled to meet at Dylan's home. It was part of their ritual.

Scott finally decided to wipe at the yolk from his face, but he did it with the back of his hand rather than the napkin that sat on the booth's Formica top. Sweat glistened on Scott's forehead. "You gettin' around okay? Need anything else?"

Dylan looked away from Scott's zombie gaze again.

"Yeah," he said. "I ride the bus, mostly. Gets me most places."

Another lie. Dylan never really went anywhere, outside of the grocery store or the Laundromat. And he never rode the bus; he drove. He had no idea why he was telling Scott he rode the bus.

Because you're a big fat liar, Joni's voice said.

Odd. At the hospital, and in the first few months since his

discharge, the drugs had quieted Joni's voice. An odd side effect. Unwelcome, really, because Joni's voice had been a comfort to him since . . . well, since joining the army. But he didn't deserve comfort. Or Joni's voice. The drugs, and the absence of Joni's constant companionship, had been a crude sort of justice. Just let the therapist, what's-her-name, get hold of that nugget.

Now, though, Joni's voice was filtering back into his mind even when he was on Perks or Vikes. Best of both worlds.

Scott nodded, mopped up some steak juice on his plate with a wedge of toast. "Whatever works for you, man. Bus'd drive me crazy. I gotta have my own ride."

Scott's ride was a beat-up old hatchback he'd bought at a surplus auction several years ago. You'd think, Scott being a bureaucrat of some kind inside the VA, he'd have more modern wheels. An office pool car, a sensible white sedan with four doors.

Scott picked up his coffee cup, drank, smacked his lips loudly. As if the people at the Sharpshooter Café brewed the richest, finest roast he'd ever encountered in his life. Maybe they did. "So you're good? Feeling good?"

"Yeah."

"Everything's looking good with your therapist and your doctor."

"Yeah."

"Still on the painkillers, though. Your doc says that's a bit of a concern."

Dylan felt his body stiffen.

"Why?"

"Addictive. Says he's going to start tapering you off them—ah, what is it you're taking?" Scott flipped open one of the folders on the table. "OxyContin?"

"Percocet." That's what his "official" prescription was for. Last month Dylan had stolen a scrip pad from the clinic, and he was now getting additional refills for Vicodin. See also: OxyContin, the drug Scott had mentioned. He'd had all three, at one time or another, during his long recovery in the hospital. Dylan saw no reason to live without them since leaving said hospital.

"Anyway, you'll feel better in the long run without the painkillers. Your leg's not giving you any ongoing pain, is it?"

"No, no."

Only partly a lie. The leg didn't hurt, but it was weak. And the weakness hurt. When you're a guy named Dylan Runs Ahead, having a bum leg is a cruel irony. So the pain he experienced in the leg wasn't a physical sensation caused by the scarred muscle or tissue. It was a pain caused by his inability. Let his therapist get a hold of that one too.

Scott pushed his chair away from the table, stood, holding a napkin in his hand. He wiped at his chin with the napkin, erasing the yellow smudge of egg yolk, then threw the napkin on the table.

Awkwardly, Dylan stood and shook hands with him.

"We'll see you next month, then," Scott said. "I'll come by the house and check up on what you're doing."

"You got it," Dylan said, noting that Scott had managed to remove all of the yolk.

He felt a twinge of disappointment; something about the yolk stain on Scott's face had been comforting and . . . right.

Let his therapist get a hold of that one.

7.

"Wake up, honey."

Honey. Quinn was fifteen years old, and this woman had called her honey. Maybe you were a "honey" at age eight, or even age ten. But Quinn was fifteen. She was practically an adult; couldn't this woman see that?

Quinn kept her eyes closed, pretending she was still asleep.

She wasn't ready to open her eyes yet. That meant starting another day, and Quinn didn't want to start another day.

Going to sleep was much better. Her favorite time, really, because her body drifted away to . . . nothingness. That's what sleep was for her. Counselors—the ones at the school she attended, and the ones at the homeless shelters she and her mom frequented—always liked to ask her about sleep. About dreams, actually. What kinds of dreams did she have? Were they frightening? Did she have trouble sleeping?

She played along with it. She told them she always felt as if there was someone waiting to snatch her in the darkness. She told them she had horrible nightmares about being chased, about falling off cliffs, about the kinds of dreams she'd read about in the books at the library. That's what they seemed to want.

But the truth was, she didn't dream. At all. And she wasn't afraid of the dark, afraid of sleep. At all. That was her time of escape. When she slept, she stopped being . . . Quinn. She stopped being anyone. Each and every day, that's what she wanted. To not be anyone at all. Each and every night, that's what sleep brought to her.

"Come on, dear. Time to get up." She felt someone shaking her arm. A worker at the homeless shelter. She could tell by the volunteer voice. Everyone who worked in these shelters used that voice. It was a few degrees higher than their normal voices, thick with fake, syrupy sweetness. Louder. Slower.

At school, she'd seen special education teachers working with disabled kids, and they used the volunteer voice too. When she was younger, the volunteer voice had confused her. But now, at age fifteen, she'd come to realize it was just the natural cadence of someone talking down to another person. Not that most people realized they were doing this; it wasn't like they were trying to be mean or anything. Actually, she knew it usually meant just the opposite: people who used the volunteer voice were trying to be *helpful* and *warm* and *caring*.

But it never made her feel helped or warm or cared for. For a time, after she understood the voice, it made her feel angry. Then depressed. Now it just made her feel empty.

She opened her eyes, did her best to offer a bright smile. That was the best thing you could do in a homeless shelter: smile at anyone who was there. It made the people working there feel good about themselves. And when the people around her felt good about themselves, they did their best to be nice to her mother.

"I know," she said. "I need to get ready for school, catch the bus."

She felt in her pocket, making sure she had the card that guaranteed her free rides on the city bus system.

When she was younger, her mom always had her change into pajamas when they came to homeless shelters. Or to temporary housing. It was part of the experience of sleeping inside.

More often, they squatted in abandoned buildings in the run-down parts of town. In the summers, sometimes in parks. Infrequently, when they managed to panhandle enough money, in a run-down motel. Motels were pajama places as well.

But Quinn had given up on the pajamas. It was much easier just to sleep in her clothes, be ready for the next day. Simple was good with her mother.

The woman who had awakened her had long, dirty blonde hair, brown eyes, a receding chin. But a nice smile. There was that.

Except the smile was fake. Quinn could tell that too.

She sat up. "Something wrong?" she asked. The woman wore a name tag that said BRANDILYN in capped letters.

Brandilyn patted Quinn's arm. "Maybe . . . maybe we could call in to school for you today."

Call in to school? An odd suggestion for a worker at the homeless shelter. Why would she want to do that? School was a warm place. They fed her toast in the morning, gave her a free lunch, took her mind off the long hours she'd have to spend with her mother in the late afternoon and evening.

Those weren't always hours she wanted to spend with her mother. For others, an evening with Mom might seem simple; with her mother, nothing was simple. Least of all the evenings.

"Where's my mom?" she asked.

"That's . . . well, honey . . . we don't know."

"Oh."

"We're looking for her."

"She wandered off again, didn't she?" Quinn itched at her arm.

"Again?"

Right. This woman was new at the shelter. Maybe a stand-in. She didn't know the long story of Vicki Simmons. Still, Quinn didn't want to go into it all with her; let someone else at the shelter fill her in.

Quinn scratched at her arm again. "She, uh . . . she has problems."

"What kind of problems, dear?"

"Mental problems." For starters. Two years ago, when Quinn was thirteen, her father had disappeared. Just walked out. Her mother—Vicki—hadn't been the same since. At first she did okay. She had a job, working in a dry-cleaning business, and she did her best to act like nothing had changed.

Well, sometimes she acted like that. Other times she went on long crying jags, lasting for a few days at a time. She just lay in bed, unable to speak. Unable to do anything but breathe. And that, just barely.

Those spells—that's what her mom had called them, *spells*— ended up costing her the job at the dry cleaner. And after that, Mom hadn't really been able to hold on to any steady work. She'd be a cleaning maid for a few weeks, or a dishwasher.

But then she'd have one of her spells, miss a shift, and get fired. Which only made the spells last longer.

One day Quinn came home from school to find her mom outside their apartment.

"Let's go," she said simply, and just like that, they left everything.

Just as her father had done.

Another one of those things Quinn hadn't understood at the

time, but had come to realize as she grew into adulthood: on that day, her mother had been evicted from their apartment. At that time, stupid little kid that she was, she'd thought they were just leaving to go somewhere else, and Quinn had been excited.

That night had been their first of many in a homeless shelter.

In the year that followed, her mother's spells became more frequent, to the point that the true spells weren't the long bouts of listlessness and hopelessness. They had become her brief bouts of coherence.

"She'll be back, dear," Brandilyn said, still patting her arm. "We'll find her."

Quinn looked at the woman before her, the woman who wore a BRANDILYN name tag and a puzzled expression, and felt a mixture of emotions beginning to bubble up inside her. This woman had no idea where her mother was, had no idea what her mother was doing, had no idea about anything. What gave her the right to say what her mother would do? Nothing.

At that moment Quinn found herself wishing, for the first time, that her mother would never come back.

Little did she know she would get her wish.

8.

Webb grunted or whimpered every time Dylan hit one of the many potholes or bumps on this stretch of secondary highway.

Thoughts of Iraq, of the 710th, of Claussen, tried to claw their way into Dylan's head. But he wouldn't let them.

Normally, the Percocets or Vicodins or OxyContins would help control those thoughts. That was part of their magic. But he couldn't sink into the fluffy, warm embrace of the drugs right now. He had to stay grounded in reality.

Still, the rusty gears of his mind wanted to explore the images that constantly wandered the hollow corridors of his memories. He could count fence posts or telephone poles, but even that effort wasn't soothing at the moment.

You there, Joni? he asked in his mind.

Always.

You've been pretty quiet since—

Since you shot two guys, then ran with the money and drugs.

Yeah.

Figured now wasn't the time for an I-told-you-so lecture.

Hard to think of a better time.

Good point: I told you so.

Now that we got that out of the way, what do I do?

You're asking me? I'm just imaginary; what do I know?

You're not imaginary; you're my sister.

You mean I was your sister.

He ignored the comment. *I could use some help here.*

You could use a lot of things. A hospital, a time machine, a get-out-of-jail-free card . . .

You're not helping.

Just feeling like I should play the role of your conscience, since I live inside your head and all.

Well, since you're into role-playing, put yourself in my place and tell me what you'd do.

I am in your place.

Joni.

Okay, I'd go with Webb's suggestion.

I don't recall Webb making a suggestion since he cowboyed up on the Percocet. Just some groans.

Medicine man.

Dylan laughed, and Webb stirred in the seat beside him, opening his eyes for a few seconds and mumbling something before returning to a stupor.

We're nowhere near the Crow rez, and I doubt any of the elders would welcome me with open arms. Especially when I bring them a white man who's been shot in a drug deal.

I'm not talking a real medicine man. I'm talking a man who deals in medicines.

Dylan paused. *Andrew.*

Yeah. Andrew.

You trust Andrew to keep something like this quiet?

Not for a second.

Me neither.

But we're not trusting him to keep quiet. We're trusting him to find some help that would be . . . under the radar, let's say.

With Andrew, it's more like under the bus.

Whatever works.

Dylan sighed, glanced at the pained look on Webb's face. *Yeah, whatever works.*

At that moment he heard a chime from his cell phone, indicating he was in range of a tower.

See? Joni said. *Almost like you're supposed to call.*

Two bars.

Okay, okay.

He dialed as he drove, knowing inside that he'd have to ditch his cell phone sometime soon. Once Krunk found out, and the guys up in Canada . . . well, he had no doubt they had access to deep resources that could trace his phone signal.

"Yeah?" said a voice on the other end.

"Andrew, it's Dylan."

"Dylan." Andrew paused, and Dylan could almost hear him smile through the phone line. "I already bought Girl Scout cookies, if that's why you're calling."

"You in Great Falls, or on the rez?"

Andrew grew up on the Fort Belknap rez, but called Great Falls home these days. Even so, he was still on the rez as much as, maybe even more than, he was anywhere else. On the rez, he was a player. Hard to leave behind power, evidently. Hard to leave behind the rez in general, something American Indians from any tribe understood.

"On the rez. Why?"

"I'm in your neighborhood."

Another pause. "Just out for a Sunday afternoon drive on the Highline? It ain't Sunday afternoon, cuz."

"I need some help."

"What kind of help?"

"The medical kind."

"What'd you do?"

"Only what I had to. But a friend got shot." He winced as he said it, picturing DEA agents listening in on Andrew's phone conversations—a distinct possibility. Probably not, though; Andrew was shady, but he certainly wasn't stupid. That's what made him dangerous.

"So you come up from the Crow rez, start shooting Assiniboine. And now you want my help."

"He's white. And I didn't shoot him."

Andrew laughed. "They don't even buy that story in tribal courts."

"We'll worry about that later, Andrew. Right now, I need you to do me a favor."

"That's me, the Favor Man. You know the Kwik Trip in Harlem? Can't miss it; it's the store with all the drunk Indians outside."

Dylan shook his head. Andrew was one of those Indians who made constant references to clichés and stereotypes, as if spouting them gave him some kind of power over them. To Dylan, Andrew's posturing smacked too much of a desperate need to be clever. Probably not a desperate need to be liked; no one really liked Andrew. But the water was rising, and Dylan didn't have any waders.

"Yeah, Andrew. I know the Kwik Trip."

"I'll meet you there. Can you make it in fifteen minutes?"

"I can make it in ten."

9.

"Wake up, young lady," a man's voice said.

Young lady. When was the last time she'd been called that? Quinn checked all seventeen years of her memory banks. Maybe she'd never been called that, truth be told. Most often, it was something like "junkie," uttered by police officers who mistook the cuts on her arms for needle tracks. More than a few junkies on the streets of Portland, to be sure, but she wasn't one of them. At least, not in the traditional sense. She wasn't addicted to crack or heroin or meth or anything like that.

She was, however, addicted to cutting herself.

Quinn kept her eyes closed, pretending she was still asleep.

She wasn't ready to open her eyes. That meant starting another day, and Quinn didn't want to start another day.

Not that sleeping was better. In fact, it was worse, much worse, than being awake. When she was asleep, her body drifted away to . . . nothingness. Just a few short years ago, she had felt the opposite: sleep was a comfort, an escape. But she had been young and stupid then, disillusioned into thinking there could be an escape, however temporary, from her life. Now she understood it was all just one long nightmare. Being nothing, feeling nothing, was much more frightening than pain and anguish. She knew, because she'd experienced them all. Give her pain any time. Sleep was death.

"Quinn, I need you to listen to me."

She opened an eye, stared at the man standing above her. She didn't recognize him, so he obviously wasn't a street regular. She knew all the dregs out there on the streets, because she herself was one of them. Had been for four years now. Two since her mom had disappeared. But she was sure she'd find her mother again soon; she checked the homeless shelters, the clinics, the hospitals, all across Portland. And even though no one ever said they'd seen her mother, no one thought her photo looked familiar, Quinn knew she was just a step or two behind. Her mother had simply gone into one of her episodes, come out of it, then been unsure where she was.

"Who are you?" she asked as she sat up.

The man was tall and thin, his features taut and sinewy. He had the look of a homeless person in this sense—he was thin—but not in other, expected ways. For instance, he wore new clothing, freshly laundered. And gloves. Not the gloves you'd typically wear to keep your hands warm, but those plastic things doctors wore.

"My name is Paul," he said, and smiled.

She pushed back the thin blanket covering her body, stood to face him. Pretty much her typical morning routine: throw off the blanket, get up, and go. She was already dressed, always dressed, and so she was ready to move. She remembered, long ago, sleeping in pajamas. Remembered her mother, her father even, tucking her into sheets that smelled like sunshine, kissing her forehead, and wishing her a good night. Her mother had even continued that bedtime routine for a time after they were out on the streets: pajamas and then a tuck-in, even though the bed sheets no longer smelled like sunshine. Eventually the pajamas faded from the picture, like so many other things.

"How do you know my name?" she asked. "I don't know you."

"You don't," he admitted. "But you should."

Quinn knew this was dangerous territory. Alarm signals should be going off inside her head—a strange man waking her in the middle of the homeless shelter, telling her she should get to know him—but nothing about him seemed dangerous. At least, not dangerous to her. Quinn was good at reading body language; her time on the streets had taught her that much. When she was panhandling, for instance, she could tell who would give her money. She knew within the first seconds of seeing the person approaching.

Besides, she'd put down men much larger than this guy calling himself Paul. She'd learned that much on the streets as well.

"Why should I know you?" she asked.

"Let me buy you breakfast, and I'll tell you about me. More importantly, I'll tell you about you."

"Right. You're gonna read my palm or something?"

"Something."

She narrowed her gaze, studied his face. He didn't seem uncomfortable being looked at. Most people, men especially, had a hard time being studied. "Just for breakfast," she said.

"At Denny's. You like Denny's."

He'd said it as a statement, not a question. Not too surprising, since they were just around the corner from a Denny's. A hot meal would be good. And it wasn't like this guy could do much to her in the middle of a Grand Slam breakfast, surrounded by dozens of other people.

"Okay," she said. "You got it."

They walked to the restaurant in silence, Paul keeping his

hands thrust into the pockets of his coat and Quinn struggling to keep pace. Dude walked fast, was all she could think.

At the restaurant, the man told her to order whatever she wanted. She figured she wanted a Grand Slam and some coffee. Paul ordered nothing. She felt guilty about that for about half a second.

"You graduated from high school this year," Paul said, no more than ten seconds after the waitress left to put in Quinn's order.

Quinn shrugged, sipped at the glass of water in front of her. "Yeah."

"You did well in school," he said. "You're smart."

She shrugged again.

"What are you going to do now?" he said.

"Eat breakfast," she said. "That's all I promised."

He smiled. "Yes, it is. But while you do that, I was hoping you might think a bit about your future."

"Don't have one. In case you didn't notice, you woke me up inside a homeless shelter."

"I don't think that's true."

Quinn had to admit she was starting to get a bit torqued. This guy woke her up at the shelter, obviously knew more than a little bit about her, offered to buy her breakfast. Okay. She knew what all those signs pointed to—she'd learned that, if nothing else, from life on the streets. But something about this guy calling himself Paul seemed . . . different.

His eyes, maybe. Many times she'd peered into the eyes of people who were mentally imbalanced, people who'd lost touch with reality, people who'd left the launch pad with the help of crystal meth or cocaine. She could tell those people were dangerous because their eyes showed . . . well, nothingness. No soul. No humanity.

But this Paul character was different. His eyes seemed alive, and that was something that made her curious. Something that even made her hopeful, she had to admit. Because when you were out on the streets, passing an endless wave of dead, soulless eyes, you had to hope you'd see something different; if you didn't, your eyes became empty, soulless coals themselves.

So yeah, she'd maybe let herself hold on to some little flicker inside. It was the flicker of hope that told her she'd someday see her mother again, the flicker of hope that told her someday, somehow, some way, things would get better.

She'd seen all that in Paul's eyes, and now she was angry at herself. Because really, there had been nothing in Paul's eyes at all; it had been her own eyes that betrayed her. Even after four years, hope was a dirty thing that mocked her.

This Paul character was no different from any of the other whack jobs she'd met on the street, and she was mad that she'd fooled herself into believing otherwise.

She stared down at the table a moment, then met Paul's gaze. At least she could knock him down a notch before leaving. She'd find a place to be by herself, maybe curl up with her trusty penknife and relieve the pressure that was now pounding behind her eyes.

"Look. Paul. Let's cut to the chase. You're a dirtbag. I mean, cruising homeless shelters, looking for seventeen-year-old girls? Stalking them, finding out where they go and what they do before you move in and offer to buy them breakfast? What comes next? After my Grand Slam, you casually mention that you have a hotel room not too far away? You're pathetic."

He showed no immediate reaction, so she continued. "I'm okay with that; I'm an expert on the subject, you might say. So here's what's going to make your story even more pathetic: I'm going to sit here and eat my breakfast when it comes, but there's no way I'm going anywhere with you when this is over. Think what that says about your life, when you can't even pick up a homeless teenager."

The waitress picked that exact moment to put down a platter in front of her, so Quinn smiled, gave Paul a quick salute, and tucked into her pile of scrambled eggs.

Paul watched her in silence for a few minutes, and she was amazed at the glee she felt inside, thinking of what must be going through his mind.

"You've been cutting yourself," Paul finally said, his voice low.

She stopped chewing, looked at him. "Come again?"

"To release the pressure," he answered. "You've been cutting yourself. You're careful—you took a penknife and some of the razors from your art teacher at school this past year when you started, and you keep a stash of rubbing alcohol to sterilize the razors and wounds—but you've been cutting yourself all the same."

Quinn felt a queasiness building inside her. The bit about releasing pressure was too . . . personal. It was a thought, a feeling, she'd never shared with anyone else. No counselor or therapist or caseworker. No one.

Paul had closed his eyes, but now he opened them again. "You think of it as deep-sea diving. You feel like you're sinking, every day, and you feel that pressure threatening to make you explode. Except it's a pressure *inside* you, and that's why you do the cutting."

This wasn't the reaction she'd expected from Paul the Stalker. She'd expected him to cry, maybe even hoped he'd cry. She'd expected him to retreat, beg her not to turn him in.

She hadn't expected him to crawl inside her head.

Quinn started to slide out of the booth, but Paul's hand closed around her arm as she did so.

Immediately she felt her anger, her pain, her hate, draining from her body. It was replaced by a sense of . . . buoyancy. Like the deep-sea divers in that movie she'd sneaked into last year. What did they call it? Equalization depth. Where she was neither sinking nor rising. Only remaining quietly, blissfully still. Until now, only cutting had produced that feeling.

"What are you doing?" she said in a whisper as she gave up the effort to leave. Suddenly, she wanted to find out more about this man calling himself Paul.

His eyes had been closed, but now he opened them to look at her again. Living eyes, not dead ones. Yes, she still had to admit that.

"I'm praying for you," he answered.

10.

As Dylan approached Harlem, hitting the speed-limit signs that slowed him from sixty-five to twenty-five in a matter of a few hundred yards, he started planning his next moves. He was going to owe Andrew for this, which probably wasn't a Good Thing. But certainly a Better Thing than having Webb die in his front seat; he'd be happy to be in Andrew's debt if it meant Webb survived.

It's not like he and Webb were BFFs, but Webb was the closest thing he had to a friend. That was his whole reason for agreeing to this now ill-fated trip: to keep an eye on Webb, who approached everything with a certain mix of childlike glee and naïveté. Webb was the guy constantly dancing on the edge of a cliff, so immersed in the moment that he was unaware of the mile-deep drop right next to him.

Biiluke, Joni said.

Dylan grunted. Yeah, *Biiluke*. The original name of the Apsáalooke, the Crow people, so-named after their ancestor chose to jump off a harrowing cliff to certain death. "I won't make many of him," Original Creator said, referring to his recklessness. So maybe the bond he shared with Webb was that feeling of a kindred Biiluke. A kindred chosen, as Claussen might have said.

It's all of that, Joni said. *Biiluke, chosen, Claussen, Webb.*

Right.

You couldn't save Claussen. Webb's a second chance to do that.

What about you? I could have saved you, Joni. Would that have kept me out of the army, out of EOD, out of—

Okay, I wasn't going to go there, but yeah: this is like your third chance. You couldn't save me, couldn't save Claussen, heck, couldn't save yourself, so you entered the army and EOD with this crude sort of death wish, didn't you? And when that didn't work out, when you didn't actually die, but only ended up crippled, you weren't any worse off. Because you were already crippled.

Yeah, you're quite the psychoanalyst. I'll be sure to pass along your theories next time I talk to my therapist.

And when will that be? Haven't you skipped out on your last few sessions?

Why would I need them, with you in my head? Can you shut up for now and let me concentrate on getting some help for Webb? You can lecture me about what it means later.

Shutting up. For now.

Two blocks away he saw the Kwik Trip looming and flipped on his turn signal. No sense getting picked up by local tribal police. Especially, as Andrew might say, with a white man bleeding all over the front seat of his pickup. He glanced at Webb again, who had awakened from his stupor a bit and now had his head resting on the dash once more.

Webb didn't dabble in the painkillers, said they took the edge off his thinking. He thought alcohol was more social, and that's what Webb was all about. Not used to Percocets percolating in his system, Webb was quiet and compliant. And this, most definitely, was a Good Thing. Dylan could think, plan his next moves, without Webb's constant chatter in his ear.

The wind leaked through the windows, creating a shrill whistle as they idled through the parking lot. On the adjacent side street, someone flashed the lights on a new Dodge Ram, conspicuously clean in the middle of the grimy Montana winter.

Dylan peered through his windshield, saw the driver of the pickup.

Andrew gave him a quick wave, started his Ram with a rumble, and pulled away from his parking spot.

Dylan followed as Andrew left town and turned onto a gravel road. Exactly 3.2 miles outside of town, Andrew's Ram turned onto a different gravel road for another .7 miles, and finally into a driveway beside a battered old trailer house.

Dylan parked behind Andrew's pickup and shut off his own, watching as Andrew slid out of the Ram and approached. Dylan rolled down the window with a few painful creaks, sitting quietly as Andrew's dark gaze took in the scene.

"Dylan Runs Ahead, the Mighty Hunter," Andrew said, smiling.

Dylan stared at the door of the trailer house, which looked abandoned. But then, many trailer houses on any rez looked abandoned. "This place a—"

"Heap Big Medicine," Andrew said.

"Shut up. I mean—"

"Yeah, his name's Couture. One a them French Indians."

"Doctor?"

Andrew smiled. "Close enough; he's a vet. Does great with horses, a regular Robert Redford."

Dylan frowned, and Andrew must have caught his thoughts.

"Relax. He does this kinda work on the side. Antibiotics, the whole deal—usually they're for cows and pigs. But all white men are just pigs, ain't that what we say on the rez?"

Dylan pushed open his door, forcing Andrew to take a few steps back. "Just help me get him inside."

"Couture knows the drill. No worries."

Dylan moved around the other side of the pickup, opened the door, slid Webb out of the seat, draping Webb's good arm over his shoulder. Webb mumbled something, but Dylan couldn't understand what he said.

Andrew watched, shuffling back and forth on his feet to stay warm.

"You gonna help?" Dylan asked, struggling to get Webb's feet under him as they moved toward the trailer house.

"You're doing fine. I'll get the door for you."

Andrew ran up the rotting wooden stairs to the trailer house's door and knocked. A few seconds later it opened, and Andrew exchanged words with whoever was inside before disappearing into the trailer.

So much for his offer to hold the door. Not that Dylan had really expected it; Andrew was one of those guys who told you all about everything he could do or would do, but rarely actually did.

Dylan worked his way up the rotting wooden steps, last painted a muddy brown sometime in the nineteenth century, grabbed the door handle, and negotiated the narrow doorway as he half carried Webb's slumping form into the trailer.

Inside, Andrew stood with a fair-skinned Indian sporting long, braided hair and a C-shaped scar on his cheek. Both held cups of coffee, and the guy with a scar took a sip.

"Over on the couch," the scarred man said with a phlegmy voice, and coughed.

Dylan struggled to the couch, noticing it was covered with a couple of black garbage bags to protect whatever thready upholstery might lie beneath. The carpet inside the trailer may have once been actual carpet, but now it was just something to collect mud. Everything smelled of stale tobacco.

Dylan put Webb down on the couch cushions slowly, letting him slump to a half-prone position before standing and turning again. His own shoulder felt a bit numb from carrying most of Webb's weight.

The scarred guy had produced a pack of Marlboros, and he offered one to Dylan. He seemed to be studying Dylan's forehead; did he have a spot of blood there without realizing it? Dylan resisted the urge to rub at it.

Andrew already had a cigarette in his mouth, unlit. Dylan paused, then decided to take one himself. He wasn't much of a smoker, but this wasn't any time to be turning down offered pleasantries.

Scarred Guy took out a Zippo, set flame to Andrew's and Dylan's cigarettes before lighting one of his own and breathing deeply. He coughed a bit of blue smoke as he cast his dark eyes at Dylan.

"Stephen Couture," he said, extending his right hand.

"Dylan Runs Ahead."

Andrew grinned. "Now we smoke the sacred tobacco, have Big Council."

Couture ignored Andrew, speaking to Dylan. "You're not Assiniboine. Not Gros Ventres, either."

"Apsáalooke," Dylan said.

"Crow."

Dylan nodded. *Crow* was a mistranslation of the Apsáalooke name that literally meant "People of the Big-Beaked Bird." Couture undoubtedly knew this, as did Andrew. For that matter, the Assiniboine and Gros Ventres people had never called themselves that; those names were misnomers as well. Only difference was, their tribes had been labeled by the French instead of the English.

"What brings you up here?" Couture asked.

"Picking up a delivery."

"From Canada?"

Dylan shifted uncomfortably. "Yeah."

Couture took another puff, considered. "Lot of folks on the Fort Belknap rez might not like that much, taking the delivery business away from them. Feel like Crows should stay south for the winter."

"Yeah."

"Lucky for you, I don't much care what folks on the Fort Belknap rez think."

"Yeah."

Webb moaned from his position on the couch, and Couture's gaze shifted, breaking the conversation. "Guess I'd better take a look at him."

Couture kneeled beside the couch, unknotted Webb's blood-stained coat from his shoulder. "Bleeding's pretty much stopped. That's a good sign. Means you didn't knick a major vessel."

"Yeah." Dylan wanted to point out that he wasn't the one who had missed a major blood vessel, but it seemed like too much effort. Instead, he took another draw of his own cigarette and glanced at Andrew, who was surveying the whole scene bemusedly.

Couture examined the shoulder, poking gently at the small hole, now turning black and bruising around the edges. Dylan noticed, for the first time, that Couture was wearing surgical gloves. Sanitary and sterile; that was obviously the rule of this trailer house. A ghost of a memory, blue nitrile gloves in the Iraq desert, flashed in his mind.

Couture stood. "Went through—won't have to fish out a bullet." Couture's cigarette was clenched in his teeth.

"Yeah."

"That your favorite word? Yeah?"

Dylan smiled. "Yeah."

Couture nodded, disappeared into the bowels of the trailer's hallway for a few seconds. He returned with few sealed packages, tore one
open as he approached Webb again. He removed some gauze and
dressed the wound, then stood and admired his work. He set the nub
of his cigarette in a glass ashtray on an end table beside the couch,
picked up the other sealed packages, and offered them to Dylan.

"You'll need to change those dressings for the next few days."

Dylan accepted the packages, nodding, and Couture brought
out a sandwich bag containing some white powder.

"Duramycin. Antibiotic for pigs—essentially tetracycline.
Usually comes in five-pound bags, but I figured you wanted to pack
a little lighter. Pigs and humans are actually pretty close in how they
react to anti—"

"So I've been told." Dylan cast a glance at Andrew's grin.

"A teaspoon in a drink the next ten days should take care of
infection—parts of his shirt and jacket got pushed into the wound,
so he'd probably get infected without it."

"Can't you pull out the fabric?"

Couture picked up his cigarette from the ashtray, clenched it in
his teeth. "His muscle's not torn up too much—likely a pretty low-
caliber gun, like a .22. If I dug around in there with what I have, I'd
probably do more harm than good. Small entrance and exit wounds,
so they should heal over just fine. His body will take care of the rest,
with a little help from the antibiotics." He held up another prescription bottle. "To help with the pain, these—"

"We've got a few Percocets and Vicodins. And Oxies."

Couture nodded. "Those should do. Keep him down to four a day, though." He scratched at his nose. "Those things are pretty addictive."

"I've been told that too." He waited for a crack from Andrew or Joni, and was surprised when none came. "So what do we do now?"

"Don't know about 'we,'" Couture said, and cleared his throat. "Me, I'm gonna have another cuppa joe and another smoke. It's my break time. You're gonna give me five hundred bucks and get your buddy off my couch so he doesn't bleed all over the place."

"Yeah," Andrew chimed in. "Evil white man ruined everything else for Indians. Can't have him staining the furniture too."

Dylan could have pointed out that Webb had stopped bleeding—the wound was barely seeping now, and bandaged—as well as the black garbage bags on the couch. But he didn't; this wasn't about what was really happening. It was about showing power. And he needed to show deference to that power.

"Thanks," he said. Then: "Can I use your latrine?"

Couture narrowed his eyes. "You military?"

"Was."

"Most people call it a bathroom." Couture pointed at him. "Purple heart?"

"What makes you say that?"

"Your limp."

Dylan shrugged, nodded.

"I got me one a those too. Operation Desert Storm. Shrapnel from an explosion. Friendly fire, of course—Iraqi troops couldn't blow up anything if their lives depended on it." He puffed his cigarette. "Come to think of it, I guess their lives did depend on it."

Dylan looked at him a moment. "Well, they can blow up stuff now." His leg flared.

Couture nodded slowly, pointed down the dark hallway. "Second door on the left."

"Wash your hands," Andrew called after him. "White Man cooties and all."

Dylan resisted a response, closing the bathroom door behind him.

Okay. Webb was gonna be fine. Probably. As for himself, he was still 50/50. Maybe even 40/60.

He fished the fresh bottle of Percocet from his pocket and popped two of them. Yeah, they made Webb fuzzy and semicatatonic, because he never used them. They'd once done the same for him. But at some point—and he didn't know that precise point—the process reversed. He needed the Perks or the Vikes or the Oxies to stay clear. Without them, his mind was muddy. And a muddy mind wasn't going to get them out of this mess. Funny how that blurred line worked in his mind. Sometimes he convinced himself he needed to avoid the drugs to think clearly; other times he convinced himself the drugs were exactly what made him think clearly. He'd played both sides of that equation just this morning.

Yes, you're a walking contradiction.

Who isn't, Joni? Who isn't?

He dug into his jeans pocket and fished out five bills—half of what he'd retrieved from Webb's rucksack before hitting the city limits of Harlem. No sense alerting Andrew or anyone else to a large pile of cash sitting in his truck.

He set the money on the counter, finally looked at his reflection in the mirror. No blood on his forehead, as he'd expected.

He splashed some cold water from the faucet on his face, ran his wet hands through his close-cropped hair. The drain gurgled with a hollow echo after he turned off the faucet.

Okay. His next step was to contact Krunk. Better Krunk should hear the whole story from him than from someone else. Not that Krunk would believe him. But Dylan might as well give himself whatever sliver of an advantage he might have. It was a good tactical move—defuse the bomb before it had a chance to explode.

That strategy had worked for him before. Many times.

Until the last time, of course, but he was playing the odds here.

Dylan grabbed the bills from the counter and opened the bathroom door again, went back into the living area. Webb was still on the couch, unconscious. Andrew and Couture sat at a small Formica table in the kitchen with their coffee cups in front of them.

Dylan put the money on the table in front of Couture, nodded. "Thanks again," he said.

Couture drank from his cup, set it back down, made no move to take the money. "*De nada.*"

Andrew giggled. "You hear that? Veterinarian Assiniboine who speaks Spanish. That's bilingual. You don't see that on the Discovery Channel."

"What do you see on the Discovery Channel?"

"Don't know. Never watch it."

"Looks like you need a new coat," Couture said.

"What?"

"New coat." He nodded at the front of Dylan's ski jacket. "You put a hole in that one."

Dylan looked down. A neat puncture, the size of a dime, laced his right pocket; some of the coat's insulation leaked out. He'd forgotten that he'd taken the first shot with the .357 through his coat pocket.

"You can take the jacket on the chair over there."

Dylan turned, saw a black nylon jacket thrown haphazardly on a flowered recliner across the living room from the couch.

"Thanks," he said, retrieving it.

"Where you headed?" Couture asked.

"Still working on that."

"You're marked," Couture said, staring.

Andrew smiled, turned to look at Couture. "Yeah," he said. "Dead Man Walking. You get a white boy shot on the rez, you're definitely a marked man."

"No, not like that," Couture said. "My grandmother, she called it the mark. But that's not really your word for it, is it?" He stared at Dylan. "You call it chosen." He took another drag on his cigarette.

Dylan felt his bad leg buckle, and his good one along with it. He stumbled, almost going down before regaining his balance. "What did you say?" he whispered, hoping he'd heard Couture wrong.

"My grandmother, she had this sense that let her . . . see inside other people," Couture said, sounding almost disinterested. "See their souls, I guess you could say. But she told me about this woman she met once, a woman she said was marked."

"What did *marked* mean?" Dylan asked.

"Meant the woman's soul was dark to her. Meant she couldn't see inside. Meant the woman was someone special." Couture exhaled a long stream of smoke. "Chosen."

"What happened to the marked woman?"

Couture smiled grimly. "She killed herself."

Andrew was oddly quiet, as was Joni. Dylan heard a strong gust of wind run across the metal roof of the trailer.

Couture motioned at him, cigarette clenched between his fingers. "My grandma knew I had the sense too. Told me I needed to watch for the day I might come across someone marked. Someone chosen. Warn them."

"Warn them of what?"

"Warn them that evil would always look for them. And always find them."

Andrew recovered before Dylan could. "Well, I guess Couture here is a big medicine man after all," he said, smiling. Except the smile looked a bit more painted on than usual. "I'd be worried about you looking into my soul, but I don't have one."

Couture shot him a hard glance. "That's why I work with animals," he said quietly. "You don't see inside them."

Couture suddenly seemed drained. He stared at his ashtray, his eyes watery and vacant.

"How about a cuppa joe to go?" Andrew asked, evidently feeling the need to change the subject, to get past the odd scene that had just taken place. Feeling the need to get Dylan out of there.

Dylan was just as happy to drop it. His leg had healed after Iraq, yes, but his memories of Claussen would never heal. Talk about being chosen only stirred up those memories.

"Coffee," he said. "Yeah, that'd be good."

Andrew rose quickly, moved to a fake-wood-grained cabinet, and retrieved a Styrofoam cup from a stack. He blew into the cup, poured some of the dark brown liquid from the coffeemaker into it.

Dylan accepted the Styrofoam cup from Andrew and took a drink, feeling the liquid warm his aching bones immediately. Or maybe it was the Percocet warming him. Didn't really matter one way or the other.

"Be right back," he said, setting the coffee on the table. "Gotta pack my cargo."

Andrew watched as he pulled Webb from the couch and half

walked, half dragged him to the door. Webb's eyes opened as Dylan struggled with the door, and he was able to stand on his own.

"Make it down the steps?"

"*Hunph*," Webb said.

Dylan took that as a yes but held on to Webb's good arm as they stumbled their way to the small Ford Ranger.

Webb cocooned himself into the passenger seat without any small talk, and Dylan started the truck again, letting it idle to bring up the heat.

He went back inside the trailer and grabbed his coffee cup.

"Thanks for the coffee," he told Couture, then turned to Andrew. "And I owe you."

"Just the way I like it," Andrew said, rocking back in the metal chair. "Make sure you give a big how-de-do to the fine folks down on the Crow rez for us."

"Maybe I will, if I ever get back there."

Andrew looked across the table at Couture, who had worked his way through most of another cigarette but remained silent. "Guess I didn't tell you, Dylan here isn't a rez boy. He's one a those urban Indians. Lives in the Big City." Andrew took another sip of his coffee. "In that case, give a big how-de-do to the fine folks in Billings for us."

Dylan, already at the front door, stopped and turned once again. "Maybe I will," he said. "If I ever get back there."

11.

Dylan met Webb for the first time in a bar. The Rainbow Bar, down on Montana Avenue next to the tracks in Billings, appropriately named because it was always packed with a rainbow coalition of people in search of a buzz. Young college students. Retired railroad workers. Hispanic migrant workers in from the sugar beet fields. And more than a few Crow and Northern Cheyenne, parading through the long, thin interior in a never-ending river of humanity.

Typically, Indians in the bar would scan, find other Indians in the bar, give a nod. Maybe even group together, exchange a few rounds.

Dylan wasn't typical. He noted the dark eyes of others he recognized as Crow, but didn't acknowledge their gestures. He wasn't really a Crow anymore. Not after leaving to join the army. Not after returning from the army unannounced to anyone on the rez. Most of all, though, not after Joni. If he were to venture back to the rez at all, and if he were to be recognized, he would just be that guy whose sister disappeared.

On top of that, Dylan rarely spent time in bars. Rarely spent time anywhere outside his house since returning from the VA hospital in

Sheridan several months ago. Venturing into the outside world took too much energy; he had to select a mask that hid the emptiness inside if he ventured into the outside world. His inside world, built around a television, a few threadbare pieces of furniture, and a bottle of painkillers, was so much more comfortable. No masks needed.

On the night he'd met Webb, though, the painkillers had ironically brought him out of his house. Somewhere, somehow, he'd lost the scrip pad he'd nicked from his doctor, and the prescriptions he had going at several different pharmacies had expired. Major painkillers such as Percocet and Vicodin and OxyContin rarely had more than one refill, which hadn't really been a problem since Dylan had lifted the prescription pad from Doctor Stewart's office. With a whole pad of more than one hundred prescriptions, he could hop from pharmacy to pharmacy; by the time he'd worked his way through all the pharmacies in the area—easily a couple dozen—he could move back to the top of the list without attracting any attention.

But the wheels had fallen off that particular plan when the scrip pad went missing. Maybe he'd dropped it on the way to the post office. Maybe he'd accidentally mixed it in with one of the trash piles. Maybe he, ironically enough, had cribbed it away in the middle of a Percocet-fueled stupor. It was harder than ever to get to that stage now, the stage that made everything unimportant, but he could still hit it now and then.

Whatever the cause, the scrip pad was gone. And shortly after that, so was his stash of painkillers. No matter, he told himself. Hadn't Scott, that eminent sage appointed to his case by the VA, told him a couple months ago that his doctor wanted to wean him off the painkillers? This was a good excuse to do that. He could do this without the Perks or the Vikes or the Oxies.

Such had been the lies he'd told himself three short days ago. He'd been fine the first twenty-four hours, something south of fine the second twenty-four, and now, sweaty and shaky. Cold. Sick. On top of it all, fuzzy and itchy.

In the midst of it, even though he didn't really care for alcohol, it became the panacea that filled his mind. Okay, so he was addicted to the painkillers, but he knew a few shots could kill the pain. Hadn't he watched more than a few folks on the rez kill their pain with liquor and beer?

He'd staggered to The Rainbow and tried to drink away the pain with middling success.

"You look like I feel," a voice said to him.

Dylan looked up, saw a guy with a full beard who looked like a lumberjack sliding onto the stool next to him. Dylan hadn't even known it was unoccupied; last time he'd looked, some drunk woman had been sitting there, working on whiskey sours. She'd held her liquor pretty well, but she kept lighting and then putting out the same cigarette as she tried to focus on her reflection in the mirror behind the bar. After the third or fourth time she'd stamped out the cigarette, it had bent and had begun to lose the tobacco inside; at roughly the same time, Dylan had lost any limited interest in continuing to watch her.

But now, lumberjack Joe was sitting next to him, waiting for some snappy comeback to his *You look like I feel* line. Fine. He could play that game.

"So how do you feel?" he asked.

The lumberjack smiled. "Like I just been run over."

Dylan returned the smile. "Then I look like I feel too."

Lumberjack Joe held out a hand. "Name's Webb."

Dylan took his hand and shook it, wishing he hadn't engaged in this conversation in the first place.

Yeah, starting a conversation was your first mistake, Joni said. *Getting hooked on painkillers, then going off them cold turkey, then trying to drown the withdrawals with liquor were all great moves.*

Shut up, Joni. I'll send you to the kill box.

Shutting up.

"I'm Dylan."

"Dylan? As in—"

"Yeah. As in Bob Dylan. My parents were big into sixties folk rock. Had a sister named Joni, named after Joni Mitchell."

Webb nodded, ordered a tap beer from the bartender.

Dylan smiled. He'd left a door wide open for this guy, that whole line about *had* a sister, and he hadn't walked through it. The natural follow-up to that statement would be to ask what had happened to the sister. But if you were the kind of person who knew it was best to keep old skeletons in the closet, you didn't peek inside other people's closets. Even when they opened them a crack for you.

"I'll buy your beer," Dylan said, pushing a fiver toward the bartender when he came back with a tall glass.

"You, sir, are a scholar and a gentlemen," Webb said, tilting his glass in Dylan's direction.

"Which is why I'm sitting in The Rainbow Bar at one o'clock on a Sunday afternoon, surrounded by all these other scholars and gentlepeople."

"Including yours truly," Webb agreed, taking another long drag on the beer. "How long you been here?"

Dylan shrugged. "Couple hours."

"How much you had?"

Dylan shrugged again. "Couple beers."

"Probably more than a couple," Webb said. "But I'm guessing beer's the least of your problems."

"And what would be the greatest?"

Webb shrugged. "You're coming down off something."

Dylan paused, decided it was time to take another sip himself.

"No worries about it, man," Webb said. "Me, I prefer to drown my sorrows. I could tell you this is my first stop of the afternoon, and that would be true." Another long drink. "But I made four stops at other places this morning. Can't say I don't worship at my favorite church on Sunday."

"Painkillers," Dylan said without really meaning to. Without really knowing why. Something in this guy made him drop his guard a bit. Maybe because he was the first person, outside of Scott the VA Swammie and Whatsherface the VA Therapist, who'd said more than two words to him in the last several months. And this guy, this Webb, wasn't getting paid to do it.

Webb turned and looked. "What kind?"

Dylan shrugged. "Whatever I can get. Percocets, Vicodins, OxyContins."

"And your prescription just ran out a few days ago."

"That's a good way to put it."

Webb drained his glass, slapped his hand on the counter. "Come on," he said, rising from the seat.

"Come on where?"

"To refill your prescription."

In spite of all he'd drunk in the last few hours, Dylan felt his mouth go dry almost instantly. "You have some?"

"No," Webb said, "but I know where to get 'em." He turned and started making his way toward the front door.

Dazed, Dylan stared at his back for a few moments before standing and following.

It was bright and sunny outside, so sunny Dylan's eyes hurt.

Of course, that could also be explained by the withdrawals. Or the beer.

"You got a car?" Webb asked.

"Pickup."

"You okay to drive?"

"Only a couple beers, like I said. Don't really have the stomach for it, I guess."

Webb smiled. "Yeah, I could tell. You lead."

Dylan paused. Should he be afraid of this guy? Yeah, probably. Most likely he was going to be rolled for some money. Maybe even his truck. He thought about it for a few moments and realized he didn't really care.

"This way," he said, leading Webb across Montana Avenue to his beat-up old Ford Ranger. The doors squeaked open, they both slid into the front seat, and Dylan keyed the ignition.

"Where to?" Dylan asked.

"Go west, young man," Webb said. "Maybe up on Poly or Rimrock."

Dylan circled back around to 27th, then went north and finally turned west on Poly.

"Figure out where we're headed yet?" he asked finally as they drove in front of the green, manicured lawns of MSU-Billings, followed a few blocks later by the green, manicured lawns of Rocky Mountain College.

"Luckily, you happen to be jonesing on Sunday afternoon, and you know what Sunday afternoon means."

"Football?"

"Not this time of year," Webb said. "I'm talking about open houses," he said, pointing to a realtor's sign.

"We're going to an open house," Dylan said. "What, you know

the guy listing this house? He can get some . . ." He paused, uncomfortable feeling himself say the word *drugs*. "He can get some stuff?"

"Just shut up and park."

A few minutes later they were walking up the steps.

"Okay, here's the plan," Webb said. "You're gonna quiz the agent, okay?"

"Quiz how?"

"However you want. The kind of stuff you'd ask if you were looking for a house. Ask about the school, ask about the taxes, ask about the colors in the dining room. I don't care."

"And what are you going to do?"

Webb turned to him just before opening the front door of the home. "I told you. I'm gonna refill your prescription."

Webb pushed the door open and charged inside. Dylan stood dumbfounded for a few moments, then followed him in.

"Hey, looks great," he heard Webb say ahead of him. "Bet your wife and kids would love it, Dylan."

"How many kids?" The realtor listing the open house was standing in front of Dylan, fake smile painted on his face. Webb had already disappeared into one of the other rooms.

"Uh, yeah," he said. "Looking to move the family."

"Great neighborhood school here," the realtor said, "Highland Elementary. You're close to downtown. Lots of renovations in this home, including the original hardwood floors." The realtor tapped his foot on the floor, as if to demonstrate the wood was, in fact, quite hard.

"You should put this on your list, Dylan," he heard Webb call from somewhere else in the house. "Tell Linda and the kids about it. I'm checking out the bathroom."

"Linda?" the realtor asked. "That's your wife?"

"Um, yeah."

"How many kids do you have?"

"Three?" he said. He winced, realizing the word had come out as more of a question than a statement.

Webb rejoined them in the front living room. "Yeah, this is a definite one to show Linda," Webb said. "Why don't you take a card from him, Dylan?"

"Sure, sure," the real estate agent said, reaching inside his jacket for a card and handing it to Dylan.

"Dylan and his family will be moving here in the next month or two," Webb said, slapping a hand on the agent's back. "We're checking out some homes for her to look at when she comes next week."

"Well, if you want to take a look at the rest of the house—"

"Don't really think we need to," Webb cut him off. "I mean, what does it matter what we think, you know what I mean? Wife's gotta like it, or it ain't gonna fly. Ain't that right, Dylan?"

"Yeah."

"But Dylan's got your card now, and he'll be calling to set up an appointment for Linda."

"Well, if I could get your name and contact information—"

"Gotta run," Webb said, cutting him off once more. "Getting him to the airport so he can fly back and meet the family. He'll be in touch."

Webb was out the door and halfway down the steps now.

"Sorry," Dylan said, following Webb out and closing the door behind him.

When they were back in the pickup, Dylan turned the crank and started the engine once more. "Wow, that was fun," he deadpanned.

Webb, a big grin on his face, held up a brown prescription bottle with a white label on it. "Hydrocodone work for you?" he said.

Dylan grabbed it, looked at the pills inside, then back at Webb.

Webb's grin was wider than ever. "Told you I was checking out the bathroom," he said. "Especially the medicine cabinet." He nodded toward the road in front of them, swept magnanimously with his arm. "So what do you say? You ready to do some house shopping? We should find plenty of open houses to hit before three this afternoon."

12.

Couture sat in silence after Dylan left, and that silence made Andrew uncomfortable. Any kind of silence made him uncomfortable; he was a man who lived amid activity. That's what juiced him.

"Thanks for the help," he said, rising.

Couture shrugged, slid the five bills off the table, and pocketed them.

Andrew took a long swig of coffee. "That's what I love about you, Couture. You're a great conversationalist."

Couture shrugged once again, seemed unable or unwilling to talk. His eyes had a watery, misty look, as if he were about to cry.

The thought of Couture crying made Andrew even more uncomfortable. He drained the last of his coffee, ignoring the grounds in the last swig, snuffed out his cigarette in the black ashtray, and stood. For the first time he noticed how cold it was in Couture's trailer. "You better start paying your heat bills, cuz. I think they turned off your gas."

Couture said nothing.

"Well. I gotta get going."

Couture nodded simply, let out a deep sigh.

Andrew left him sitting there in his melancholy, shrugging on his jacket as he made his way to his Dodge Ram. He'd washed it just this morning, and now it looked like a new snowstorm was close. Typical. Still, when he got back to the Falls, he'd spin it through the wash. He liked to have a new rig, a clean rig, especially when he was on the rez. People took notice, and Andrew was a man who knew that notice equated with power.

It was good for business.

Before heading back to Great Falls, though, he had to make a few phone calls. Mobile reception out here was spotty at best, so he'd just zip back to Kwik Trip, make his calls at the pay phone there.

He started the truck, hit the gas hard so he could admire the throaty rumble of the dual exhaust, shifted into reverse, and backed away before spinning around.

A few minutes later he rolled into the parking lot at the Kwik Trip, a ghost of a smile on his face.

This was a very nice surprise Dylan had dropped in his lap. A birthday gift and a Christmas gift all wrapped up in one nice package.

Dylan, calling in a favor. And he'd responded. Aside from that odd reaction, the babble from Couture, he had a new lever he could call in on Dylan Runs Ahead. That lever would come in handy sometime.

But there were other favors he himself had to repay; such was the life of a man with a lot of business contacts.

He wasn't an importer, like Krunk down in Billings. Or an exporter, like Prince Edward up north of the border. Didn't specifically handle contraband merchandise at all. But those kinds of people were his best customers, because Andrew was . . . well, he was an information merchant, wasn't he? That's what his business was: buying, selling, exchanging information.

There were many, many people out there searching for the kind of information he could provide.

Dylan had called on him as a "cousin," as a fellow Indian, to provide such services. He'd done as much. Probably saved the white boy's life. But when the two of them had walked out of the trailer, their transaction had ended.

Now Andrew had other information that could be shared. Could be sold.

He looked at his mobile phone. No service, even back in town. Probably because of the snow that was starting to fall—often, out here, he was lucky if he had one or two bars. He crawled out of his truck, went to the pay phone. Pay phones weren't all that bad. He rather liked using them every now and again, though they were something of an endangered species.

On the rez, though, pay phones were still vital links.

He picked up the black receiver, admiring the cold, solid heft of it in his hand, pulled a calling card out of his wallet, punched in the code, and connected.

13.

Quinn was running her fingers over a needle embedded in the fleshy part of her stomach when the cell phone rang.

The ring was "Thus Spake Zarathustra," the familiar tones of the music from that old movie *2001: A Space Odyssey*. Quinn loved that movie, loved the open, airy feel of it. At the beginning, the people in the space station floated, free from gravity, free from pressure.

Quinn grabbed the phone and flipped it open. "Yeah."

"Quinn. How are you?"

When Andrew talked, Quinn always had the impression he was the only person in on some kind of joke; it was as if Andrew were always on the verge of laughing, even when he was trying to be serious. Wind blew into the mouthpiece of Andrew's phone, creating harsh bursts of static. Obviously, he was outside.

"What do you have, Andrew?"

Information, obviously; that's what Andrew's calls were always about.

"Right to the chase, Quinn. That's what I like about you. No great-weather-we're-having, just right into what-do-you-have."

Quinn hadn't looked outside recently, but it had been snowing at last check. "We're not having great weather."

Andrew's laugh sparkled on the line. Come to think of it, Andrew wasn't just on the verge of laughing all the time; he really did laugh all the time. Part of what made Andrew so interesting. Not trustworthy, of course, but interesting. Which made him a good source of information—Andrew always had an ear to the ground.

"You remember we talked about a mutual acquaintance," Andrew said. "Dylan Runs Ahead."

Quinn sat up straight. "I remember." Actually, Quinn had about a dozen people across the state keeping tabs on Dylan Runs Ahead. The only chosen in Montana right now, and the first one Quinn had been asked to monitor. So far, HIVE didn't know who he was—even Dylan didn't know who he was—but he was becoming more mobile now. That brought in so many variables Quinn couldn't control.

"Told you I'd call if I heard from him," Andrew said.

"And you did."

"He left just now."

"Great Falls?"

"Harlem. I'm over on the rez."

Quinn had made the right call, tracking Greg to Great Falls and neutralizing him. But the timing was poor, because it had kept Quinn from tracking Dylan on his drug run, making sure he made it back to Billings without causing a ripple.

The fact that Andrew was calling meant there was a ripple now. Maybe even a wave.

"Tell me about it."

"He called me out of the blue. Needed a bit of help. That's what I am, you know: a statewide help desk."

She could hear his smile through the phone line. "What kind of help?"

"Showed up with a white guy. Needed some . . . medical assistance."

"Medical assistance for what?"

"A gunshot wound."

Alarms went off inside her head. "He got shot?"

"No, no, not Dylan. His buddy."

Webb, the guy who had made the drug run with Dylan. This wasn't good; it meant Dylan and Webb would be on the run.

And often, people who ran ended up running into traps.

For several months Dylan had stayed quiet, confined to his home on the south side of Billings, popping his pills and sinking into oblivion.

Which had been simultaneously easy and aggravating. Easy because a man who never went anywhere, never did anything, was simple to keep out of trouble. Aggravating because knowing he was chosen made her impatient. So many times she had wanted to burst into his home, shake him, and tell him that he needed to make things happen, that being a chosen meant he was destined for big things.

But she couldn't do that. She couldn't activate a chosen; only God could. People inside the Falling Away had tried to enlist the chosen to their cause, and instead only caused their ruin. Sometimes the chosen were overrun by the disease before they could accept what they were. Sometimes they simply disappeared, unable to grasp what it all meant. Sometimes the chosen had killed themselves, seeking escape once they realized the full magnitude of what they represented.

Now Dylan was on the move. The drugs had gone from help to

hindrance. A local dealer, guy by the name of Krunk, had sent Dylan and his friend out on an assignment in exchange for free scrip drugs.

Which had made her assignment much more difficult.

"You still there?" Andrew asked.

"Sorry. So what did you do with Dylan and his buddy?"

"I took them to see a friend named Couture."

"And what's Couture's story?"

"He's a vet."

"As in veteran, or veterinarian?"

Andrew laughed. "Both, actually. But he's a good Indian. Knows how to keep quiet. Too quiet, actually."

Quinn sighed. Andrew always treated their conversations like a game.

"Okay, so what happened?"

"Couture patched up his buddy and sent them on their way."

"That's it?"

"Yeah, that's pretty much it."

"Nothing out of the ordinary? Nothing . . . strange . . . happened while you were there?"

"Other than a white boy with a gunshot wound getting treated by an Indian veterinarian?"

"Other than that."

"Well, Couture had . . . kind of a bad reaction to Dylan."

"What do you mean?"

"I don't know. Maybe not a bad reaction, but . . . scared. Yeah, that's it. Like he was scared."

"Why, do you think?"

"Well, he kind of went a bit sixth sense on him. Said he was . . . what did he call it? Marked. Chosen."

Quinn's face began to tingle. "Chosen?"

"Told Dylan bad people were gonna come after him."

Quinn took a deep sigh. There were a small number of people who could sense the undercurrent of this world's physical reality. Many of them, like her, were part of the Falling Away. Those outside the Falling Away invariably succumbed to their neuroses and compulsions, never fully understanding why they felt driven to escape what they sensed. This Couture was obviously one of these anomalies.

"You've never talked about your friend Couture before."

"Because he's not a friend. Just a business contact, you understand. I got more business contacts than friends. Part of my curse."

"You said he's an Indian?"

Andrew laughed. "Yeah, Couture's an Assiniboine."

Quinn nodded silently. "Dylan say anything about where he was headed?" she asked.

Another tittering laugh from Andrew. "Nah, but I bet he's headed back to Billings. Crawl into his hole."

"How long ago did he leave?"

"Fifteen minutes, tops."

Quinn wasn't so sure Dylan was headed to Billings, but she didn't have any better information to go on. If he was, Harlem was probably about eighty miles east of the cutoff at Eddie's Corner. Great Falls, where Quinn was still cleaning up after neutralizing Greg, was about eighty miles west. With any luck, Quinn might catch them there.

"Okay. Thanks, Andrew. What do I owe you?"

Andrew paused. "I'm thinking of a quid pro quo here. A *Quinn* pro quo." A giggle at his own pun.

"Just spit it out, Andrew."

"Let's just say, he might be carrying some cash."

"You're thinking you might get some reward money out of this? That what you're getting at?"

"Yeah, yeah. Me being a good citizen and all."

"I can probably swing a Good Citizenship Award." Quinn had no intent of doing so, didn't care how much money was involved. But it was best to let Andrew think he'd been a good dog, that he had a nice juicy treat coming.

"Appreciate it."

Quinn hung up the mobile, stared at it for a few moments.

Dylan Runs Ahead was running.

And Quinn would be running behind him.

14.

Andrew wasn't done after hanging up with Quinn. Not at all. Information falls into your lap, you start working all the angles you can. He smiled, picked up the phone, dialed again.

"Hello?"

"Krunk, how you doing this fine morning?"

"What do you want, Andrew?"

"Oh, it's not what I want. I'm calling about something you might want."

"What's that?"

"Dylan."

Andrew noted a brief hesitation before Krunk answered. "What about him?"

"It seems Dylan and his buddy, whatever his name is, ran into a bit of trouble this morning. Think they might be . . . ah, what should I say? . . . a little scarce. They were working for you, I believe."

"And what makes you say that?" Krunk asked.

Andrew felt his smile falter a bit. He'd expected an expletive-laden reaction from Krunk, not a quick game of Twenty Questions.

"Please," he said, recovering. "A magician tells you how he does the trick, it kills all the magic."

"Not interested."

"Really?"

"Really. Dylan's not going anywhere. He knows better than to double back on me."

"Well," Andrew said, leaning back in his chair. "Your faith in Dylan is admirable."

"Good-bye, Andrew."

Andrew sat for a moment, listening to the connection drop after Krunk hung up.

Well. He'd miscalculated. Obviously, Krunk didn't value the information he'd been given. Bad move on Krunk's part.

Andrew scratched absently at his face for a few moments. Dylan was claiming he'd run into a bit of trouble. Obviously, a deal gone bad. Nature of the business; it happened sometimes. People decided they wanted to go into business on their own.

If Dylan and his buddy had walked away—even though his buddy had a gunshot wound—that meant whoever they'd met had *not* walked away. Dylan Runs Ahead, getting all entrepreneurial, decided to take the cash and drugs and disappear with them. Krunk didn't want to believe that, well, that was Krunk's own downfall. He'd always felt Krunk was a little too soft anyway. Someday that softness would kill him.

Well. His information was still just as valuable. Maybe even more valuable, whispered into other ears. Neither Dylan nor Krunk knew just how deep Andrew's network of information ran; no one really knew. For instance, though he didn't know the specifics of this morning's drop—other than the scattered bits Dylan had shared—he had a very good idea who had been on the other side.

Fine. He might be a red-skinned Indian, but he was also a red-blooded American. He'd given Krunk first crack, but he was an equal-opportunity broker. Time to make a call north of the border, see if the Canadians wanted to pay to play.

He punched in his call code again, dialed a new number from his memory. This time a rough, cracking voice answered.

"Prince Edward," Andrew said through a smile.

Everyone in the trade called him Prince Edward, because he'd originally grown up on Prince Edward Island before relocating to British Columbia. Few people knew Prince Edward's real name, Andrew himself being one of those few.

"What's on your mind, Andrew?"

"Well, I've just seen a Very Bad Thing, and I feel a need to make a confession. I'm Catholic, you know. Most of us Indians are."

"What sort of confession?"

"I must confess I heard that you had a delivery that was supposed to go south this morning. Trouble is, it *really* went south."

"I ship a lot of merchandise, Andrew. You know that."

"Yeah, well, this merchandise was scheduled for delivery over Port of Turner way. Let's just say your delivery service didn't absolutely, positively get the packages there. Shoulda used FedEx."

The line was quiet for a few seconds. "Let me call you back."

"Sure, sure. I'm not on my mobile right now, though. Let me give you the number." He read the number off the faceplate of the phone, and Prince Edward hung up.

He considered another cigarette, then decided against it. Especially not out here in the wind, which would burn through the tobacco in just a few minutes. Really needed to cut down on the cancer sticks, anyway; these things would kill you.

Right now, Prince Edward would be trying to raise his two

lackeys, putting out feelers for confirmation of their border transaction. He would get none.

Two minutes later the pay phone clattered with a sickly ring.

"Yes?"

"Andrew. I checked my records, and I don't have confirmation those packages were delivered. I'm listening."

"Yes, yes, of course. Matter of fact, I happen to know the packages have been intercepted by an alternate delivery service, but they . . . well, I can't say they'll get it to the place you're going. Not very reliable themselves."

"So what can you do for me?"

"Well, I think I can make other arrangements. Maybe get the packages to their proper destination."

"And what would this cost me?"

"We can talk about that later. Right now, your customer satisfaction is all I'm worried about."

"Okay. I want a call when you've received the . . . uh . . . shipment."

"No problem. No problem at all."

Andrew hung up the phone and smiled to himself. Just one more call to make. He dialed the number, waited while it rang a few times.

"Hello?"

"Doze, how you doing?"

Doze was a computer geek over in Helena, a young twenty-something who loved tracking down information online for a little extra spending money.

"Hi, Andrew. Where are you? Sounds windy."

Andrew smiled. "I'm an Indian, Doze. I'm one with the wind."

Doze laughed. "What can I do for you?"

"Glad you asked. Remember you told me awhile ago you could track cell phones? Their signals?"

"Sure."

"Even when they're out of range?"

"Well, no. Not really. You have to trace their location when they make a call, pinpoint them by triangulating from the tower picking up the call."

"Right. So you can just . . . monitor the phone number, get a read on its location when it makes a call?"

"Sure. Once they make a call, we know they have a reception."

Andrew smiled. "That's just what I wanted to hear, Doze. Let me give you a number; I want you to tell me where it is the next time it makes a call."

15.

Dylan needed to call Krunk and give him the news. Soon. He glanced at the analog clock on the dash of his old Ford Ranger. It had stopped working long ago, stuck at roughly three thirty for at least a couple of years. Usually that was fine with Dylan; he had no real interest in counting the hours and minutes of his days.

But right now time was vitally important.

Neither he nor Webb wore watches. His cell phone was out of range again, and wouldn't come back into range for ... well, who knew how long? Out here on the barren Montana prairies, where you might expect a cell phone signal to carry forever, there was just one problem: no towers.

Which was usually okay, since there were no people either.

Say it was eleven a.m. Probably wasn't that late yet, but just say it was for the moment. Their exchange up north had happened at about eight by his best guess, which meant he was no more than three hours out. Probably less.

Would Krunk know by now? Probably not. Chances were, the two Canucks hadn't been discovered yet. Probably hadn't even been missed. Maybe two hours before the Canuck contacts started to miss their mules, another couple hours before they'd be found dead in the drifting snow. Figure five hours before the Canadians made a call and hooked up with Krunk.

Trouble was, he didn't want Krunk to get the news from the Great White North. If Krunk heard two of his Canadian counterpart's guys were found dead in the snow, with the $50K in cash and drugs missing from the scene . . . well, Krunk was no mathematician, but he could add two and two.

It would be better if Dylan could break the news to Krunk himself. Guys decide to hink a drug drop and head off with all the cash and merchandise, the last thing they're gonna do is make a call and tell the mark about it afterward. So he had that going for him. If he broke the news, Krunk just might—*might*—believe his story. Krunk heard the news anywhere else, Dylan was sure both he and Webb would be dead mules within a day.

So. First, he had to make that call to Krunk. Mobile phone was out, and he probably should ditch it anyway. Figured he'd use a public phone somewhere. Café, bar, something like that. Out here in the sticks, you could sometimes still find pay phones mounted next to bar bathrooms, placed there so men who drank too much could call for a ride.

Not that men who drank too much in these parts ever did call for a ride. But the phones were there, just the same.

He gave up counting the fence posts beside the road (he'd gotten to 1,784 before giving up) and looked at the horizon ahead. A white cloudy sky met the ribbon of grimy highway in the distance. He separated his field of vision, subtracting the sky from his vision, leaving the land and highway in front of him. The straight road ahead split the bottom half of his view into two parts again, so he concentrated, erasing the land on the right side from his consciousness.

You're doing it again, Joni's voice said inside.

Doing what?

The kill box.

When Dylan had been in Iraq, the kill box referred to a specific zone targeted for massive attack. In the time since, Dylan had come to think of it as a dead zone inside his own mind—a zone where he sent any thoughts he wanted locked away. Memories of his time in Iraq, especially memories of the explosion that tore up his leg. Some memories of the rez. Most true memories of Joni. Even now, when the imaginary Joni inside his mind didn't want to shut up, he banished her to the kill box for a time.

Suppose I am.

Is it helping?

He smiled, took a deep breath. *Yeah. Yeah, it is. You should know.*

He felt her return the smile inside.

Whatever works, right?

Whatever works.

Where are you going? Joni asked.

You should know that too. You're inside my head.

I'm just trying to start a conversation here. Keep myself out of the kill box.

You never go to the kill box for being quiet.

Yeah. Well, I'm not exactly a quiet personality; that's why you keep me around.

Okay. We're heading to Malta.

Because?

Because I need to deal with Krunk. He finds out what happened, he's gonna send the goon squad after me.

I thought you were the goon squad.

Just a mule, Joni. Just a limping mule.

So Malta's the answer.

I don't know. Figure I can drop the drugs and the money there, get in touch with Krunk, maybe make him think I'm making a break for the Dakotas.

But you're not going to the Dakotas.

No. I'll double back west. Then maybe south.

To where?

Still working on that.

You could go the rez.

No, I can't. You know that. You of all people.

Okay, let's just concentrate on Malta.

That's what I'm trying to do, but you won't shut up.

Fine. Go back to your little subtractions, if you think those are so much better than talking to your sister.

No need. Only about five miles to go.

About?

Okay; 5.3 miles exactly, according to the odometer and the mileage posted on the last highway sign.

There we go; that's the obsessive-compulsive brother I know and love.

Joni went quiet, so he turned his mind back to planning. Drop the drugs, drop the money in Malta. Call Krunk. If Krunk had the contacts to trace his call—not really much of an *if* in Dylan's mind—it would be easy enough to trace his route. Just like he'd told Joni: maybe, just maybe, Krunk would think they were heading east, escaping to North Dakota and points beyond. Might give him a few days.

Dylan saw a building on the flat horizon: a squarish structure covered in barn wood, a large vinyl banner proclaiming WELCOME HUNTERS COLD DRINKS affixed to the outside.

Dylan wheeled into the parking area at the front of the building, coming to a stop beside the only other car: an old white Plymouth Acclaim with peeling paint.

He still hadn't seen any signage telling him the name of this particular bar or lounge, but it didn't really matter. Out here, they probably didn't even need a name; it wasn't like there was a lot of competition for the drinking dollars. With this location, they'd easily cater to those on-the-go outliers who couldn't hold their thirst another five miles until they got to Malta itself. Five miles less driving to town meant a one- or two-beer head start. And five fewer miles to drive back home, or wherever you were coming from.

"Be right back," Dylan said to Webb as he stepped out of the pickup.

Webb probably didn't hear; he was totally out of it, had been in a deep sleep ever since curling into a fetal ball. Dylan half wished the Percocets would still do that for him.

Snow, mixed with the red-clay mud of the parking area, stuck to Dylan's work boots as he opened the squeaky door on the front of the bar and entered the dark cave.

A guy behind the counter was reading a newspaper. He looked up, nodded, went back to reading the paper. Dylan tried not to pay any attention to the odor of stale beer that had soaked every inch of the place.

Dylan stamped his boots. "Need to make a phone call," he said.

"Back by the bathrooms," the guy behind the bar said, nodding his head toward the rear of the building.

Just as predicted.

16.

"I don't like the idea," Dylan said, staring at Webb. Webb had essentially moved into his house a few months ago without any real invitation. And that was okay; Dylan liked the company.

"'Course you don't like the idea," Webb said, not looking away from the television. "You don't like any idea. You're like Mikey, that kid who hates everything except Life cereal."

"What you're talking about isn't Life cereal."

Webb turned and looked at him for the first time. "No, it isn't. It's just a year's supply of happy pills for you, and a nice score in cash. Or would you rather keep hitting the open houses, trying to figure out which real estate agents haven't seen you blitzing through before?"

In the few months since they'd met, Webb had taken him on several open house raids, finding partial prescriptions left in medicine cabinets all over Billings. Dylan was amazed how many people kept old scrips in their homes, amazed he hadn't thought of it.

Equally amazed Webb had.

"I don't trust Krunk," Dylan said, trying to switch tactics a bit.

"Yeah. And I'm thinking of nominating him for a Nobel Peace

Prize. It's not about trusting him; it's just about making a quick trip to the border, making an exchange, then bringing it back. Couple grand for what really amounts to a night of work." Webb turned back toward the television. "Not like I haven't done it before."

Dylan knotted his eyebrows. "What do you mean?"

"I've known Krunk a couple years. Done errands for him before, now and then. He's fine."

Webb was the kind of guy who jumped into everything with both feet. That was interesting to Dylan, because really, he hadn't been around that kind of energy since Joni. It was vicariously invigorating, in a way, to be around someone who would do anything, anywhere, at a moment's notice. Freeing, in a way.

At the same time, Webb's spontaneity also meant recklessness. True, in the time since he'd known Webb, the man seemed to get away with everything. He lived a charmed existence, talking his way out of every sticky situation. Talking his way into every interesting opportunity. And he'd brought Dylan along for the ride.

Now, unless Dylan went along for this ride, made a drug exchange with some Canadians, Webb would do it alone.

Ever the protective big brother, Joni said.

And I'm so good at it. Look what it did for you.

"Okay," Dylan finally said. "Let's call Krunk and tell him I'm in."

Webb turned back and flashed his grin again. "Hey, we got this," he said.

"Yeah," Dylan said. "I just hope it doesn't get us."

17.

Quinn hated sleep, hated the idea of sleep, yes. But now, after meeting this guy who called himself Paul, after eating only a few bites of her breakfast, after feeling his hand on her arm and feeling her thoughts and feelings shift inside ... she almost *wanted* to sleep. Her mind was sharp, sharper than it had been for as long as she could remember. And a strange excitement danced inside, something like what she'd felt as a young child on Christmas morning, lying awake in her bed, wanting to rush into the living room and see the wonders but holding back because there was something special about that feeling.

Her mind, her core, were energized and revving. But her body felt drained. An odd mix of sensations.

After the breakfast, she'd stumbled back to a nearby hotel room with Paul—ha ha, wasn't that funny, because she'd said that was the last thing she'd ever do—but after their exchange in the restaurant, she knew he presented no danger. Instead, he presented ... newness. Something different.

"You okay?" Paul asked as he seated her in an ugly green chair near the room's dark television.

"Yes. No."

He smiled. "Natural reaction. We all feel it at first. It's like, inside you feel electric and alive. Outside, your body doesn't feel electric; it feels electrocuted."

"We?" she asked.

"I'm part of a group called the Falling Away. And I think you're next."

"Why do you think that?"

"Because you're meant to be. Because you were chosen."

"By?"

He smiled. "We'll get to that in a minute. Right now you're thinking, how does this guy know so much about me? About the way I feel, about the cutting, about everything inside? I know for two reasons. First, because I've been through it myself. Not exactly the same thing, but similar. So I know what it feels like to be standing where you are right now, feeling . . . well, like I said before: feeling like you've been electrocuted.

"In a way, that's what's happened: your body, your soul, has been through a literal shock to the system. It's been . . . I guess *purged* would be the right word for it."

"Purged?"

"Means it's been—"

"I know what purged means. I just graduated from high school, as you pointed out. What I don't know is what you mean by purged."

"I mean, you've been bottling up these emotions, these feelings of disgust and self-hatred and, well, sometimes rage. Rage against yourself, rage against others. It's a disease, Quinn, and I've pulled that disease out of you."

She eyed him, saying nothing. "And what's the second reason?" she asked.

"Hmm?"

"You said there were two reasons why you knew so much about my life. What's the second reason?"

"Oh," he said matter-of-factly. "God. God led me to you, and now He wants me to lead you to Him." He stood, went to the sink, peeled off the surgeon's gloves he was wearing. He washed his hands, lathering up his arms to the elbows, dried them with a towel he selected out of an open suitcase on the floor, produced fresh gloves, and put them on. Then he returned.

"That's it?" she said. "All of this for some quick give-your-life-to-Jesus spiel? As if that explains everything?"

"It's not a spiel, Quinn. It's . . . it's an awakening. God's chosen you to be part of the Falling Away, and has been preparing you for it since . . . well, since you were born. Only now, you're ready to find out. To discover why. That's why I'm here."

Quinn shook her head. She felt more tired than ever.

"You can't argue with the evidence inside you, Quinn. When I touched you, when I prayed for you, it drew out all that pain."

She nodded, weakly. Yes, she did have to admit that. It was the one reason she was in this room now; she'd felt . . . something. Even before she'd asked what he was doing, she knew inside that he was praying for her. And she knew that it was working. It had been physical. Real.

"When I prayed," Paul continued, "I drew that disease out of you, I drew it into me, you might say. And to help me cope with those thoughts, those emotions that were bottled up inside you, I have to go through my own . . . well, my own ritual." He held up his gloved hands. "You've been wanting to ask me about the gloves, haven't you?"

She nodded. Even that took physical energy she didn't have.

"I'm what you might call a germophobe. A clean freak. I don't like physical contact—which, in a funny way, makes it hard for me to do what I do. But the irony is, it also makes it possible for me to do what I do."

"And that is?"

"Ever read the Bible?"

"Not really."

"You're not alone. You'll find the Falling Away in Second Thessalonians: 'Let no one deceive you by any means; for that Day will not come unless the falling away comes first, and the man of sin is revealed, the son of perdition.'"

"I don't get it."

"Hang with me. That verse is talking about . . . well, it's talking about a lot of things. But the Day it refers to—the day that will not come unless the falling away comes first—is a right relationship with God. So the falling away, in the literal sense, is about us, as humanity, falling away from God. Falling away from what is right. Hitting bottom, if you will. That's happening all around us, and it's been happening since . . . really, since the beginning of mankind."

"I still don't get it."

"Okay, okay. The Falling Away is happening all around us, every day. Hatred, bitterness, pain: it's everywhere, because we live in a world that's cracked and broken. It's not meant to be this way. And we in the Falling Away are doing all we can to help repair those cracks and breaks."

"By?"

He sighed. "Well, that's the other part of the phrase, the other meaning of the Falling Away. We want people to see the reality of what's around them, open their eyes to what they should be seeing: a world that's hurting and needs redemption. We want the illusions of hatred and suffering to fall away, in a sense. Because falling away from the lies that surround us means falling into the hands of God. That's from Hebrews—"

"Okay, okay. I get it. You're a religious wing nut, telling me I just need to pray and everything will be all right."

"Oh, I didn't say everything will be all right. But let me finish. It's not what you're picturing; we don't lock arms and sing happy songs and talk platitudes. In the Falling Away, we're an army, down in the trenches. We're . . ." He paused, cleared his throat. "We're exorcists, in a sense."

Quinn laughed. "Exorcists? You're crazier than I thought."

"No, Quinn. It's the world that's crazier than you think. What I just did to you was, very literally, an exorcism: you've been carrying around your guilt and your pain and your suffering and your longing for your mother. Those are all symptoms of a spiritual disease. People get coughs and aches and pains, they're perfectly willing to take medicine to heal their physical bodies. But when they start having symptoms of spiritual disease, they ignore them. Because the world believes the lie that there's no such thing as spiritual disease."

"So how do you get this spiritual disease?"

"It's from the evil that's leaking into our world. It's from demonic activity—which is why I'm talking about exorcism."

"So I was possessed by demons?" She laughed; she couldn't help it.

"No. Possession is a whole other level. I'm saying the disease is spread by demonic activity. The demons are the source of the original infection, but they don't hop from human to human, possessing them. That's not the way it works. Especially because humans themselves are so good at spreading the infection."

"So you're saying demons are all around us."

"No, I'm not. I'm telling you we're surrounded by the spiritual disease they create. People think of angels versus demons as some kind of war going on, and that's not right at all. It's more like a virus, and you can be infected without ever coming into contact with a demon itself."

"I'm not buying."

"It's a lot to take in, I'll give you that. It seems so foreign, so wrong, so unbelievable. But that's because we live in a world that doesn't want to believe those things are possible. Which makes the disease so easy to spread."

"I think you've taken your germophobe thing to a whole new level. You need to talk to a psychiatrist or something."

"See, that's why I'm talking to you." He held up his gloved hands again. "These gloves, the germophobe thing you talk about—that's my compulsion. That's how I control the thoughts that try to take hold. That's how I ward off the disease. And you're the same. But you don't wash to relieve the pressure. You cut."

"I'm not immune; you just said it."

"No one's immune. But you can learn to control it, like I did. All of us in the Falling Away, we have these compulsions that help us filter out the evil, once we learn how to use them. It's that odd dichotomy, really: we're almost magnets for pain and suffering, but because we have ways to control it, there's a design to it all. Think of yourself: You've been homeless for four years. Your father walked out on you and your mother, and then your mother disappeared. That's more pain than most people go through in a lifetime. But once again: you're a magnet for it, because you were built to handle it. It might seem impossible, but—"

"But with God, all things are possible. Blah, blah, blah."

Paul smiled. "Matthew 19:26. And you said you never read the Bible."

18.

Dylan found the phone, a giant *JOE SUX* scratched into the black metal of its faceplate, and dialed his contact number for Krunk.

"Yeah?"

"Krunk. It's ... uh ... Dylan."

"Dylan. Where are you?"

Dylan closed his eyes, leaned against the cold metal surface of the phone. Was there an edge in Krunk's voice, or was he just being paranoid?

Probably just being paranoid. And OCD.

The plan had been for him and Webb to call Krunk when they were an hour outside Billings and arrange delivery of the drugs. Of course, that plan had been shot full of holes since it was made. Literally.

"I'm sorry, Krunk, but I'm having to improvise here."

There was a pause on the other end of the line. Dylan thought he could hear Krunk breathing, but it might have been the static of an old analog connection on an ancient pay phone.

"Improvise? You been reading a thesaurus?"

"We had a little problem on the exchange."

"Define 'little problem.'"

"Big."

"I'm listening."

"Our two—" Dylan paused, unsure how to continue. Did Krunk record his conversations? Possible. If not, it was also certainly possible the DEA or some other government agency was tapping his calls. Not that Dylan had any evidence of this, but the guy was probably the biggest mover of scrip drugs in the whole state of Montana. A fish that big, well, even the government would start smelling it after a time.

He backed up, started again. "Our friends from up north decided to change the terms of the deal at the last minute." He listened to the wheezy breathing for a few more seconds. Or static.

"What were their new terms?"

"Their new terms were, they wanted to take our money and keep their merchandise."

Dylan heard Krunk mutter something he didn't quite catch, followed by: "So what happened?"

"I . . . uh . . . couldn't accept those terms. So I did a bit of on-the-spot renegotiating. Unfortunately, Webb got caught in the negotiations, but he'll be fine." He winced, realizing he'd used his real name and Webb's real name on a phone call that was possibly being recorded. So much for his cloak-and-dagger skills. That's why he'd been an EOD tech in the army; he was better at working with his hands.

"So where are you now?"

"Ah . . . I'd prefer not to say."

"You'd prefer not to say, because . . ."

"You know why, Krunk. A deal like this goes sour, I end up with the money and the merch, a guy like you might start to suspect I was planning this all along."

"And were you?"

"I didn't want to do this, remember. I just tagged along to keep an eye on Webb."

Krunk drew in a deep breath. "Yeah, I remember."

"Even worse, your—ah—counterpart up north is probably going to assume the same. Think his boys were golden, no way they'd be trying to rock the boat. So he's gonna be looking for us. Which is why it's best not to be found."

"But if you really didn't do it, just come in and give me the money and the merch. I can smooth this over."

"Which is why I'm calling. I told you I didn't want any of this. So here's what's happening. There's a bar about five miles west of Malta, called the—" He turned, looked at the guy reading his paper behind the bar. Above the shelves holding bottles of liquor was a sign saying LIQUID LENNIE'S: FREE DRINKS TOMORROW.

Dylan cleared his throat. "There's a bar called Liquid Lennie's. Ever heard of it?"

"No."

"Well, you aren't alone. It's a little clapboard shack alongside Highway 2 on the Highline. One of those places for the local yokels and the hunters when they're in the field."

"Malta? What are you doing in Malta?"

"I'm not in Malta. But I was. Just shut up and listen."

Dylan could almost hear the wheels spinning inside Krunk's head. Good. If Krunk thought he was past Malta, he would likely think Dylan was heading east—maybe to the Dakotas. But Dylan wasn't going to continue to Malta or anywhere else east of here;

after this call, he would double back and head west. With any luck, Krunk would start casting his nets in the wrong direction.

"You go ask the guy behind the counter at Liquid Lennie's. He's keeping Webb's rucksack with your money, and the backpack."

"What's the guy's name?"

"Which guy?"

"The guy at Liquid Larry's."

"Liquid Lennie's. Don't know. Just have your guy tell him he's picking up something left by Dylan. He'll know what's happening."

"Okay."

"Now, Webb and I agreed to the delivery for two-and-a-half each. I took that out of the . . . uh . . . proceeds. Also, five hundred for some stuff I had to take care of with Webb, and a grand for the guy at Liquid Lennie's. But the rest is there, in Webb's rucksack."

Dylan paused, knowing Krunk was calculating in his mind; if he was any good with math (and Dylan was pretty sure Krunk knew his math), he knew there'd still be $43,500 left in the rucksack.

"Okay. I also took some merch—five packages total—to get me by." Five bottles of Percocet would be a typical five-month supply. It might last him four weeks, if he conserved. "But everything else, you're gonna find at Liquid Lennie's."

Krunk exhaled loudly, obviously not pleased with recent developments. "And you just left all this with the guy at Liquid Lennie's? Maybe Lennie himself? Who's to say he's not gonna run with it?"

"Guy's not stupid. You think he wants in the middle of this?" Dylan had no idea this was the case, not having talked to the guy behind the bar.

"You already brought him into the middle."

"I gave him a thousand bucks to hold on to a couple packages. That's how involved he is."

"He Indian?"

Dylan's turn to sigh. "Yeah, he's an Indian. Why, does it make a difference?"

"Not really."

Dylan waited, but Krunk had nothing else to add, so he continued. "I'll call you in a week, make sure we're square."

Krunk grunted on the other end of the line.

Dylan shifted, his injured leg getting sore from standing. "Look, Krunk, I didn't want any part of this. You know that."

"Yeah."

"And I went out of my way to make this drop, to call and let you know before you found out from—other people."

"Yeah."

"So I'm hoping you'll remember that. Keep me in the loop, give me a heads-up when you hear something."

A long pause on the line. Dylan turned and looked at the empty bar behind him. The man with the newspaper flipped the section he was reading and refolded it.

"Yeah," Krunk said. "You stay under a few weeks and check in. This works out the way you say, we're square."

After he heard the click of the call disconnecting, Dylan replaced the phone on its receiver and limped back to the counter. His leg was stiff. Might be time for a few more Perks when he got back to his truck.

He sat at the bar, waited for the guy reading to finish and make eye contact.

"What'll ya have, cousin?" the guy asked. His face was pock-marked, as if sandblasted by the constant wind of the high plains. Maybe it was. His hair was in two long braids, draped over a navy blue hooded shirt.

"Gimme a six of something to go."

"Coors?"

Dylan shrugged. "Yeah, that's good." One or two of the beers might take the edge off Webb when he got back to the truck—more from the familiar ritual and taste of beer than from any alcohol.

"Ask you for a favor?" Dylan said as the bartender pushed a paper bag with the beer in it toward him.

"Shoot."

Dylan flinched at the word, then did his best to recover and pulled ten hundred-dollar bills out of his pocket and put them on the counter. The bartender glanced at the cash, but didn't seem particularly moved; he locked gazes with Dylan once more.

"Guy's gonna come in here soon—maybe even today—asking for some packages left by Dylan. You turn them over for these ten bills."

The bartender's *Billings Gazette* was folded on the bar beside him, exposing a story on the front page about wolves in Yellowstone Park. He gathered up the bills, stuffed them into the front pocket of his hooded sweatshirt. "No problem."

"Two bags. I got 'em out in the truck."

The bartender picked up the paper again, made a show of reading the next story. "I'll lock 'em in the back."

Dylan pushed out the front door and reentered the bright white landscape outside, carrying the package of beer. He was surprised to see Webb up and awake in the front of the truck.

He opened the truck door and dropped the six-pack into Webb's lap.

Webb flinched, then cursed. "I got shot this morning, if you don't remember."

"I shot back, if you don't remember." Actually, Dylan had been the first one to pull the trigger, but this didn't seem the time to start splitting hairs.

Webb looked at him, his eyes watering a bit. "Yeah, I remember."

"Have a drink," Dylan said as he fished the antibiotic from his coat pocket. "Put some of this in it."

Webb held up the bag of powder and examined it. "What is this?"

"Antibiotic."

Webb pulled a can out of the brown bag, opened it, and gulped a few swallows. He wiped at his mouth with the sleeve of his good arm. "Rather have this antibiotic."

"Then give yourself a couple of shots. I'll be right back."

Dylan closed the door and pulled the backpack and rucksack from the truck bed. For a moment, he considered what to do with his .357. At some point, when the Canucks had been found, the gun would tie him to the scene of the crime. If he left the gun in the rucksack with the money, he'd be rid of any physical evidence that might put him there.

Other than blood from Webb, left on the ground.

But snow and wind would likely take care of that within a few hours. Probably had by now.

Still, if goons were going to come after them, and he knew in his heart they probably would, he might need the revolver, as well as the half box of ammo under his front seat.

Dylan sighed, draped the backpack over his shoulder, and picked up the rucksack. He left the revolver in the right pocket of the new coat Couture had given him. He couldn't give it up right now.

Inside, the bartender had finished his reading and was washing some glasses in a tub of soapy water. "Drag 'em back there," the bartender said, jerking his head toward the rear of the bar.

Dylan did as instructed and waited while the bartender came to the back, drying his hands with a towel. He pulled keys from his jeans pocket, studied them a few moments, selected one, and slid it into a padlock on the door. Like everything else inside the bar, the door was covered in old barn wood.

Inside the room were crates, cases of beer and liquor, a desk in the corner with sheaves of paper stacked on top.

"Be okay in here," the bartender said.

Dylan pushed the packs inside and backed out of the room. "Like I said, might be someone here as early as today."

The bartender watched him in silence for a few seconds, and Dylan realized he'd been unconsciously rubbing his hands on the front of his jeans. As if he could ever get those hands clean.

He stopped, ran his hands through his own close-cropped hair, stopped once again as the braided bartender looked at him.

"Surprised if they weren't," the bartender said as he relocked the padlock and turned to head back to the front of the building.

"Why's that?" Dylan asked, following.

"Guy pays me a grand to watch something, probably twenty times that in the package." The bartender was back behind the large bar now. "Today's economy, no one wants to leave twenty grand just lying around for long." He smiled for the first time.

Dylan nodded. This guy was about $30K off on his estimate, but he'd be all right. He knew how the real world operated. Still—

"Look," Dylan said. "I don't think you'll have any problems. Quick in, quick out. Just—"

"He white?"

"What's that?"

"The guy coming to get the packs—is he white?"

Dylan paused, considering. "I don't know who it will be, but I'm guessing he'll be white." Dylan had an odd sense of dèjá vu. "Why? Does it make a difference?"

The bartender smiled. "Might not make much difference to you, because you think you're white. But to me, yeah, it makes a difference. I'll be fine." The bartender returned to washing glasses that didn't need to be washed, so Dylan stepped outside.

Back in the pickup, Webb was working his way through a second beer.

"Careful," Dylan said as he started the truck and hit the wipers a few times to whisk away the flakes deposited on the windshield. "A lot of beer with those painkillers might be a bad mix."

"That's what I'm counting on," Webb said.

Dylan turned onto the road and wheeled them south on Highway 191. Webb looked out the window as they drove, staring at nothing. Mainly because there was nothing to stare at. Unless you counted snow. At least the highway was clear.

"You dropped the drugs and the cash."

Dylan glanced over, but he could only see the back of Webb's head. Webb had wrapped his good arm across his chest, gently supporting his wounded shoulder.

"Yeah," Dylan answered.

"And you called Krunk."

"Yeah."

"What'd he say?"

"About what you'd expect."

Webb shifted, grunting with the effort. "We coulda disappeared with that."

"Disappeared to where?"

"I don't know. But $50K and a bunch of drugs can buy a lot of magic."

"Not enough magic."

Webb was quiet for a few more minutes. "Krunk say anything about the Canucks?"

"Like what?"

"Like anything."

The windows were beginning to fog over a bit, so Dylan turned up the heat another notch.

"Said he'd let us know if he heard of something happening."

"And you think he will, him being such a thoughtful guy and all."

"Well, I don't much like the alternative."

"You're saying that like there is an alternative."

"That's my point: there isn't."

Webb let out a long sigh, popped open another Coors. He chugged half the can in a long draw, shifted in his seat again. "Could my life suck any worse?"

"I don't think you really want to know the answer to that."

19.

Andrew had parked his pickup in the lot for Fiddler's Foods in Harlem. He often parked here, because it was the one place in town where he could actually get two bars on his cell phone. In about half of Harlem he could pick up one bar; in the other half, no signal. But here, in this exact spot outside Fiddler's, he could pick up two bars.

And so, when he was waiting for a call on his cell phone while stuck in Harlem, he often parked here. Gave him a chance to show off his pickup, anyway.

But this waiting sucked. He'd waited here for—quick check of the dash clock—he'd waited for more than an hour now, and Doze still hadn't called with a location on Dylan's position. Dylan was now an hour away from him, and Andrew didn't know which direction. Maybe he should have just followed him.

Abruptly, the phone rang in his pocket. Had to be Doze.

He fished the phone out of his pocket, glanced at the number, smiled.

"Hello?" he said, pouring the sugar on his voice.

"Andrew," Krunk said.

"Well, Krunk. What a surprise. You hear from your boy Dylan?"

"Hmm? No, no. After we talked, I remembered I got something needs to happen over by Malta. Figured maybe you'd know someone."

"Malta?"

"Yeah. Some packages I need picked up."

"I know people in Malta."

"Someone who can get there soon, make sure I get those packages?"

"Of course."

"Okay. It's a bar called Liquid Lennie's."

Andrew smiled. "Liquid Lennie's. I know it."

"You get someone there, tell them to pick up the packages, call me right away."

"Your wish is my command."

Andrew hung up the phone, thought for a moment, started his pickup. He didn't buy Krunk's snow-job story about "remembering" something that needed to happen in Malta. He had a very good idea what the packages in Malta were and where they'd come from. Dylan was being a bit more clever than he'd ever given him any credit for; he'd dropped the money and drugs in Malta, called Krunk to break the news about the deal, played the old "I'm being straight with you" routine, told Krunk to find the stuff in Malta.

And Krunk, soft as he was, stupid as he was, had called Andrew right back.

Dylan's present had just become the gift that keeps on giving.

He could be in Malta soon.

20.

Alone in a stall of the restroom at Eddie's Corner, Quinn studied the paper clip.

Quinn had left Great Falls right after Andrew's call, before the pressure inside—caused by Greg's cleansing—could be released. And so, during the drive to Eddie's Corner, Quinn had been forced to listen to the whispered voices, the lies drawn from Greg's mind. Distracting, because what Quinn really wanted to listen to was the police scanner, hoping to pick up something about a red Ford Ranger.

Not that Quinn wanted, specifically, to hear mention of Dylan's truck. That would mean Dylan was causing even more ripples. Ripples that could work their way back to the HIVE.

So in a way, it was good that Quinn was here in the restroom at Eddie's Corner, an odd outpost/convenience store/truck stop in central Montana. It meant there were no mentions of Dylan on the traffic scanner. It meant, maybe, there was time to stop Dylan and Webb.

It meant Quinn could stem the pressure, the constant pressure, building inside.

The paper clip wavered in her hand for a few moments.

Most people might think it would be too difficult, too painful, to embed bits of metal beneath your skin. Paper clips. Staples. Broken bits of glass. Even small nails.

But Quinn knew this was not true. Pain was an illusion, a cruel parlor trick meant to keep you from seeing what was truly behind the curtain. Pain turned your focus inward, if you let it, kept you from seeing truth. Pain, in the right context, was cleansing. That's what the embedding was all about.

That's what the Falling Away was all about. Quinn's purpose, Quinn's reason for existing.

After sucking the disease from someone else's body, after uttering the cleansing prayers, your own skin was bloated, rotten from the sickness. Embedding brought down the swelling, relieved the pressure. It released the true pain—the deep, dark pain of lies—and reset your body. Made you sharp and clear. Prepared you for the next assignment.

Quinn had discovered the need for release long ago, while still on the streets of Portland. At the beginning, simple cuts were enough: nicks on the flesh, usually the stomach or the upper arms, sometimes the legs. Just a quick slice, nothing too deep, and the pressure came draining out. The world around you reset. Colors returned, everything came into focus.

But the cutting had opened a deeper vein, hadn't it? A vein that led her to Paul. Or more appropriately, led Paul to her. He showed Quinn that the compulsion inside could have a purpose outside.

The rest of society, Quinn had learned, knew nothing of the Falling Away. They only lived in the Fall. Which was what made them so susceptible. They walked around in their everyday existences, constantly complaining about finances and jobs and stress and pressure. Eventually they grew to hate their lives, hate themselves, and that's what opened them to the disease.

But society in general didn't know anything about the transforming power of true pressure. Not even close.

Quinn had seen a movie about deep-sea divers around the time the cutting became necessary, after panhandling a couple bucks on the street. It had been cold and rainy on the streets of Portland that day, and the movie theater held the promise of darkness and warmth for a few hours. And it had always been easy to get into the theater; more than once, she'd slipped past the kid at the ticket counter.

On the screen, these divers, these men and women, sank to the depths in giant suits made of armored metal; the suits were necessary because the pressure of their surroundings, thousands of feet beneath the surface of the ocean, would crush a normal human body. Without the diving suit, the body would just collapse, fold in upon itself.

Quinn had felt a certain camaraderie with the deep-sea divers, instinctively knowing, as the movie progressed, that it was possible to feel that kind of bone-crushing pressure above sea level. In fact, it was quite possible to have that kind of pressure build up inside you, threaten to inflate your skin to hideous, balloonlike proportions, and eventually make you explode. The opposite of deep-sea divers, really; for them, the outside pressure threatened to collapse their bodies. For Quinn, the inside pressure was the danger. Maybe someday, without a deep-sea diving suit, Quinn could just sink beneath the surface of the ocean. Find the equalization depth, the perfect balance between the ocean's pressure and Quinn's own body pressure.

Cutting had been the only way. At least to start. After a time the cuts weren't enough; maybe they were too superficial, too easy. Deep cuts didn't seem to do any better, and Quinn instinctively knew this was . . . dangerous. Quinn wasn't crazy, not in that huge, put-me-in-a-padded-room-because-the-little-green-guys-are-out-to-get-me way. Only in this small way. Quinn knew when the cuts were going too deep, going too far.

One day, working at the ankle with a pocketknife (Quinn didn't know why—the ankle was a bad place to cut, because it was all bone), the tip accidentally broke off beneath the skin. Just a nick of the tip, really.

Quinn had stared at the knife, stared at the oozing wound . . . and felt the pressure deflating. Almost heard it leaking away.

That had lasted a couple months, much longer than any of the superficial cuts had ever lasted. So when the pressure became overwhelming again, when it threatened to swallow everything, Quinn found a staple, flattened it, and pushed it into the fleshy part of the left palm, just beneath the thumb. Once again, the pressure began to equalize, almost instantly.

It had been all embedding since then.

The voices inside began to cycle to a higher volume, individual lies combining to form waves that crashed over Quinn's mind, threatening to drown it completely.

Quinn had to find Dylan, neutralize him before he was discovered by HIVE, because Dylan entering the HIVE was far more dangerous than any of the mindless drones the community spat out. But first, she had to relieve the pressure.

Quinn began to unfold the paper clip.

21.

Just past Lewistown, Dylan started mapping his next route. He had options, limited as they were, from here. South . . . well, that would take him toward Billings. Too expected. Probably better to continue west toward Great Falls. He knew a couple people there; maybe he could get in touch with them, find a way to hole up for a few days.

Sure, he'd dropped the money and drugs. He'd even told Krunk, truthfully, where to find them. But he didn't believe for a second Krunk would just leave it at that. Or whoever got hinked on the deal in Canada.

That's why it was important for Krunk, or anyone connected with Krunk, to think he was running east. Then they wouldn't be looking for him in Great Falls. Yeah, Great Falls would be good.

If they could just get somewhere safe, somewhere underground, for a few days, they might have a chance to figure out their next steps.

"You gonna stop at Eddie's Corner?" Webb asked, yawning. Some of the color had returned to his face.

"For what?"

"I don't know. For a few minutes."

Something caught Dylan's eye in the rearview mirror, and he glanced at it, frozen by what he saw there. "I think we're going to be stopping a lot sooner than that."

Behind them, a Montana Highway Patrol cruiser was flashing its lights, signaling them to pull over.

Webb turned and looked, then groaned. "This day just keeps getting better and better."

"What happened to Mr. Glass Half-full?"

"The glass got shot this morning."

Dylan pulled to the side of the road, activated his emergency flashers, watched as the trooper opened his car door.

Dylan rolled down his window as the trooper approached.

"License, registration, and insurance, please," the trooper said as he bent and looked through the window. All business. The trooper was tall and thin, face marked by acne scars, hair shaved military-style under the wide-brimmed hat that was part of the uniform.

A soldier wannabe, Dylan guessed immediately. Good chance he'd tried to join up at some point, but had been rejected for poor eyesight or some physical condition before sliding to plan B at the patrol academy. Dylan knew this type pretty well, had run into more than a few of them in bars around Billings. When he started chatting with them and they found out he was a vet, they were always good for a few drinks. The kind of guys who said "thank you for your service" with every round and regaled you with the stories of their own coulda shoulda woulda, if they'd only been allowed to serve their country.

Mostly harmless, in a bar setting. But they tended to gravitate toward law enforcement, border patrol, maybe even security guards. They had a serious need for any position that let them wear a uniform. They craved the authority it represented because it slaked their internal insecurities. By wearing the clothes of a person who was Large and In Charge, they themselves would grasp control, power, and respect.

Their fatal flaw, of course, was an overarching need to be liked by others in uniform. Maybe Dylan could use that to his advantage.

"Anything wrong, sir?" he asked. "I don't think I was speeding."

"License, registration, and insurance," the patrolman repeated, leaning to get a better look at Webb.

"Sure, sure," Dylan said. He leaned across the seat, felt his seat belt holding him back, unbuckled it, and opened the glove compartment in front of Webb, fishing out the license and registration. He handed them to the trooper. "Had this pickup since high school, you know," he said, trying to make casual conversation. "Sat for a couple years while I was in the army. Couldn't just get rid of it after I was discharged."

The trooper was studying the registration and insurance, and didn't rise to the bait. "Can I see your license?" he asked without looking up.

"Sure, sure." Dylan retrieved his wallet from his back pocket, pulled it out of the sleeve, and handed it to the trooper.

The trooper studied Dylan's license behind his dark sunglasses, the lenses clouding with each breath from his slightly opened mouth. In this kind of cold you didn't just breathe through your nose; if you did, your nasal passages became tunnels of ice.

"You're a vet, then?" he said, looking at Dylan. Or so Dylan thought; it was difficult to know with those big sunglasses.

Bingo. "Yeah. One tour of duty in Iraq. One Purple Heart." Dylan smiled. The Purple Heart was a good bit; it would be the hook that landed the trooper.

"Hold tight for a moment, gentlemen," the trooper said finally.

"I'll be right back." He returned to his cruiser, obviously wanting to run a check on Dylan's license and paperwork.

"You weren't speeding," Webb said slowly. "Your reg and insurance legit?"

"Of course."

"No outstanding warrants for me. You?"

"No. No outstanding warrants."

"We're golden then. We just play it cool . . . if you have to, let him say we were speeding and pay the ticket so he hits his monthly quota."

"Don't think we're looking at a speeding ticket," Dylan said, watching the patrolman's activities in the rearview mirror. He was still on his radio.

"Yeah. Fine. Whatever. We're still golden."

Dylan shook his head. "Look at the floor, genius."

Webb's gaze dropped to the floor, where the torn and muddy paper bag from the bar now held just two cans of Coors. Webb had dropped each of the four empties on the floor in plain sight.

Dylan saw him pause, as if trying to catch a whiff of alcohol. Pretty hard not to. "No big deal," Webb said. "I'm the one drinking—you haven't had any. That's why you're driving."

Dylan shrugged.

"So you don't think you have one of those trustworthy faces," Webb said.

Dylan wasn't sure if he detected any sarcasm in the statement, but he answered anyway. "I think I got a face that's Indian, right on a driver's license next to an Indian name: Dylan Runs Ahead. The military service might do us some good—that's why I hit it pretty hard. But I'll bet you money this patrolman grew up on a farm somewhere in the middle of nowhere, and I'll also bet he didn't have many Indians in his close circle of friends."

"You're not drunk. I'm not even drunk."

"No, but that doesn't keep him from giving me a field sobriety test. Or, if he wants, hauling us into Lewistown for blood tests. Maybe no DUI, but it's hard to get away from a DWI."

"DWI?"

"Driving While Indian."

Webb paused. "Even so, you haven't been drinking. So you're good." As if repeating the same line over and over gave it more force.

"Well, Webb, we got some scrip bottles from Canada stashed in here, couple thousand in cash. You got some antibiotics for pigs, along with a gunshot wound in your shoulder. I got a .357 in my pocket, and I'm sitting on a box of ammo."

Dylan heard Webb's breathing stop for a few seconds, then return at a faster pace.

"No, no, no," he said. "We're okay." But he didn't sound okay.

In the rearview mirror, the trooper had stepped out of his cruiser and was walking back toward the truck.

"Yeah," Dylan said as he watched the patrolman approach. "Everything's great." He rolled down his window once more, looked at the patrolman.

"Can you step out of the car, please?" the patrolman asked.

Well. So much for Dylan's amateur psychoanalysis of the trooper. The whole vet thing hadn't made any difference at all. Or if it did, it hadn't made as much difference as the Indian thing.

"Sure, sure. What, exactly, is the problem?"

"I see some empty beer cans in vehicle, sir. That gives me probable cause to administer a sobriety test."

"It does," said Dylan amiably. "But I can demand a blood test."

The patrolman seemed to rock on his heels for a few seconds. "That means we go to Lewistown."

"You do your field sobriety test, you'll just decide you want to haul me into Lewistown for processing anyway." Dylan smiled. "I'll wait for the blood test and save us some trouble."

Dylan now sensed the proper handle for the particular trooper, and it wasn't the handle he'd first envisioned. Trooper Evans, as his name badge indicated, had probably confirmed Dylan was an honorably discharged vet when he ran his license, and that hadn't made any difference in his demeanor. He was your basic By-the-Book Guy. By-the-Book Guys were always concerned about their own record of conduct.

Dylan went for the throat. Nothing to lose. "Can you tell me, Trooper Evans, why you pulled us over this morning?"

"Speeding." Patrolman Evans scratched at his nose. Classic behavior for a lie.

"I don't think so," Dylan said. "I bet you didn't have your radar on, but even if you did, we were safely under the limit, especially with the conditions. I think your dash cam will probably back me up on that."

Trooper Evans glanced back at his cruiser, then back to Dylan's face again, eyes still hidden by the dark lenses of his sunglasses. Probably thinking about the dash cam in his car, which automatically recorded every stop he made. Probably wishing the cam wasn't recording this particular stop.

"I think," Dylan continued, "maybe you saw an Indian behind the wheel of a pickup, and you thought you'd make a stop based on that. Don't know what they call that in highway patrol circles, but my attorney likes to call that racial profiling."

He paused, and the patrolman ran a slow hand across his mouth.

"So, you tell me, Trooper Evans. You think you got probable cause, I demand a blood test. We can all head to Lewistown, and you can do a blood test and find out I don't have a drop of alcohol in my system, and then I think I'll have pretty good cause to call my attorney. Or we can all forget this ever happened, and the problem goes away for everyone."

Trooper Evans took a deep sigh, looked down the empty highway ahead of them. He crouched down a bit farther, looked at Webb, who had gone as white as the snow swirling outside the windows.

"Okay," the patrolman finally said. He handed back the license, registration, and insurance card. "Thank you for your service," he said icily. He tapped the roof of the pickup and turned to walk back to his cruiser.

Without waiting, Dylan wheeled out onto the highway and accelerated. No need to wait around for the patrolman to rethink his position. Or to get mad enough to forget reasoning. Bubbas like that weren't always the most logical creatures.

Webb breathed for the first time in five minutes. "Thought you were going to get us shot there."

Dylan smiled. "Too late for you," he said.

"Funny. You're a regular Jim Carrey."

Dylan glanced in his rearview mirror, watching the patrol car fade behind them.

Webb made a show of picking up his Coors empties and putting them back in the paper sack, maybe just to keep himself occupied. Dylan noticed he kept his injured right arm close to his body, not using it, but not seeming to grimace too much.

"So what now?" Webb asked after he pushed the empties under the seat.

"Good question. I'm open for suggestions."

"Gotta lay low."

"I know."

They drove in silence for a few minutes, light snow swirling around them. Even though the empties were under the seat now, Dylan could still smell the sharp tang of beer in the cab—a smell that gave him no desire for a drink. Oddly, though, it made him crave another Percocet. Or two. He briefly considered fishing the bottle out of his pocket and popping a few pills to take off the edge, but resisted. For now.

"Can't be with anyone we know—we'll be too easy to find," Webb ventured.

"I know."

"So where's that leave us?"

"Right where we are."

22.

Andrew stepped through the front door of Liquid Lennie's and looked around. Two guys bellied up to the bar, getting in their morning quota. Behind the bar sat Eddie, reading the newspaper. Probably for the third or fourth time of the day.

He approached the bar, nodded. "Eddie."

Eddie looked up from his paper. "Andrew. What brings you over this direction? Not your usual paper route."

Andrew nodded at the *Billings Gazette*, folded and refolded on the counter. "Looks like you're already a happy subscriber, anyway. I'm actually here to pick up something."

Eddie barely registered a reaction. "From Dylan?"

Bingo. "Yeah. From Dylan."

"Come on back." Eddie led him to the back of the bar, unlocked a door, showed him the rucksack and backpack on the floor.

"Well," Andrew said. "Looks like Dylan was planning to do a little hiking in the wilderness. Maybe the weather caused him to change his plans."

"Surprised you're here for the pickup, cousin."

He looked at Eddie. "Why are you surprised? You know I get around. I have business over this direction. Not always over to take care of it myself, but you know, sometimes you go the extra mile. Give it that personal touch." He slipped the rucksack over his shoulder, picked up the pack, heard the contents shifting inside.

"Well," Eddie said, "this Dylan guy said he figured a white boy would swing by to pick up this stuff."

"You know the White Man, Eddie. Can't ever trust him."

Eddie laughed, followed him out of the back room, locked the door again.

"I'll be right back," Andrew said. He hefted the bags out the front door, barely raising an eyebrow on the regulars' faces. As if people walked through this bar all the time lugging backpacks.

Andrew locked the merchandise in the front of his Ram, turned, and went back inside.

"Any mobile phone reception around here, Eddie?" he asked.

Eddie shrugged. "Here and there. Mostly there."

"Okay, I'm just gonna make a call in the back here, then." He went to the pay phone by the restrooms, picked up the receiver, punched in the code for his calling card, and rang Krunk's number.

"Hello?"

"Krunk. Andrew here."

"Whatcha got?"

"Well, that's just the thing. I got nothing. My contact in Malta went to Liquid Lennie's just like you said, called me back, cussed me out for playing a joke on him."

"A joke?"

"Said the bartender told him there wasn't any kinda package waiting for anybody. Thought I was pulling a fast one on him. I know the bar, so I made some calls, got in touch with Eddie—guy who tends bar there, and happens to be on shift right now—and he told me the exact same thing. So, what gives? You trying to trick your friendly neighborhood Indian Andrew, make him chase his tail? You made me look bad."

On the other end of the line he heard Krunk's heavy, phlegmy breath quickening. Andrew turned, nodded at Eddie behind the bar.

"Okay, Andrew. Sorry about the mix-up. I'll take care of it."

The line clicked dead.

This was working out very well for Andrew indeed. Soon Dylan would use his cell phone, and Doze would track it. Doze would call him, let him know where Dylan was. Then he would turn Krunk loose on Dylan, but when Krunk killed Dylan, he wouldn't find any of the money or the drugs. Mainly because they were sitting in the front seat of his pickup.

After that, he'd just make another quick call to Prince Edward up in Canada, tell him Krunk had found Dylan, taken the money and junk from him. Sit back and watch the fireworks fly.

It was perfect, all so perfect. And all Andrew had to do right now was drive back home to Great Falls and wait for all the pieces to fall into place.

23.

Quinn turned the defrost knob another notch on the ancient green Plymouth Satellite, trying in vain to keep the cold from seeping into the vehicle's many cracks and leaks.

Sure, Quinn could choose a new vehicle. Something white and nondescript—a Toyota Camry or a Ford Taurus—that was forgettable and therefore invisible. Certainly it would make sense, considering what she did. But Quinn held on to the aging Satellite; the old bit of Mopar Muscle was solid, despite its many age-related flaws and odd color. She couldn't just abandon it, leave it to rot into nothingness.

Quinn turned up the volume and adjusted the squelch on the police scanner, making it easier to hear over the roar of the defroster.

Dylan was on the run, for sure. If he went east to the Dakotas, or even north to Canada (something Quinn doubted), it would take her a few days to find the trail and catch him. Bad.

But if he were headed anywhere else, he would probably go through Eddie's Corner. At the intersection he'd be able to turn south, catch the I-90, or head farther west to the heavy woods of western Montana. So really, sitting and waiting at Eddie's Corner was all she could do today. Maybe, just maybe, it would be a matter of the right place at the right time.

She had been listening to all the emergency frequencies, hoping for anything that might offer a clue. None had come in the forty-five minutes since she'd been here at Eddie's Corner. Another hour, at the most, Quinn would have to assume Dylan was headed east, try to track him into the Dakota Badlands.

The scanner emitted a burst of static, followed by a man's voice calling dispatch. Quinn listened, picking up the letters MHP from the transmission. Montana Highway Patrol. A plate check on a red Ford Ranger.

A red Ford Ranger. Quinn smiled, turned the defrost down a notch to hear the scanner clearly. The trooper listed his location as five miles west of Lewistown on 191/87. That was only a few miles away. Yes, they were running Quinn's direction . . . just an hour or two behind her guesstimation. A detour? A stop? No matter. There would be time to find that out later.

Depending on how long the trooper took to issue a speeding ticket, Dylan was within twenty minutes of Eddie's Corner. Smiling, Quinn eased the Satellite into gear, wheeled out of the parking lot, and headed east. She didn't want to wait and meet them at Eddie's Corner, where truckers and locals congregated; it would be too . . . messy . . . to work in front of an audience like that. Better to meet Dylan on the road.

And ironically, it would all happen within just a few miles of the HIVE community.

Crazy how life worked sometimes.

24.

Dylan and Webb passed a sign telling them they were five miles from the junction with Highway 3. Eddie's Corner. The last several miles, since just before they'd hit Lewistown, the snow had become heavier; it had slowed them down on the way into Lewistown, but since turning west and heading for Eddie's Corner, the road had cleared. Evidently the snowplows were working this section, which was probably why Friendly Trooper Evans had been working it as well.

Ahead of them, a car's emergency flashers began to resolve in the haze of snow. The first car they'd seen on this lonely stretch since leaving the patrol car a few miles back.

They both stared, slitting their eyes to get a better view as they approached. The car, an odd green seventies-vintage four-door, was parked on the other side of the road, its hood up and the driver's door hanging open.

Dylan slowed as they came closer to the vehicle.

"What are you doing?" Webb asked.

"I'm gonna stop, see if anyone needs help."

"Yeah, we're regular Dudley Do-Rights. Whenever we're not transporting thousands of dollars in drugs or shooting people."

Dylan ignored Webb and kept a light foot on the brake. Behind the open door of the puke-green vehicle, a figure came into view: someone on hands and knees, hunched over as if in pain.

"Great," Webb said. "Looks like someone had a bit too much barley soda, and now his stomach is hitting reverse."

A puddle of pink stained the snow in front of the figure, wrapped in a hooded black parka. Webb was probably right.

But just as Dylan thought it would be better to drive away from this mess, not get involved with someone who'd brought this upon himself with too much liquor, the figure lifted its head.

A woman's face peered at them, blood streaming down her forehead. Dylan instantly realized the snow on the ground was stained pink from the woman's blood, not vomit.

Once again, scenes of Iraq came flooding back. How many people had he seen, soldiers and civilians, bloody and injured in the pothole-laden streets of Baghdad? Too many.

The woman raised her hand to them in a weak plea for help, tried to stand, slipped to the ground again.

"I think she's hurt," Webb said. Captain Obvious.

"Yeah. You still just wanna drive by?"

Webb stayed quiet as Dylan pulled the truck to a stop and opened his door. "Hey," he said, looking at the woman. All he could see was the top of her head now, the dark hood, as she hunched in the snow on all fours. She offered no response; she might not have heard him over the wind. He raised his voice. "You okay?"

She turned her face to Dylan, fixed an oddly vacant stare on him. "Yeah. I . . . I don't know what happened."

Dylan stepped out of the pickup, walked across the pavement.

Maybe it had been plowed recently, but new snow was already laying white fingers across the road in small drifts. "You must have had an accident. Looks like you hurt your head."

He kneeled beside her, moved slowly, touched her shoulder. He knew from experience that you didn't just walk up to an injured person and start pressing and prodding. Often, pushed into a momentary panic by injuries, people started flailing, creating more injuries for themselves. Or you. It was dangerous, in the way that trying to save a drowning person can be dangerous. One wrong move and you could be pulled under.

"You're probably in shock," he said.

She flinched at his touch, but made no move to push away his hand. She put her hand to her head, came away with a bit of blood on her ungloved fingers, stared at it intently for a few seconds. To her credit, the sight of her own blood didn't seem to be pushing her over the edge.

Dylan had been examining the scene, and nothing seemed to fit together. The woman's head injury and the broken-down car seemed to be pieces from different puzzles. Looking at scenes such as this, analyzing what had happened, came naturally to him now; programming that had been drilled into his brain after hundreds of missions in Iraq. You looked for things that didn't fit.

"Can you remember what happened?" he asked.

She shook her head. "I . . . car stalled, so I pulled over to take a look and . . . can't remember."

He looked at the open hood. "Epilepsy?" he asked, thinking she might have had a seizure, hit her head.

She shook her head, stared at the ground again.

"Diabetic?"

"No."

Okay. Maybe she'd accidentally hit her head with the hood while opening it. Old cars like this tended to get a bit of rust in the metal, became harder to work.

But if that had happened, why wasn't she still out by the hood? Maybe she'd crawled back to her door?

"I . . ." she said. "Maybe you could give me a ride. We're pretty close to Eddie's Corner, I think."

"Yeah, yeah. Sure. You've probably got a mild concussion—you'll want to get checked by a doctor. You never ignore head injuries."

"Okay," she said. "If you can just help me to your truck."

"Yeah. Just take my arm." She looped her arm through his as he started to guide her across the highway.

"Dylan," Webb shouted from his pickup.

Dylan looked at Webb, still perched in the front seat of the pickup, and followed his gaze to the road behind them. In the distance, a vehicle was approaching. After a few seconds, Dylan recognized it: the highway patrolman. Friendly Trooper Evans.

This initially struck Dylan as good news, a rare bit of fortune in this already-long day. Trooper Evans could take over, get the woman some medical attention. They could continue on to . . . whatever they were continuing on to.

But as the cruiser flashed its lights, as Dylan took stock of his current situation, he knew that was all just wishful thinking. Trooper Evans didn't need a possible DUI to haul them back to Lewistown now. He had an injured motorist, and good reason to think the motorist had been injured in an accident or near-accident with Dylan's pickup. He had more than enough, racial profiling or not, to haul them to Lewistown, and Dylan was quite sure Trooper Evans would be more than happy to take that chance. Especially now.

The woman, for her part, had stopped when she saw the patrol car's red and blue lights strobing. She gazed at the approaching vehicle as she and Dylan stood, arm in arm, in the middle of the highway.

Time seemed to stop as the highway patrolman rolled up behind the pickup. His door opened, and Trooper Evans crouched to the ground behind the door, gun drawn.

"Everybody just stay right where you are," Trooper Evans said.

"No problem," Dylan called.

"Ma'am," Trooper Evans shouted. "If you'd just step away."

"I—it's okay," she stammered. "He's going to—"

"I have reason to believe these two men are dangerous. Please step away."

"No, no," she said. "You don't—"

"Step away now," Trooper Evans interrupted, more forcefully.

The woman looked at Dylan, then down at the ground. He heard her mutter something under her breath, then raise her own hands and begin walking toward Trooper Evans. She moved steadily, forcefully. The hesitation, the confusion she'd exhibited, drained away instantly.

One more piece of the puzzle that didn't fit.

"Okay, ma'am. If you'll walk this way, please step behind me and get in the backseat of my vehicle." The trooper's gun was still trained on Dylan, who stood in the roadway with his hands on his head.

She approached Trooper Evans, walked behind him.

"I'm sorry, ma'am," Trooper Evans said, his gaze and his gun never wavering from Dylan. "I can see you've been injured by these men, and I'll be able to offer medical assistance once we have them in custody. I called for backup already."

"Look, Trooper Evans," Dylan tried. He noted that the woman, now behind Trooper Evans, had not entered the car as instructed. Instead, she stared at Dylan, the blood on her face now beginning to dry and crack in the strong Montana wind.

Trooper Evans, obviously caught in the heat of the moment, hadn't noticed her movements behind him. He was too focused on what was in front of him. Too focused on showing Dylan who was boss after all.

"What would your attorney call this, sir?" Trooper Evans said. "I'd say this is very probable cause, wouldn't you? I'd say there may be a few things in that pickup of yours you don't want me to see. Some dope, even."

"I'm trying to cooperate," Dylan shouted.

"Then drop to your knees."

Dylan did as instructed.

"Now, to the other gentleman inside the pickup," he said. "If you'll step out of the vehicle slowly, and—"

As Trooper Evans spoke, Dylan watched the woman. She nodded at him, almost imperceptibly, then dropped to her knees and overtook the trooper, cutting him off in midsentence. Dylan heard the sounds of a struggle, then saw the trooper's weapon clatter across the pavement of the road. Immediately after, the trooper's legs began flailing beneath the car door.

He didn't wait any longer. When the woman refused to get into the patrol car, he started realizing why the woman's stalled vehicle and her injury were two puzzle pieces that didn't fit. By the time the woman attacked the trooper, he'd figured out that this woman was an elaborate trap to get him and Webb. Krunk, maybe the Canadians, someone, had put her on their trail. And he'd come dangerously close to escorting her into his own pickup.

He scrambled into the open door, slammed it shut, and slipped the truck into gear. Any moment, he half expected to hear gunshots, but none came.

Spinning the tires, he angled the pickup onto the roadway and watched the scene behind begin to recede.

In that scene, caught in his rearview mirror, the woman ran from the patrol car to her own. A few moments later her car executed a three-point turn and began to follow them. He saw no movement or sign from Trooper Evans, only the thrum of the cruiser's lights alternating red and blue, the headlights winking on and off in a steady pattern.

Webb was babbling gibberish Dylan couldn't understand, and the headlights on the green car chasing them were flashing, as if signaling them to stop.

Yeah. Like he was going to do that.

Dylan went as fast as he dared in the conditions, but she was steadily gaining on them; the green puker obviously had some old Detroit V8 power under the hood. His Ranger was just a 4-banger, and she obviously had little regard for the snowy road.

"Shut up," he said to Webb, mainly because it was the only thing he could do to control the situation that was increasingly spinning out of control around him. Falling snow raced by their windows vertically as he pushed the speedometer past eighty. Not exactly ideal conditions to be hitting eighty, but the highway was a straight shot through this area, and a thin layer of fresh sand even coated the road surface for traction.

Fresh sand, Joni's voice said in his mind. *That's a good sign.*

How so?

Had to come from somewhere, didn't it? Think about it.

Dylan looked at the roadway ahead, created an imaginary line where the yellow line of the highway would be if it were visible; he colored the left half of his field of vision black inside his mind, as if subtracting it from view, then divided the right half of his vision into two halves itself.

I said think about it, not do your psycho kill box stuff.

This is how I think. I—

And suddenly, he saw what Joni was talking about.

"We can't outrun her," Webb said, interrupting his internal conversation with Joni.

"I know."

"So what are you doing?"

Dylan tapped his brakes, felt the pickup slide a bit before the tires gripped. Behind him the woman hit her brakes and slid as well.

No go. Would have been too easy to get her to slide off the road with such a simple maneuver. He had four-wheel drive, which helped his traction, but was also a detriment: it brought down his top speed dramatically. If he ran this fast for much longer, he'd likely drop his drive train on the highway.

He slammed the pedal down farther and did his best to ignore the speedometer. They were going way too fast for conditions, way too fast for his old Ranger. The stench of panic filled his nostrils, a stench he recognized from his tour of duty in the sandy desert. But just as quickly, he pushed it back down. When you were EOD, panic only got you killed. This situation was no different.

The puke-green car started to pull up beside them, and Dylan recognized what the woman intended to do: if she could bump into the pickup at just the right spot, behind his door, she could spin them out of control. Her own car, heavy early-seventies Detroit iron, would win that battle over his lighter half-ton pickup with no payload in the back.

Dylan hit the brakes again, harder this time, and the woman overshot the pickup, glancing across their front bumper and sliding sideways in the middle of the road.

The front of the pickup arced to the right as Dylan felt the tires on the right side come off the ground for an instant. He corrected and turned into the swerve—the opposite reaction for most drivers—and felt the pickup right itself. Punching the gas again, he regained speed and passed the green car as it came to a stop backward on the highway.

Somehow the woman had managed to stay in the road. Dylan caught a glimpse of her bloody face, her vacant eyes, as he sped by. Behind him, the woman wasted valuable seconds getting her car turned again before giving chase once more.

Just as she started to gain ground, Dylan saw what he'd been hoping for: ahead of them, the hulking form of a giant MDT snowplow pushing snow off the roadway in a giant plume while throwing down sand behind it.

Hallelujah, said Joni in his mind.

Amen, he answered. *Think it'll work?*

No.

Thanks for the vote of confidence.

Dylan pulled up behind the snowplow, blinded by the billow of snow leaping from the giant blade.

"You're gonna hit him!" Webb screamed. But at the last moment, calculating the distance of the woman closing the gap, Dylan slipped out into the passing lane.

He hoped no vehicles were approaching from the opposite direction. If there were, he'd drive into a head-on collision; this chase would end suddenly and messily. But would that be so bad? Problem solved.

He saw the surprised plow driver through the windshield, gesticulating wildly as they passed.

Dylan floored the gas to get around the plow as quickly as possible, relieved to see no other vehicles on the horizon as he broke the plane of cascading snow from the plow's blade. He popped back over into the right lane just ahead of the plow, took a breath, and hit his brakes hard again.

Behind him, the driver of the snowplow also hit his brakes. His huge plow needed much more room to stop than their compact pickup, and would need to make an evasive maneuver to avoid hitting them.

That's just what Dylan was hoping as he punched the gas and squirted away again, fishtailing for a few moments as the four-wheel-drive bit into fresh snow untouched by the plow.

The plow's driver had somehow lifted his blade, and its giant V-shape came agonizingly close to their rear bumper before the plow swerved to the left and into the passing lane they'd just occupied.

On the outside of the plow, the green car, trying to pass and keep up the chase, was forced into the ditch. Its front bumper pushed up a fresh cloud of white as it bounced off the road and came to a shuddering stop.

Dylan accelerated again, leaving the plow and the green car behind forever.

He hoped.

25.

"I think you're ready," Quinn heard Paul say. She opened her eyes, brought herself back. Next to her, his hands still on the motionless body, Paul was staring at her. Inside the hotel room where they hunched in the darkness behind drawn curtains, a mist of water covered the ceiling and walls. Outside, the dry Arizona heat was parched, devoid of any moisture. But inside this room it was moist, wet, sticky. That's the way the exorcisms always worked.

"Ready for what?" she asked, even though she knew the answer.

"To go out on your own."

Paul took his hands off the man who called himself Brandon and stood with some effort. Quinn remained on her knees, kept her hands on Brandon, continued uttering prayers. She didn't need to, specifically; the exorcism, the purging, had already drawn the disease from Brandon's body. The moisture that now clung to the ceiling and walls was the evidence of that cleansing. But she didn't want to move yet; once she disconnected, once she stopped what she was doing, she would begin to feel all the pain and hate she'd drawn into her own body. She would begin to feel the pressure build, and she would have to relieve that pressure.

Behind her, she heard Paul check the shades on the hotel room's window, let them close again. Then he settled onto one of the beds.

"Been wondering when it was going to happen."

Paul sighed. "Yeah. Probably should have happened before now. You've been ready."

At last she stood and turned to look at Paul. He was already feeling the effects of the cleansing, she could tell. His face was gaunt, ashen; his hands, even beneath the nitrile gloves he always wore, were dry and cracked. Soon he would need to shower, scrub himself, replace his clothing with fresh items he kept in sealed packages.

She was a natural, just as Paul had promised. Often she could recover without embedding. That was, in many ways, why embedding was better than cutting. Many times she could relieve the pressure created by the disease just by pressing on one of the objects beneath her skin. No fresh wounds. In the last year she'd only embedded two new objects; both she and Paul knew it was because she was harnessing the power of what they did. Which was why both she and Paul knew it was time for her to go out on her own.

They were in Phoenix, about ninety miles from the headquarters of a cult calling itself 2012.

Cults tended to fall into different categories. Some were wish-fulfillment cults, trading on the hopes and dreams of people who felt something was missing from their lives. Some were doomsday cults, focused on the end of the world and the need to hoard supplies. Some were escapist cults, trying to create their own artificial existence away from outside eyes.

Most cults, of course, shared many of those characteristics.

But 2012 was mostly a doomsday bunch; they believed the world would end in 2012, as foretold by the Mayan calendar. Out in the middle of the Arizona desert, they built bunkers and stored supplies, biding their time. Or waiting for it to run out, as the case may be.

Currently, Paul and Quinn were two of about a dozen members of the Falling Away who were monitoring ten cults in the western United States. There were many more cults than these in the region, of course—probably dozens—but these particular cults were of interest to the Falling Away because they were demonic infestations. Literally.

At the center of any demonically infested cult, you always found a powerful, magnetic leader—made powerful and magnetic by the demon he or she carried inside.

Be they wish-fulfillment cults or escapist cults or doomsday cults, the demon-infested compounds had one major function: they sent out infected members, who would in turn infect other people.

Quinn smiled. Out on the interstate just a few months ago, she'd seen a bumper sticker: LOVE, NOT HATE. That's what the Falling Away was about, really; killing the disease carried by cults before they could spread it to others. Killing the hate.

Paul spoke again, drawing her out of her reverie. "I've talked with some of the others. We think you should monitor the HIVE."

"Up in Montana?"

HIVE was mostly an escapist cult, appealing to people who wanted to leave behind their corporate lives and return to nature. Of the ten cults she had studied while training with Paul, HIVE was the fastest growing.

"Yeah," he said. He smiled feebly. "Get out of this heat."

She nodded, secretly started to press at a small paper clip

embedded in the meat of her palm. The growing pressure inside subsided.

"But there's more to it," Paul said.

"More to what?"

"HIVE. The reason we need you there."

"What's that?" The Falling Away was a small group, really. Quinn had only met a few of the other members, and Paul himself only knew about a dozen people in the organization. They were spread thin, and getting thinner all the time. Recruitment wasn't exactly easy; members had to have odd compulsions they could turn into tools for coping. And the welcome speech about demons and infectious spiritual disease wasn't exactly an easy sell. Quinn knew that, all too well; she'd heard that speech a couple years ago now, and she still had a hard time believing all of it.

Even though she experienced it, time and again.

"There's a chosen in Montana now," Paul said simply.

She felt her breath catch. "A chosen?" People who were called chosen had many things in common with those who were in the Falling Away, but they tended to be even larger magnets for pain and suffering. Chosen were particular targets for demonic cults, rare prizes.

At their most basic level, chosen were puzzle pieces in human form. They fit part of a larger picture, and if they found their place— if they discovered who and what they were—they held great power. But more often, chosen people went through life never fitting in with their surroundings, because they never discovered they were part of the larger puzzle. Far too often, they were destroyed by the power inside them.

"Man or woman?"

"Man. His name is Dylan Runs Ahead."

"An American Indian, then."

"Yes."

It made sense; genetically, it was more likely in Native Americans. But still, chosen were rare; she'd never known of one, and Paul himself, after some fifteen years in the Falling Away, had only met a couple.

"Do you think HIVE knows about him?"

"I'm sure they do, Quinn."

"So they'll be after him."

"You have to keep him away from HIVE. But you have to stay away from him yourself, you know."

"I know." Part of what made protecting chosen so difficult was never being able to tell them who they were; they had to discover it for themselves. In the past, the Falling Away had tried to warn them. In every instance, the chosen had been destroyed—often by themselves.

"And you have to do it by yourself. I can't help you. No one can help you."

"It's my cross to bear," she said, smiling.

It was an operating principle for the Falling Away: all members flew solo, after their apprentice period. All human systems of organization tended to break down, become infected by the Fall as they grew. The Falling Away's defense against this was utterly simple: they operated without any official organization. Occasionally they would communicate, trade data and movements. But they were not an army in any real sense of the word. They were all independent mercenaries, trusting that God's plans would lead them, elusive though they may be. Paul hadn't been led to her by his own plans, but by God's. And she wouldn't be led to Montana by her own plans.

Quinn thought of the verse of the chosen, the verse Paul had said to her many times during her training: "It is a fearful thing to fall into the hands of the living God." Hebrews 10:31.

Job, a chosen in the Old Testament, had discovered the truth of that. Joan of Arc, another chosen, had discovered it.

Now, Dylan Runs Ahead needed to discover it.

26.

Behind Dylan and Webb, the plow and green car had disappeared from view. They were alone on the highway. They had to go slower now on this unplowed stretch, their tires spraying fine particles of snow as they drove through several inches of fresh-fallen whiteness.

"What just happened?" Webb asked, his voice cracking.

"You wondered if things could suck any worse," Dylan answered.

Webb ignored the dig. "She . . . she killed that patrolman."

"I don't think so. I didn't hear any shots; did you?"

"No. No, but . . . we gotta . . . I don't know . . . report it."

Dylan looked at him. "Yeah, that's just what we wanna do. Go to local police and start talking. We can tell them all about your bullet wound, and I can show off my shiny .357 Mag."

"Okay. Yeah. Right." Webb had been reduced to one-word sentences, which was something of a rarity.

Dylan returned his attention to the road. Or what little bit of the road he could see; in front of the plow, the snow was piled three or four inches deep again.

By now it was likely the two Canucks up north had been missed.

Maybe even found. And whether friendly Trooper Evans was alive and well or dead and not-so-well, he had backup on the way. Plus a dash cam capturing an image of his pickup and plates. Even now, there was probably a bulletin going out, telling law enforcement from the local to the federal level to be looking for a red Ford Ranger in central Montana.

All in all, probably not one of Dylan's better days.

You have to ditch the pickup.

You have a keen eye for the obvious, Joni.

Just saying.

Great idea. I'll just pull to the side of the road, and we'll jump out and start walking. In the middle of a snowstorm.

Take this back-country road; you have to get off the highway.

"Yeah," he said, slowing as they came to the road and then turning south. Nothing down this road except a few farms, he guessed.

"What was that?" Webb asked.

"Nothing," Dylan said, realizing he'd answered Joni aloud.

"No, I'm used to you muttering to yourself. What I meant was, what was that turn? You think we're not going slow enough on the highway, so you want to lock in the hubs and go cross-country?"

"We gotta get away from the highway. They'll be looking for us."

"But . . ." Webb went quiet, obviously having a hard time coming up with a good *but.*

Dylan promised himself, if he somehow got out of this alive, he'd swear off guns forever. He'd had enough of them by the time he was discharged from the army, a fractured shell of his former self. But he'd still believed they were a necessary evil in some situations.

Too bad necessary evil often led to a lot of unnecessary evil.

Gun saved your life this morning.

And your point is?

You wouldn't be here if you didn't have a gun.

No, that's my point.

Oh, enough with the woe-is-me, I'd-rather-be-dead crap. Shoulda got that out of your system after Iraq.

Shoulda got you out of my system by now, too, but I still let you hang around. Just shut up for a few minutes and let me think on my own.

They continued down the secondary road, coming over a slight rise as they drove. In the distance, a red barn wavered in stark contrast to the blanket of white, huddled with a couple of other outbuildings and a dilapidated old windmill. Beyond that, perhaps another quarter mile away, a lonely farmhouse stood with trees planted around it as an ineffective windbreak.

Dylan pulled on the turnout that led to the red barn and outbuildings, coming to a stop in front of a barbed wire gate. He opened his door and started to slide out of the cab.

"How do you know no one's at the barn?" Webb asked, a little too shrill. Webb was holding his arm stiffly against his side again; the flood of adrenaline had likely seeped most of the drugs out of his system. Probably time for another bump soon.

For him, or for you?

Joni, you want me to throw you in the kill box?

Okay. Shutting up.

"Look at the snow," Dylan said to Webb. "No tracks."

He opened the gate, returned to the pickup, and drove it through before going back to reattach the gate. The lack of tracks told them no one had been at the barn this morning. But the downside was anyone coming down this road would now see their own tracks.

Dylan bounced down the rutted path to the barn, parking beside the windmill at the back. From the secondary road, the view of the pickup would be blocked by the barn; from the farmhouse in the distance, it would be hidden by the framework of the windmill. He hoped. He shut off the pickup and they sat for a few moments, listening to the tick of the engine cooling and the ever-present whisper of the winter wind in the cracks of the cab.

"So we're just going to hole up in a barn now?" Webb asked. "It's like one of those old escape movies from the fifties. The only thing missing is we're not handcuffed together, and we don't have a pack of bloodhounds tracking us."

"Yeah, then things would be perfect."

"What's that old saying about bad luck and no luck at all?"

"Just that: a saying. Let's check out the barn."

Webb swung out of the pickup slowly, and Dylan went to make sure he could stand and walk. He checked the pickup for their cash and belongings, few as they were. The gun was still in his coat pocket, and he fished the shells from beneath the seat. Webb noted the box of ammo without comment.

"You've never spent much time on a farm, have you?" Dylan said as they tramped through the snow to a rickety door with white, peeling paint.

"Sorry," Webb said. "More of a city mouse."

Dylan opened the door, went inside the barn, wishing for a flashlight. At least they were here in daylight; with the reflective snow and the light from the sun, hidden above the bank of storm clouds, the barn had plenty of cracks to let in light.

"Well, being a country mouse myself," he said as his nostrils filled with the scent of hay, straw, and mildew, "I know that barns can hold more than just hay."

They crept into the barn's interior, past a horse stall that obviously hadn't been used in the recent past. No tack on the walls. On the other side of the stall, to their right, bales of hay were somewhat haphazardly stacked toward the ceiling. A good sign. That meant the hay was for cattle, and they hadn't seen any cattle on the way in. The cattle were in pasture on some nearby acreage . . . which meant the hay had to be transported.

They moved to the left of the horse stall, past a partial wall. And there they saw what Dylan had secretly been hoping they would see: a battered, old yellow Ford pickup, seventies vintage, parked in its own cramped stall.

That wasn't quite right; what he'd been hoping to see was a new turbocharged Dodge Ram, something like the rig Andrew drove; but in a pinch, the old yellow hay truck would do.

"What's that saying about bad luck and no luck at all?" Dylan parroted back to Webb.

Webb stared for a few moments. "Yeah. Lucky us. I shoulda bought a lottery ticket this morning. You really think the keys are in it?"

Dylan let out a quick laugh. "Think Farmer Joe here is worried about fugitives dropping by to steal his old truck? My old man had a pickup a lot like this—didn't even need a key after so many years. Actually started the thing with a screwdriver jammed into the ignition."

Dylan moved to the door of Old Yeller and peeked inside. A fine layer of dust and hay covered the ratty bench seat inside. The key was in the ignition, just as he'd suspected.

"All aboard," he said to Webb as he settled into the squeaky driver's seat. He could feel broken springs beneath him, even through the old jean jacket that was obviously being used as seat padding.

Webb opened the door with his good arm, stumbled into the pickup, turned to close it behind him with some effort.

Dylan retrieved his bottle of the Perks, shook one out, paused, shook out a second.

"Now's not really the time for you to start hitting the happy pills," Webb said.

"No." Dylan offered the two Perks to Webb. "But it's time for you to hit them. I can tell you're starting to hurt more."

Webb looked at the pills a moment, as if they were alien objects from an alternate universe, then took them and slowly dry-swallowed them.

"Thanks," he grumbled.

"Dylan Runs Ahead, Portable Pharmacy," Dylan answered.

"I don't mean just for that," Webb said, staring at the layer of dust on the metal dash. "I mean for everything. You could have left me."

Dylan's mind flashed on the Iraqi desert, fuzzy images of medics bending over him. Not for the first time, he wished the medics had left him there to bleed out. Sure, he would have died. But died a hero. Perfect and blameless in the eyes of his country. In the eyes of his family.

Maybe that would have made up for Joni.

Instead, the medics had saved him. He'd repaid that favor by becoming a painkiller junkie, and now a fugitive. What was that old saying about bad luck and no luck at all? Oh yeah. Much more than a saying.

Chosen. First from Claussen in Iraq, then from Couture today. Yeah, he was a real chosen one.

"But you didn't," Webb continued. "I owe you."

Uncomfortable with Webb's feelings of thanksgiving, Dylan changed the subject. "Check the jockey box," he said.

"The what?"

"The jockey box. The . . . uh . . . glove compartment."

"Jockey box? You really call it that?"

"Country mouse, like I said."

Webb leaned forward, flipped the lever on the glove compartment. More dust, a few wayward pieces of hay, and a tin of sardines.

"You're kidding me," Webb said.

"Take the hay out to the cattle, probably a few miles from here, spend the morning feeding them, you might want a snack. Farmers and ranchers are all the same at heart."

Webb shook his head, retrieved the sardines, blew the layer of muck off its surface before unwrapping the plastic and popping open the lid. Instantly, the fishy aroma filled the cab, and Dylan's stomach leaped to attention.

Webb offered the first bite, and Dylan worked a slimy fish from the packed oil. Webb followed suit, hungrily licking at the oil on his fingers as he chewed.

"Don't even like sardines," Webb said and smiled.

"Who does?"

They ate in silence, finishing the whole tin before Webb dropped it on the floor, where it readily mixed with an assortment of refuse already there.

"Just hope it isn't our version of the Last Supper," Webb said.

"Yeah, well. It's fish. Good and biblical for you."

They both chuckled, then laughed. Laughed because they had to laugh. Laughed because they were terrified, and neither one of them wanted to explore the only alternative to laughing.

After a few moments, the silence returned. Only the sound of the wind making its way through the cracks in the barn.

"So where do we go from here?" Webb asked.

"Well, I think we can hang here for a while. Maybe even should."

"What about Farmer Joe?"

"He won't be out here again until tomorrow morning."

"Really? How do you know that?"

"You have cattle, you feed first thing in the morning. It's late afternoon now, already getting dark; he already did his feeding for today."

"But you said it yourself: no tracks in the snow."

"Well, Einstein, it's been snowing pretty steadily the last few hours. Any tracks he left this morning were covered. If we're lucky, Farmer Joe even went into town to do some chores, get some supplies."

"Lewistown?"

"Probably," he said absently, his mind making new connections. Lewistown.

The giant windmill behind the barn.

A few dozen miles past Lewistown was the town of Judith Gap, not far from the HIVE compound and its huge array of wind turbines. The modern equivalent of the windmill.

Bingo, Joni said inside his mind. *I've been thinking that myself, but didn't want to interrupt you from my little shut-up corner here.*

You really think I'd fit in with some wacko cult?

Hey, you got all the goods. You talk to your imaginary sister inside your head. You do your stupid subtractions and kill box to block things out of your mind. Any cult would be proud to have you. 'Course, you could also take your chances with the psycho chick bounty hunter who tried to run you off the road.

"Hey, you still with me?" Webb asked.

He turned and looked at his friend, sighed. Did they really have another choice?

"Feel like joining a cult?" he asked Webb.

27.

"You okay?"

Quinn looked at the snowplow driver, who had opened the door of the car and was crouching beside her. His dark beard was flecked with gray, and he wore one of those ridiculous fur-lined caps that made her think of Siberian peasants.

Of course, central Montana's winter-swept plains probably weren't all that different from Siberia this time of year.

"You're bleeding," Snowplow Driver said.

She touched her forehead, looking at the fresh blood now trickling from the self-inflicted cut just above her hairline. Evidently, it had reopened when she slid off the road. It had been awhile since she'd cut herself, and she'd really felt nothing inflicting this latest cut. But she'd needed to do it for the whole wounded-motorist-stranded-in-a-snowstorm routine.

That part, at least, had worked fine.

She stared at the wet blot on the fingers of her gloves, as if this were the first time she'd seen blood. The first time she'd seen her own blood.

"Must have hit my head," she said, trying to smile.

"Let me help," Snowplow Driver said as she swung her legs out of the car. She leaned on him and they both stood, their feet sinking into the snow of the roadside ditch.

"You better come with me," he said. "Get that looked at by a doctor." He pulled on her arm like an eager puppy.

"Okay," she said. As if she had any other choice. "Just let me grab my things." She pulled her case from the backseat, and Mr. Snowplow tried to be all gallant, carry it for her.

"I got it," she said. A member of the Falling Away could never be separated from her case; that was one of the primary things she'd learned during training. When she died, she'd do it with her case in her hands.

"Whatcha got in there?" he said. He offered his hand and helped her out of the deep snow of the ditch, into the slightly less deep snow of the unplowed road surface.

"Tools for work, mostly. Some clothes." No need to tell him her main tool was a gun.

"What kind of work do you do?"

She stamped her boots, smiled. "I'm a cleaner."

"A cleaner? And you carry your own . . . tools?"

"It's a dirty world."

The driver knitted his eyebrows for a second, then shrugged. He crossed the road, leading her to the giant orange truck with a huge V-shaped blade attached to the front. He helped boost her into the passenger seat and crossed back to the opposite side, closing his own door behind him and settling in.

"Better buckle up," he said. "Don't want to hit your head again."

She smiled, pushed a strand of hair that had fallen from her greasy ponytail behind her ear, found the seat belt, and buckled it.

He shifted the huge vehicle into gear and began moving forward. After a few seconds, he reached for the two-way radio on his dash.

"What are you doing?" she asked, keeping her voice flat.

"Gotta call this in," he said. "You'll need to get your vehicle towed, and . . . well, you'll need an ambulance. I'll see if they can meet us up at Eddie's Corner, so—"

"I don't think you'll want to do that," she said.

He narrowed his eyes, looked back at the unplowed highway ahead of them. "Why not?"

"They . . . well, you know I'd never try to pass a snowplow usually."

She waited for him to look at her and nod, acknowledge her follow-the-rules gesture.

"But you did."

"Like I said, usually I wouldn't. But this wasn't usual. The two guys in that pickup shot a state trooper a few miles back."

He did a comic double take, and for a moment she thought he might actually swerve off the road. "What?"

"I was headed to Great Falls, where my next job is, and . . . I guess I just happened to be in the wrong place at the wrong time. I saw them shoot him, right in the middle of the highway. So when they took off, I tried to catch them, and . . . well, that's when they slipped around your plow."

"So I should definitely call them in."

"Yeah, yeah, you should," she said. "But I stopped to check on the trooper after they shot him. I told him I'd try to call on his radio, but he said I shouldn't. Said the two guys had a police scanner in their pickup, so they'd hear anything we said. So I got his cell phone out of the car, and he called his dispatch on that instead."

She almost wanted to shake her head; this story was piling up thicker than the snow outside. But the snowplow driver would believe it, she knew; people wanted to believe lies. Human nature. It's what happened when you were part of the Fall, rather than part of the Falling Away.

"Was the trooper okay?"

"What?" She licked her lips. Oh yeah. The trooper. "I think he'll be fine—troopers wear bulletproof vests, you know." She didn't know this, was actually pretty sure that wasn't the case. But she guessed this doe-eyed snowplow driver didn't know any better.

"Maybe we should go back and check on him."

She panicked. "No, no. I mean . . . I know they were sending an ambulance for him. We'll probably pass it on the way. Keep plowing to help them get there faster."

She saw his eyes flicker for a moment, overcome with thoughts of being a further hero. "Nah," he said. "They'd send the ambulance from Lewistown—behind us. Closer."

"And you already plowed that section. Good thing."

He smiled grimly, a bit of pride dancing in his eyes.

"Anyway, if they're scanning police frequencies, I bet they can pick up your two-way too."

"Yeah," he said, buying into the lie.

"I think we should just head to Eddie's Corner, meet the officers there. When we called his dispatch on the phone, they said they were gonna set up a roadblock there."

"The trooper had a cell phone?"

"Most people do."

"Sure, sure. But he picked up a signal out here?"

Oops. "Well, it was closer to Lewistown, you know. Probably got a signal from the towers there." Her pile of lies was in serious danger of collapsing under their own weight, but she only needed to keep it going a few more miles.

"It all happened pretty fast," she said. "But we're just a few miles from Eddie's Corner. We can wait that long, can't we?"

He rubbed at the cap on his head, causing the earflaps to move up and down like duck wings. "I suppose you're right," he said. Then he turned and smiled at her. "Good thing you were there." His tone of voice made it obvious he wished he'd been the one to be there, tantalizingly close to his fifteen minutes of fame.

"Yeah," she answered, wiping at the blood on her face with the back of her hand. "World needs more Good Samaritans like you and me."

28.

The gate at the HIVE compound seemed abandoned, but as Dylan and Webb eased to a stop, they saw a man in a stocking cap come out of the small guard shack and approach their old truck, a mittened hand raised in greeting.

"Evening," the man said when they'd stumbled their way to him. "Rough night to be without four-wheel drive."

Dylan glanced at Webb, who had gone into stony silence at least twenty minutes ago. Maybe from pain in the shoulder, maybe from the cold. In retrospect, the cold may have been a blessing, numbing him against some of the pain.

"Rough night to be without heat either," Dylan said. The old yellow Ford's heater screamed, but didn't put out much in the way of warm air. Luckily, they'd driven less than an hour in it.

"So what brings you out?"

Dylan took a deep breath. "We're here to join." In the distance, they saw a snowmobile move across the horizon in the haze, its headlight looking more like a flashlight in the purple twilight.

The man smiled, his white teeth oddly gleaming. "Well then. We better get you inside."

Dylan watched him go back inside the shack and exchange some words with the other guard. The partner looked out the semi-frosted window, waved, picked up a two-way radio, and spoke into it as Guard #1 came back outside.

"We'll give you a ride inside," he said with a pleasant smile. "And we'll take care of your, ah, truck here."

"It's not really my truck."

The guard's smile never faltered, as if he'd expected this answer. "That's why we're going to take care of it."

Dylan and Webb slid out of the truck and stood, stamping their feet against the cold as the headlights of a vehicle approached from the main compound.

"So that's it?" Dylan asked. "We just walk in, no questions asked?"

The guard smiled again. "You wouldn't be the first. That's the way I did it, and I wasn't the first either."

A Jeep came to a stop in front of them, and the guard opened its back door and motioned them in. Webb slid in the nearest side, and Dylan walked around the other side to get in behind the driver. Instantly, the warmth of the heater began thawing his bones. New Jeeps beat old Fords any day.

Without a word, the Jeep's driver executed a turn and drove back to the main grouping of buildings, stopping in front of a long, thin structure that looked something like a motel.

The guard turned and looked at them from the front seat. "We'll put you up in a guest room tonight—you'll probably want a hot shower and a warm bed." He opened his door, then opened Webb's door behind him. Webb offered Dylan a weary look and slid out.

After a few moments, Dylan opened his door, grabbed his small fanny pack with the drugs and money stashed inside, and followed Webb and the guard to a door on the first level of the motel. Or dorm. Or whatever.

Inside, the room was barren, but clean and warm. No art or decorations adorning the walls, but the twin beds on opposite sides of the room looked inviting. A desk, with a small illuminated tabletop lamp, sat in the right corner of the room, next to a pocket door.

The guard pointed at the door. "Through there and down the hall to the left, you'll find a bathroom and showers. We're getting you some fresh clothes."

Webb went to the nearest bed and collapsed onto it.

Dylan exchanged a look with the guard and nodded. "Thanks," he said.

"That's what I'm here for," he said. He retreated through the entry door to the blowing wind outside again, closing it behind him. Dylan went to the door, meaning to lock it, and discovered there were no locks of any kind. Well, that shouldn't be any surprise; this was a commune, after all. Everyone shared everything, from what he knew of the place.

Dylan went to the desk, sat down in the office chair, picked up the book. *HOPE IS VIA EARTH*, the hardback cover said in all caps.

He thumbed through the book, filled with writings from Li, the Great Sower. Color photos broke up the text, images of people plowing fields, constructing giant wind turbines, loading boxes onto trucks. All of them smiling beatifically. He skimmed through the pages, getting the general gist of the story. Earth was green and healthy and vibrant before the "pestilence of mankind" began to poison it. Only by recycling and generating clean power and focusing on returning earth to its natural, preindustrial state could mankind make up for its past sins.

A knock on the door interrupted him, and he jumped. On the bed, Webb was already in a deep sleep; evidently, the knock wasn't enough to wake him. Probably for the best.

Dylan put his hand in his pocket, slipped his finger inside the trigger guard on the revolver. He approached the door cautiously, wanting to ask who it was but feeling like it would be oddly out of place here.

After debating a few moments, he opened the door. Standing in front of him was a chiseled figure with a bald head, brown skin, and deep, peering eyes. The cold weather didn't seem to be a problem, as the person wore no kind of coat or hat.

"I brought clothes," he said, holding out freshly laundered jeans and flannel shirts.

"Sure. Uh, I mean, thanks. Come on in." Dylan backed away, letting the stranger into the room. As if he could keep anyone out anyway.

When Dylan closed the door and turned back to the room, the figure had already placed the pile of clothes on Dylan's bed, then seated himself next to the clothing.

"My name is—" the figure began.

"Li," Dylan finished. "The Great Sower." He'd seen photos in the book on the desk. Before that, even, he'd seen photos of Li in local newspapers and television broadcasts; the HIVE community garnered a fair amount of regional media interest.

Li smiled. "And you are Dylan Runs Ahead."

"I didn't expect you to be the Welcome Wagon."

"Why not?"

Dylan shrugged. "I don't know—Great Sower, you know. You should be great sowing, or whatever."

"And you don't think this counts as sowing."

Dylan nodded at Webb, who still hadn't moved since crashing on the bed. "Me and Webb, we're kind of bad seeds."

He crossed the room back to the desk and sat down in the chair, not wanting to sit by Li on the bed. Too near. Too personal. Too close to those eyes.

Li smiled. "No such thing as a good seed, when we talk about humanity. We lost that when we turned away from Earth."

Dylan smiled. "You've got the sound bites down, I'll give you that."

Li returned the smile, and Dylan felt his own fade. The combination of Li's penetrating eyes and smile made him look like a hungry predator.

"Oh, it's not just a sound bite. Here at the HIVE, we get back to humanity's roots—literally. We came from the land, and we are worthless until we return to the land."

"So the path to enlightenment is a healthy bit of self-hatred."

Li pursed his lips. "You're something of an authority on that subject, I suspect."

Dylan, uncomfortable with the conversation, tried to shift the subject. "So you're probably wondering why we're here."

"You're running."

Dylan stayed quiet, staring for a few moments into Li's eyes. Even in the low light of the tabletop lamp, Li's smile sparkled in his eyes.

"Yeah," he finally said.

"Also part of the sorry state of earth. Humans run from themselves. Even when they think they're running from something else."

Dylan, unsure how to respond, nodded and cleared his throat.

"You can stay as long as you want. Of course, you can leave any time you want as well—but I don't think there's anything waiting for you out there, is there? Nothing good, anyway. And in here . . . well, I think you may be surprised what we can do for you."

"Like what?"

Li rose from the bed and walked to the front door again. Dylan, uncomfortable, stood from his own chair as Li turned to face him again. "We'll talk more tomorrow."

"Okay," Dylan said.

Li opened the door and was gone as quickly as he'd come.

Dylan wished again for a lock on the door but did his best to ignore the unease inside as he transferred the clothes Li had brought from his bed to the desk. A shower could wait until morning. Right now, like Webb, he needed sleep more than anything.

He undressed and slid into the bed, welcoming the feel and smell of the crisp sheets and a warm blanket.

Within moments, he was out.

29.

It hadn't been difficult for Quinn to shake the snowplow driver. When they reached Eddie's Corner—so named, she'd always assumed, because the guy who started the lone fuel station/convenience store here years ago had been named Eddie—the snowplow driver expressed surprise at not seeing vehicles from the highway patrol or other law enforcement agencies.

She'd been prepared for that. "They probably already made the bust," she said. "I bet they were here fifteen minutes ahead of us, and they're probably on their way to Billings to book 'em on federal charges."

The driver eyed her suspiciously as he brought the snowplow to a stop on the east side of the service station, put it in park, and left it idling. "Maybe I should call in now, though," he said. "Let them know where I'm at, find out if they've heard anything."

"Good idea," she said, opening the door. "I gotta use the facilities; be right back."

He had nodded as he picked up his two-way. She shut the passenger door and walked to the front of the building, continued past the front entrance without hesitating, and went to the large parking lot on the west side of the building, where most of the people making a pit stop at Eddie's Corner parked. She knew, even before reaching the other side of the building, that she would find a car with the keys in it; Montanans, as a rule, weren't worried about people stealing their cars, and at a place such as this, when they were just running inside for a pack of cigarettes or a quick bathroom break, many of them were unlikely to take the keys and lock their vehicles.

She did even better than that. Parked in the front row, running, was a silver Pontiac Grand Am. When it snowed and blowed, many folks played even faster and looser with their vehicles; they left their cars running while they went inside.

Mr. Silver Pontiac Grand Am had obviously made this mistake. Quinn slid into the front seat and backed out without hesitating. The question was: Where was Dylan? Headed to Billings? Maybe, maybe. An injured animal often returns to its den when hunted by a predator.

She held on to that hope as she pointed the Grand Am south.

30.

Quinn's first destination in Billings was a quick drive-by at Dylan's home. She saw no activity, which came as something of a surprise.

It was a good bet that the friendly snowplow driver she'd abandoned at Eddie's Corner had spilled his guts to his bosses at MDT, the highway patrol, Fergus County sheriff, and even the FBI. They would have been able to talk to the state trooper she'd incapacitated, review the footage on his car's cam, and track Dylan's plates back to his home address in minutes.

She'd expected a whole alphabet soup of law enforcement agencies to swarm Dylan's home long before she hit Billings city limits, and because of that, she'd also expected to see some evidence of them doing a full search at his house. Yellow tape, the whole CSI thing going.

She wheeled around the block, drove two more blocks, and parked. Well, maybe that was a good sign. Maybe law enforcement had simply staked out Dylan's house, hoping to catch him sneaking back home. It would be stupid for him to do, granted, but people under distress did stupid things. Certainly, she didn't expect him to come back here. Billings . . . maybe. His house? No way.

Still, if the place were simply staked out, it meant he wasn't in custody yet. So she had a chance to find him before they did.

Law enforcement would also be trying to figure out who the mystery woman was in Dylan's whole scheme, of course, but she wasn't worried about that. The Plymouth Satellite had been registered under a ghost name for years, and her real name—Quinn Simmons—wasn't on any government registry anywhere. No social security number, no driver's license, no nothing. She was, in a very real sense, nonexistent. One of the perks of becoming part of the Falling Away.

It was a shame she'd had to leave behind the beloved Plymouth Satellite, but she'd check and see where they towed it. She had a key; she'd be able to boost it back once everything cooled.

Enough of that. She needed to concentrate on the task at hand, get a lead on where Dylan and his friend Webb might have gone.

Inside, pressure was beginning to build. She'd lost them mere miles from the HIVE, and that was the most unsettling part. If Li found them, and if Li then found out what Dylan was . . .

No time for that. Only time for thinking. Dylan wasn't stupid enough to go to his home, but he'd look for familiarity. Krunk? No. If Webb had been shot, that meant something had gone wrong with the drug deal. Krunk was the last person they'd want to talk to.

But she could start with the neighborhood. She was parked on the south side, just a few blocks south of the tracks that ran through downtown Billings.

Dylan wasn't much of a drinker, she knew, but he did venture to the Western and Rainbow bars on occasion. She could at least start there, see if she could pick up any information that might help. Then she'd tap into a few people she knew in Krunk's network, find out if they'd dug up any leads.

She opened the door of the stolen car, got out, and hiked a couple blocks to the Montana Rescue Mission. Funny how she found her way to the homeless shelters of any city she visited. For two years with her mother, and then two years on her own, those shelters had, in fact, been her one and only home. Even today, whenever she walked into a shelter anywhere, she felt as if she could sense her mother's presence.

"I said, can I do anything to help you?"

Quinn came out of her memories, shook her head, looked at the young woman at the intake desk of the homeless shelter. Doing her best to look pathetic, Quinn asked if she could get some clothes.

The woman looked at her, obviously noting that her clothes were in good condition. "A jacket, I mean," Quinn said. "Something hooded—it's cold out there."

The woman smiled, and she found Quinn a dark green hooded sweatshirt with a Rocky Mountain College logo on the chest.

"Great. Now, uh—"

"Go ahead," the helpful young woman said. "You're safe here."

"Well, I'm wondering. Do you have reading glasses? My eyes aren't so good."

"Reading glasses?"

Quinn offered her own broad smile. "For reading my Bible."

The woman seemed taken aback for a moment. "Yes, yes. Of course."

"If you could find reading glasses, it would help me a lot."

"Certainly. We'll get you some reading glasses, then get you something to eat. How's that sound?"

"Sounds great."

An hour later, after eating, Quinn slipped out of the rescue mission with her fresh hooded sweatshirt and reading glasses.

The glasses were the kind of large, wire-framed monstrosities she'd hoped for; they magnified her eyes, changing her appearance, while the hood hid her hair. She'd listened to news radio while driving the stolen car to Billings, expecting to hear some update on the state trooper debacle, but none had come. Not yet, anyway, but it could happen at any time. If they had a clear image of her from the trooper's dash cam, her face would likely start to show up in news outlets.

She made her way to the Western, just two blocks away, and walked through the front door.

A few people glanced at her as she sat at the bar, but no one took particular interest; she looked like another wayward drunk off the street, which was what she'd intended.

"Cold out there," the bartender said to her. He was bald, with a graying mustache and the top of some kind of tattoo showing above the collar of his neck. Looked like maybe the tattoo was a dagger, with just its handle showing.

"Yeah," she said. "But no snow. That's good."

He nodded. "Getting hammered through the central part of the state, I hear. Seemed to miss us."

Pleasantries about the weather dutifully exchanged, the bartender paused so she could order.

"I'll take a draft," she said. "Whatever's cheap."

He smiled. "It's all cheap."

Thirty seconds later he returned with a frosty mug of pale beer and put it in front of her, then took the five-dollar bill she'd placed on the counter and made change. She left the change sitting there and sipped at the beer. She hated beer, but it was the kind of thing you drank in bars like this. Especially if you were here late in the evening, when all the serious drinkers were in attendance. The amateurs had long since gone home.

A battered television, mounted on a homemade shelf at the

end of the bar, presented a car chase. *COPS: World's Wildest Police Chases*, some kind of show like that.

"Whatcha watching?" she said to an old-timer sitting on a stool a few spaces away. He seemed intent on the program.

"Idiots running from cops."

"Been there," she said.

The old-timer cast an eye at her. "You mean running or watching?"

She smiled. "I think I'd better take the fifth on that one."

He shook his head, turned his attention back to the TV. "No good comes from running, I can tell you that. Always get caught."

"If it's the Mounties."

He furrowed his brow.

"The Mounties. Canadian police, you know: the Mounties always get their man."

He still seemed confused, then a look of understanding dawned in his eyes. "You must be talking about those Canucks got killed this morning."

Okay, so it was obvious the old-timer had no clue about the Mounties. "What happened to them?" she asked. "Car wreck or something?"

He shook his head again. "Don't you ever watch the news?"

"Not really."

"Some guy killed a couple Canadians and a highway patrolman. They're after him now."

She felt the breath constricting inside her chest. In her palm, the embedded paper clip began to itch, but she did her best to ignore it. "Killed a highway patrolman? Where?"

"The Canucks were . . . I don't know. Up by the border some-where. Got the highway patrolman just outside Eddie's Corner."

Had to be her highway patrolman. Quinn had not shot the highway patrolman, merely disabled him with a choke hold. Her mind was already telling her what had happened, but she didn't want to believe it. Couldn't believe it.

The old-timer waved at the bartender. "Hey, Dave, you put that on CNN for a second?"

"Why? You got a crush on the weather girl?" Titters around the bar.

"Just change the channel."

This bar didn't seem like the kind of place that ever flipped the television to a news channel—more like professional wrestling and NASCAR—but Quinn said nothing.

The bartender grabbed a remote and clicked it through several channels, coming to a stop on a blonde-headed news anchor. A crawler appeared across the bottom of the screen, something about a fire at a factory in Tennessee.

"Just wait," the old-timer said.

Quinn tried another sip of the beer, but it tasted like vinegar.

"There! There!" the old-timer said.

Quinn looked at the screen, caught the CNN update saying authorities were searching for fugitives in the murder of a Montana highway patrolman and two other unidentified Canadian citizens.

"You see?" the old-timer asked.

She nodded to him slowly, but her mind was racing. A dead highway patrolman. And two others. Canadians. She already knew Dylan and Webb had run into some trouble dealing with Canadians; Webb had been shot. Coincidence?

No. Not at all. It could only mean one thing, the thing she had dreaded since this whole long tailspin of a day began with Andrew's call.

If the patrolman had been shot, that meant someone else was on the trail now. HIVE. Somehow they'd got a whiff of Dylan while her back was turned. And now, they'd want to sink their teeth into him.

Quinn closed her eyes, pushed on the paper clip in the fleshy part of her palm, welcomed the pain.

31.

The next morning Webb looked infinitely better. Especially after popping a few more Perks to quell the shoulder pain. Even the wound looked better as they dressed it; Dylan had expected a hot, reddened mass of flesh, having seen more than his share of bullet wounds. But Webb's wound had actually seemed to shrink overnight, healing without the normally attendant inflammation.

Maybe everyone should be taking pig antibiotics. Or Percocet. Or both.

They sat in their room exchanging quiet conversation as daylight began to glimmer. The storm had broken, and the day dawned crisp and blue outside the small window.

"So what now?" Webb asked, dressed and sitting on his bed.

"This is as far as I planned."

"Little bit further than I planned."

Dylan smiled. "Okay, me too. But I didn't think you'd want to hear me say that."

Webb tested his shoulder, didn't seem horribly troubled by a limited range of motion. "So now we're ... what? Cult members, I guess."

"Beats being mules."

"So far. They haven't asked us to drink goat's blood or anything."

"They won't."

"How do you know that?" Webb was looking around him, as if searching for an item that would ground him in his current reality.

"I don't. Just trying that glass-half-full thing for a change."

"And how's that working for you?"

"I'll let you know."

A knock came at the door. They exchanged a look; Webb shrugged. Dylan rose and went to the door, opened it.

A tall woman stood in the doorway, dark hair spilling over her shoulders in thick curls. On her face was a smile almost as bright as the morning sun behind her. "I'm Elise," she said. "Your S.O.B." As if that explained everything.

"S.O.B.?" Dylan asked.

She laughed easily. "Sorry, guess I didn't say what that was. Special Orientation Buddy. S.O.B."

Dylan turned and looked at Webb, who shrugged once again. At least with his good shoulder.

"How about if I come in, for starters?" Elise asked.

"Oh, sorry. Sure, sure." Dylan backed away, and Elise stepped inside, stamped her feet on the rug by the doorway, closed the door behind her. "Beautiful day outside. Almost like we special-ordered it for you two."

"Did you?"

Another laugh. "Well, just part of my job as your S.O.B."

"Sit down," Dylan offered, and Elise crossed to the end of the room, settled easily into the chair at the desk. She was tall, thickly built; Dylan could picture her in armor and a helmet as a Valkyrie. Or maybe an Amazonian warrior.

Methinks someone's developing a little crush.

Shut up, Joni.

"So . . ." Webb said. "What exactly does an S.O.B. do?"

She ran a hand through her hair. "Yeah, I know," she said, "you're thinking S.O.B. is corny, maybe a bit—what?—precious. But that's part of the whole thing. People come in here a little scared sometimes, don't really know anything about us, think we're going to whisk them away to some secret ceremony. The S.O.B. part is unexpected, so it's—"

"Disarming," Dylan said.

Elise looked at him, nodded. "Yeah. Disarming." They were all awkwardly quiet for a few moments.

"I guess," Dylan said, trying to fill the space, "we didn't officially introduce ourselves. I'm Dylan, and this here is Webb."

"Nice to meet both of you. Officially."

"So what happens now?"

"You get the grand tour."

"Don't you want to know why we're here?"

She furrowed her eyebrows, looked at Dylan. "You're here because you're supposed to be."

"How do you know that?"

"Well, why else would you be?"

Hard to argue with that kind of logic.

She smiled. "I guess what I'm saying is, it doesn't really matter. We all come in here, unsure what to expect, but maybe hoping for something better, right?"

"I could go for some better," Webb said.

"There you go," she said. "So let's just go with it, assume you're here because you're supposed to be here. It's my job to show you around, give you an idea what we're all about."

Dylan cleared his throat. "Well, I have to be honest: I'm not exactly what you'd call a True Believer."

"What do you mean?"

"I mean . . . I suppose most people are here because they're ready to change their lives and all."

"Really."

Dylan wasn't sure if she meant that as a question or a statement.

"Me and Webb," he said, "we're here because we got a whole mess of trouble following us."

She nodded. "Well, Li says even when we're running from something else—"

"We're running from ourselves," Dylan finished. "I got that bit of fortune cookie advice last night."

"So Li visited you already?"

"Brought us these clothes."

Her smile widened. "Well, there you go. That's why you're here. To get away from whatever's following you. Maybe to get a fresh start."

Once again, hard to argue with that kind of logic.

Elise pushed a wayward piece of dark hair behind her ear again. "First, let me get a few big misconceptions out of the way. We're not Amish, or anything like that. We don't ride around in buggies. And no hippie-dippie treatment; some people expect us to sit around a big campfire, tripping on acid."

"Or drinking goat's blood," Webb said helpfully.

Dylan shot him a harsh look, but Elise laughed.

"Well, we only drink goat's blood when it's a full moon."

"So how do we start our big S.O.B. tour?" Webb asked.

"Well, it's morning, which usually means breakfast. No goat's blood on the menu, but we have the more mundane fare: pancakes, hash browns, eggs. Even our own fresh fruit during growing season."

"I hear that's the best time to grow," Webb said.

Elise cocked a finger at Webb, smiled, went to the door. "Let's go," she said. "Unless you've already eaten."

They followed her past a building with large windows; Dylan was about to ask what it was when Elise spoke again.

"This is our community center," Elise said. "Kinda like the town hall, if you like."

Dylan had to admit, as they walked, the place didn't look much like a stereotypical cult compound. It looked more like a planned community scooped from suburbia and dropped onto the Montana prairie. The buildings shared an architectural vision of some sort, incorporating large, rough-hewn timber framing and bright white stucco. The effect made it seem like a small community, a place you could call home, and Dylan was quite sure that was no accident.

Inside the dining area, a cathedral ceiling held the large rough-hewn beams overhead, punctuated here and there by gently turning fans. Skylights let in natural light from the sun, while odd lights he'd never seen before hung from the ceiling at strategic locations, illuminating tables and common areas with a warm, inviting glow. The entire room was enveloped by the sweet smell of fresh bread, and laughter filtered toward them.

"LED," Elise said, noticing him staring at the lights. "Much more efficient, much more natural. We're all about that here."

Chain restaurants would kill for this kind of ambience. Dylan had to admit, each new glimpse of the HIVE was more and more impressive. Unexpected. Somehow . . . genuine. All the more impressive because very few things struck him as genuine these days.

They followed Elise through a cafeteria line, heaping their

plates with eggs, hash browns, fresh fruits, pancakes. The beverage station even had a machine that ground and brewed individual cups of coffee. Dylan carried Webb's plate on his tray so his friend could rest his shoulder.

After his time in the military, Dylan knew how difficult it was to keep up with food service for large groups, and the HIVE seemed to do it effortlessly.

They sat at their own individual booth. Webb hungrily took his plate from Dylan's tray, first bites shoveled into his mouth before they even sat down.

Dylan tasted the coffee, let himself close his eyes for a few seconds and enjoy the feel of hot liquid in his mouth.

"So I'm guessing this gets a passing grade," Elise's voice said.

Dylan opened his eyes, turned to Elise seated beside him, and let out a sigh. "You had me at fresh-ground coffee," he said.

"Good recruiting tip. I'll tell Li."

He set down his coffee. "So, uh . . . if you don't mind my asking—"

"You're wondering about Li."

"Among other things."

She took a bite of hash browns, shrugged. Across the table, Webb was polishing off some scrambled eggs.

"He's what Oliver Stone might call a mystery wrapped inside an enigma," she said.

"Also known as: the Great Sower."

"You've obviously seen the Guide."

"Did a little bit of reading last night."

"So what'd you think?"

Now Dylan shrugged. "I don't know. Seemed a little over-the-top."

"Sometimes that's the only way to shake up the status quo."

"That one from the Guide too?"

"No, that's a pure Elise-ism."

"Maybe put it in the suggestion box for the Great Sower. You might get a Junior Sower badge or something."

"Already got that," she said. "I'll show you sometime."

Dylan blushed and felt Joni stirring inside, wanting to say something. *Not now, Joni*, he warned, and she went still again.

Dylan drained the last of his coffee thirstily, looked around the dining room at other tables, other people laughing and smiling. Maybe they had good reasons to keep those grins on their faces all the time; maybe, odd as it might sound, they were smiling because they were happy.

Elise noticed him surveying the surroundings. "Not exactly what you expected from a cult, huh?"

"You call yourselves a cult?"

"No, but a lot of people outside do. People who don't understand what we do. What we are."

"Well," he said, "if it is a cult, I just might be ready to drink the Kool-Aid."

Elise did that push-a-lock-of-hair-behind-the-ear thing again. "Or at least the coffee," she said.

32.

After breakfast, Elise informed Dylan and Webb she had the whole day to show them the compound and help them get their bearings. Following the orientation, they would again meet with Li, the Great Sower.

She started by offering them computer-printed maps of the main section of the community, which was labeled on the page simply as HIVE Village Center. Dylan studied the general layout. In the middle were the dining hall and the community commons, with other buildings radiating away from them along a series of roughly concentric circular streets and paths. Various buildings were labeled as homes, greenhouses, production, storage, resources, livestock, entertainment.

"What do these labels mean?" Dylan asked as they walked down a cobblestone path. Even though a light dusting of snow covered the frozen ground, the path was clear.

"Which ones?" Elise asked without stopping.

"All of them. Production, storage—what gets produced and stored?"

"Ag, mostly. Remember, this is all self-sustaining, so we grow our own grains, veggies, fruits, raise our own livestock. Even create our own power with the turbines—and what we don't use, we sell. Don't tell me you've never seen HIVE community eggs or milk on the shelves."

"Well, sure, but I mean: it's all on this map? This looks pretty small. Maybe a couple hundred acres."

Elise stopped, turned, cocked her head. "Well, of course it's not all on this map. We have thousands of acres of cropland, open-range leases, that kind of thing. You're just looking at the community itself."

"How many acres?"

She shrugged, started walking again. "Don't know. Like I said: thousands. Does it matter?"

"I guess not, but . . . I mean, that has to be a lot of money. To buy and build."

"I suppose. But a lot of the early people came from family farms, brought their acreage into the cause. Some brought money. And of course, it's all built on a sustainable model. The turbines, for instance, are long-term leases from a power company back in . . . Minnesota, I think. Actually, not just a power company; they're a holding company for a couple pharmaceutical companies, some bioresearch companies—all of it pushing green technology, sustainable technology. Li's in pretty tight with them. They put up the capital to build the turbines; we get power and a percentage of all the profits. Li's pretty brilliant about building partnerships."

They came to the door of one of the large, timber-framed buildings.

"Just Li?" Dylan asked as Elise opened the door.

"Of course not," Elise said. "Everyone here is part of it, offering different skills. Think of Li as the general; he's got other officers overseeing troops in all different divisions."

A military analogy for the army vet, said Joni inside. *She's good.*

She doesn't even know I was in the military.

What makes you think that?

We just met.

I know, but . . . be careful.

Being careful.

"Okay," Elise said. "Right now we're standing inside one of the packaging buildings, as your map will tell you. Any guesses as to what gets packaged?"

Ahead of them, several smiling workers checked eggs in cardboard cartons, stacked the cartons on wheeled pallets, then wrapped the pallets in paper. Once the pallets were filled, the workers pushed them toward a large overhead door at the far end of the building. A few of the workers noticed their visitors and waved a greeting.

Elise didn't wait for an answer. "Great thing is, the whole operation is environmentally friendly, sustainable. We reuse everything: the pallets, the cartons—ask people to return the cartons for a nickel each, and a ton of them come back—"

"I know," Dylan said. Part of what had made the HIVE community a media darling was its huge effort to encourage consumers to return cartons, bags, and other containers for reuse.

"Even the packaging elements themselves," Elise continued. "Most pallets get wrapped in cellophane, but we use this unique fiber paper that's made from one-hundred percent postconsumer materials. Actually make the paper here and sell it to other places."

"This place is obviously a lot bigger than it looks from the outside," Webb said.

Elise smiled. "Oh, it's definitely more than meets the eye."

"Great," Dylan said. "So Woodsy the Owl and the Sierra Club love you guys. I get the idea."

"I don't think Woodsy has a middle name. It's just Woodsy Owl," Elise replied.

"Yeah, amateur," Webb piped in.

Dylan paused, listening as a vehicle pulled to a stop outside. Part of the gig for an ex-EOD: he was always hyper-aware of approaching vehicles.

The door behind them opened and two men entered the building, both of them with close-cropped hair, military style. The same kind of hair Dylan had worn during his time in the service.

"Sorry to interrupt," the first one said, "but we'll have to cut the tour short. I'm Jeff, and this is Randall. We're going to take you to a safe place."

"A safe place?" Webb asked.

"Local sheriff, a couple FBI agents in tow, at the front gate. Just a guess, but I'd say they might be looking for you two."

Dylan exhaled. "I don't think it's a guess."

Webb seemed to be on the edge of hyperventilating, and Dylan himself felt his heart trip-hammering.

So much for that idea, Joni, he said inside his mind.

Which idea?

The one to come here to the HIVE. Took the law all of about twelve hours to find us.

They haven't found you yet.

For their part, Elise and the two men didn't seem at all concerned; their plastered smiles never faltered, as if this were just another day in paradise.

In their minds, it probably was.

"Relax," the first guy said as he studied their reactions. "You guys think you're the first Butch Cassidy and Sundance Kid to visit? We're just taking a slight detour. Like I said: a safe place."

The two men turned and walked out the door; Webb followed immediately. Dylan started to go as well, but he felt Elise's hand on his arm. He turned to her.

"Things are about to get . . . confusing," she said. "But just roll with the punches. I know you can."

"Yeah, well, let's hope so," Dylan said. He didn't like how this was developing, but he didn't see a way out of it at the moment.

"I know so," Elise said. "It might get weird, but . . . just trust me."

"Yeah, because my life up until now has been so boring and normal."

Outside, Jeff and the other man pushed Dylan and Webb into an SUV, followed by a quick trip down one of the village's main arterial roads. They turned on one of the outer roads that circled the Village Center, as the HIVE map labeled it, then came to a stop beside a garage of some kind.

The doors opened, and the four of them piled out of the SUV.

"This the place?" Dylan asked Jeff. "Doesn't look very big."

Jeff chuckled, led them around the back of the outbuilding where four snowmobiles were parked. He disappeared inside for a few moments, returned with two helmets, handed one to Dylan. The other man, Randall, retrieved helmets for himself and Webb.

"HIVE is more than just the Village Center where people spend most of their time," Jeff explained. "Cattle, fields, even turbines spread out over thousands of acres. We use ATVs in the warmer months, but in the winter snowmobiles are much faster. All electric, of course; we have plenty of electricity."

Dylan wanted to tell him he'd already received that particular chamber of commerce speech from Elise, but he stayed quiet.

Jeff unhooked a sled from the back of the nearest snowmobile, then put on his helmet. He keyed the ignition and the snowmobile came to life with a steady whir, something that sounded like the old slot car set Dylan had played with as a kid. Only louder. The helmets' dark, full-face visors made communication impossible, so Jeff motioned for Dylan to hop onto the back of the snowmobile.

Dylan pulled on his own helmet and strapped it; behind them, he saw Webb and Randall mounting a second snowmobile. Webb had been uncharacteristically quiet; maybe his arm was hurting.

A voice came into his head, and Dylan realized it was Jeff speaking to him through a helmet-to-helmet intercom. "Be there in a couple minutes."

Jeff angled them away from the community. They sailed across the fresh snow, the whole landscape sparkling like crystal around them. Clean. Fresh. A fitting start for Dylan's next steps. He was nervous, yes, but also excited. Odd. He hadn't popped a Perk or Vike for . . . how long? Normally, he could count the hours between pills on one finger.

Eventually Jeff pulled up to the base of one of the giant turbines and killed the engine. Dylan slid off the seat and pulled off his helmet, and Jeff followed suit.

Dylan turned back, looking at the Village Center on the horizon behind them. For a moment it reminded him of that scene in *The Wizard of Oz* where Dorothy and her ragtag bunch first catch sight of the Emerald City in the distance. But in this case, instead of endless fields of poppies separating them, it was a huge expanse of white, glowing snow, punctuated by the bases of other turbines.

"Magical, isn't it?" Jeff said, standing next to him and admiring the view. "Summer, it's a carpet of green. Fall, when the grain stalks are high, it's gold. No matter what time of year you're out here, you realize what a true escape from reality this whole place is."

Dylan turned and smiled. "Sounds like just what I need," he said.

"I think so," Jeff replied. He went to a door at the base of the turbine and keyed in an entry code.

This struck Dylan as odd, because it was the first bit of security—aside from the guard gate out front—he'd seen at the HIVE.

"The door," he said, walking up behind Jeff.

"What about it?"

"It's locked. No locks in the—whatever you call it—the Village Center."

Jeff nodded. "Farther away we get from the central district, the more the real world—what everyone else likes to call the real world—starts to take over. Gotta lock up access to the turbines to keep out the vandals. Drunk kids, thieves, that sort."

The door opened, and Jeff let Dylan in first. He turned and keyed a code on the pad, relocking the door behind them. "Down the steps," he said.

Dylan made his way down a flight of about a dozen stairs, and they came to another door on the landing at the bottom, also keypad protected. Jeff squeezed by, punched in another code, and the new door opened automatically. Inside were two smiling nurses who greeted Dylan warmly and asked him to take a seat in a black vinyl chair.

Dylan felt uneasy. He was underground, behind two locked doors. Trapped. But he knew that was just the paranoia in his system trying to take over. Let it go. Just let it go. These people were helping him, after all; he'd come to them after shooting two men near the Canadian border, then running from a Montana highway patrolman and one of the state's biggest drug traffickers.

Oh, and also a bounty hunter.

Not many places, outside of the rez, they'd welcome you if you did that. And even the Crow rez, he knew, wouldn't welcome him specifically.

He took a seat, and one of the nurses slipped a cuff on his arm to check his blood pressure. He glanced at Jeff, who still wore his permagrin.

"You're fine," Jeff said. "Lisa and Nancy are here to take care of you. Just take your vitals, do a few tests."

The second nurse produced a syringe.

"What's that?" Dylan asked uneasily. After spending several months in the VA center in Sheridan, Dylan had developed a natural distaste for anything medical.

Lisa—or maybe it was Nancy—patted his arm. "Mild sedative," she said. "Help you relax, get some rest. You've got some big work ahead of you. You'll just feel a little pinch."

The nurse pushed the needle into his vein, and within seconds the world around him began to swim.

"I—" he started to say, but he lost the thought before his tongue could form it. Suddenly all he wanted to do was close his eyes, close his eyes and sleep.

So he did.

33.

Dylan opened his eyes, waited a few seconds for his vision to come into focus.

He was in a room. He was lying on a soft bed, a light blanket draped over him, a pillow beneath his head. Next to him, a lamp on an end table emitted a soft glow. Somewhere outside the open bedroom door he heard the sounds of a television.

He waited a few seconds, pushed away the blanket, swung his feet to the floor. When he sat up, black dots swam in front of his eyes. He took a few deep breaths and felt good enough to stand.

He expected his bum leg to radiate waves of pain when he put weight on it; after all, it had probably been several hours since his last Perk. Probably. He'd lost his sense of time since . . . well, since entering the HIVE.

Okay. The bedroom door opened in toward him. And with the television blaring in the other room, he obviously had someone guarding him. Maybe he could knock the lamp off the night table, create a crash, hide behind the door, and jump whoever came to—

"You're up. Good." It was Jeff's voice, but oddly tinny.

Dylan followed the sound of the voice and saw a screen on the far wall of the bedroom. Jeff's smiling face was on the screen.

"'Up' is a relative term," Dylan said, rubbing at his head.

"Everything's relative if you don't have the big picture."

"And what's the big picture?"

"Ah," Jeff said, obviously enjoying himself. "You're getting there."

"So the small picture involves you injecting me with some kind of drug, knocking me out, and throwing me into a room with video surveillance?"

"Well, there's where you're looking at the small picture. The big picture is: we're starting you on detox, keeping an eye on you to monitor your withdrawals."

Dylan looked around. "Detox."

"Those prescription drugs are the worst. You're in a safe, controlled environment; you'll have regular medical care and checkups; and most important, you'll be away from the outside world for a few days."

Why isn't that making me feel any better? Joni's voice asked inside.

Webb's form appeared at the open door of the bedroom. "Hey, man."

"What about Webb?" Dylan said to Jeff's form on the surveillance image. "You've got him locked up down here, and he doesn't have a drug problem."

"Alcohol's a drug, isn't it?"

Dylan looked at Webb, who shrugged. Yeah, Webb did like to hit the demon drink a bit too much, he had to admit.

"Besides," Jeff continued, "he has a bullet wound and needs medical supervision as well. You've got plenty of food and supplies. You'll be fine."

"Other than being locked up and held hostage."

Jeff shook his head. "You think we're holding you hostage?"

"Sure. Make a deal with the feds, hand us over."

"What would we get out of that?"

"I don't know. Ask the feds. Course, I'm sure you already have."

"Ah. Well, like I said, you don't have the big picture yet. I told you we had you in a safe place. A place no one can find you. You two have been—well, you've got yourselves into a bit of hot water. It's going to take a few days for the water to cool down. In the meantime . . ."

Dylan waited for him to finish the sentence, but he didn't.

"Look," Jeff said. "We're the good guys. We're here to help. Right now, you're coming down off some powerful painkillers, and it's messing with your brain. That's to be expected. Once you're past the actual detox process, you'll see this for what it is."

"And what is it?"

"It's our gift to you."

Dylan took a deep breath. "Given freely, out of the kindness of your hearts."

"Like I said, this isn't the first time we've had Butch Cassidy and the Sundance Kid join our ranks."

"That's assuming we agree to join your ranks."

"You will. You'll come to share the vision of the Great Sower. At HIVE we realize that individually we're nothing. But collectively, we're pointing toward harmony with Earth. That's what it's all about."

"Yeah, I remember reading that in the welcome brochure."

"Like I said, you're not seeing the big picture. You think you're trapped here. You ask me, you're trapped everywhere else but here."

The monitor went dark, but Dylan noticed a camera mounted in the corner of the ceiling, red light blinking steadily.

Webb was scratching at his forearm. "I think that went well," he said. "I can tell you two are going to be fast friends."

"That's me. I make friends everywhere I go."

"Those cameras are everywhere inside our digs. Every room."

"Surprise, surprise."

"Might as well come on out, have something to eat. We got a kitchen, full fridge and freezer, satellite TV."

"And they give us the first month's rent for free."

Webb smiled. "Well, it beats sardines in the front seat of Farmer Joe's old Ford."

Dylan sighed, motioned for Webb to lead the way back out into the apartment. In the front room, Dylan sat on the couch, stared at the television screen. Mr. Clean was showing a middle-aged housewife how scrubbing toilets could be rapturously easy.

Webb returned, a plate and glass of milk in his hands. He put them on the coffee table in front of Dylan, sat next to him on the couch.

"I made you a sandwich, figured you'd be up soon."

Dylan felt his stomach grumble, picked up the sandwich, and took a bite of whole wheat and chicken. He had to admit, it tasted great. The milk was cold, smooth, and fresh.

"Gotta be early afternoon," he said around a mouthful of sandwich. Webb picked up the remote and hit Info; the screen displayed the time as 1:37 p.m.

Dylan nodded. "So we've been down here, I don't know, a couple hours."

"Yeah."

Dylan took another bite, stopped. "Wait a minute. You carried in a plate and a glass."

"Yeah, I'm multitalented."

"What I mean is, you used your bad arm."

Webb rotated his shoulder a bit. "Tell you the truth, the arm's not feeling so bad. Nurses came in, checked the bandages earlier; it looks a lot better than I thought it would."

Webb picked up the remote, reclined on the couch, put his feet on the coffee table.

Dylan felt his temper flare. "So that's it?" he said. "Here's a sandwich, Dylan, I'm gonna watch TV, and oh, by the way, we're being held hostage?"

Webb shrugged. "Pretty much."

"None of this bothers you?"

Webb shook his head. "I'll tell you what bothers me. Getting shot by a couple of tripped-out Canadians. Driving through snowstorms, getting chased by a bloodied psycho."

The commercials ended, and Webb turned up the volume. On the screen, a young woman sat in a room, surrounded by half a dozen people who told her what they were going to do if she didn't go into rehab.

"This," Webb said, holding up the hand that still held the remote and gesturing to the room around them. "This doesn't bother me in the least. It's like the dude said: safe. Frankly, seems like a pretty good place to hide while we wait for the heat outside to cool down. And even if I did want to get out of here right now, how would I do it? And where would I go? Back to Billings?"

Dylan sighed. "I don't know," he said quietly.

"No, you don't know. So if you'll just shut up, I'd like to see what happens to Erica here."

Dylan sat quietly for a few moments, watching the TV. Erica's mother said she was going to kick her out of the house and cut off all contact if Erica didn't accept this gift freely offered to her today.

"This that *Intervention* show?" Dylan finally asked.

"Yeah. Erica, here, is bulimic. Also, she's developed a taste for meth."

Erica, tears streaming down her face, agreed to the rehab. Her family and friends erupted in joy, wrapping her in a tight group hug.

"That meth's bad stuff," Dylan said as they watched Erica being whisked to the airport, where she would catch a flight to a detox clinic in the Arizona desert.

"Yeah," Webb agreed, his eyes still on the TV. "Should stick to scrip drugs."

The next five minutes recounted Erica's experience at the rehab clinic. A follow-up said she'd been clean and sober for eight months, and had reunited with her kids.

"Lookie there," Webb said. "A happy ending. All she had to do was roll with the punches."

Dylan looked at Webb, then back to the TV, which had started the intro segment to another episode of *Intervention*. Obviously a marathon.

Okay, okay. He got it. This was his intervention, of sorts. His mind had rebelled against that, but maybe it was just the drugs talking. Maybe these people really were trying to help him, and he was just playing the part of the drug-addled addict.

Roll with the punches. Isn't that what your Amazon girlfriend said?

Yeah, Joni. That's what she said.

Dylan picked up his glass of milk and drained it. "Okay, Webb," he said. "I'm rolling."

34.

Quinn pulled to a stop on the lonely, snow-covered road and turned the key to shut off the old Chevy's big-block engine. She sat in silence for a few moments, listening to the slight breeze outside, letting the rays of the sun warm her through the pickup's windshield.

The old 4x4 Silverado had only cost a couple grand; she'd seen it advertised in the *Thrifty Nickel* in Billings, and talked the guy down from three grand by flashing two thousand in cash. Not that it mattered. She could have spent ten times that if needed. One benefit of being a part of the Falling Away: an unlimited expense account.

Dylan was inside the compound. She was sure of it. She just needed to find him.

Getting in and getting out with Dylan in tow, however—that was going to be a bit tricky, and the plan was only half formed in her mind. Which was why she was here.

She forced open the door of the Silverado, slipped her portable scanner into the pocket of her camo jacket, looped the rabbit earpiece around her left ear, and pulled her hood over her head. Next, she grabbed her field glasses and a 12-gauge shotgun (another quick buy found in the *Thrifty Nickel*), then locked the pickup. Her tool kit was wedged behind the seat; she didn't feel comfortable having it out of sight, but there was really no way to carry it and maintain the illusion.

It was the middle of the fall/winter pheasant season in Montana, and she was a pheasant hunter.

Her feet created small sprays of white as she hiked through the fresh powder, making her way toward the phalanx of giant turbines in the distance. The HIVE compound was largely surrounded by federally owned land operated by the Bureau of Land Management; bird hunters were welcome on BLM lands.

She continued hiking for another ten minutes, making her way across the open range and keeping her eyes on the wind turbines, praying silently with each step.

Finally, at the barbed-wire fence lining HIVE property, she stopped and scouted the view ahead with her field glasses. To any casual observer—and to security cameras on the HIVE compound—she would look like just another hunter glassing the landscape for pheasants. Nothing out of the ordinary.

But she wasn't hunting pheasants. She was hunting a man named Dylan Runs Ahead, somewhere in the hundreds of acres rolling away from her current position. She put a gloved hand into her pocket and turned on the portable scanner; several seconds later she picked up a short-wave transmission from inside the compound, someone reporting a security check at Turbine 19. Over the past two years she'd listened to their short-wave transmissions inside the compound—the open, unsecured transmissions of general chatter, as well as the secret number-encoded transmissions.

With the luxury of time, she'd been able to crack their encryptions.

Her scanner's built-in digital recorder would help her capture any secret transmissions for later decoding.

Of course, she'd never monitored and recorded HIVE activities from their fence line before. But this was a special situation, and she needed to get a better visual reference than anything she'd previously gleaned from Google Earth and other satellite tracking of the compound.

She looped the field glasses around her neck and began walking again. She could walk the fence line for the next few days without attracting any kind of suspicion. Watching. Listening. Learning.

Soon she would know where Dylan was hiding.

35.

Dylan was feeling less trapped, and more . . . was *free* the right word? Maybe not free, but relieved. Yes, they'd been shanghaied, and yes, they were hostages—two things he thought he'd never quite get over—but he had to admit, they were much better off in here than they were out there.

Out there they'd be hounded, maybe even caught, by law enforcement officials and agents from just about every government entity you could name. In here, as Webb had pointed out, they had a well-stocked refrigerator and pantry, as well as cable TV. For 90 percent of America, that's really all you needed out of life. Why should they be any different?

And maybe, just maybe, there was something to this whole old-world-meets-New-Age cult thing. Maybe working the earth, getting back to the basics, joining a larger cause, would cleanse him inside.

He certainly needed cleansing.

Claussen had said he was chosen, spouted off about the Bible and humankind falling from grace. Maybe this was his chance to reclaim that grace. Maybe this was his "chosen" assignment. The thought made him smile, made him feel a sense of belonging he hadn't felt since the violent end of his army career. Made him actually long to see Claussen, hear him pray.

It was 7:59 in the morning, according to the digital clock on the satellite receiver. Was it the *next* morning? Two mornings after? He couldn't be sure; time ceased to exist when you were in a giant box with no windows, and he'd drifted into and out of sleep several times. As if he were on drugs of some kind, even though he knew he was going through detox. A little bit of irony, there.

Webb was in the shower yet again. In their time here, hours or days, Webb had showered several times. The first few had been difficult, as he tried to figure out a way to avoid getting water directly on his wound and bandages. But after Dylan created a mini-sleeve out of a bread bag and a roll of duct tape he found in one of the kitchen drawers, the floodgates had literally opened for Webb.

Dylan suspected his friend was trying to clean something no shower would ever wash away.

"Morning, Dylan." A woman's voice. He looked at the nearest monitor, saw the unexpected image of Elise.

He smiled. "Elise. How's my S.O.B. doing?"

She returned the smile. "You're keeping your sense of humor. That's good."

"You're talking to me over a grainy camera, while I'm locked up in some hole. Humor's about all I got."

"I told you things would get weird. I also told you to trust me."

"Because you're a trustworthy S.O.B."

"Exactly."

"Okay, well, all's well aboard the good ship this morning, so you can note that on your report and go back to . . . whatever else you do here."

"What about Webb?"

"He's in the shower. I'm trying to decide between QVC and the Home and Garden channel."

"Right. Because you love home decoration, jewelry, and fashion so much."

He looked at the bare walls of the apartment. "Well, the art is tacky. And the window treatments—oh, wait, that's right. This place doesn't have any windows, because it's underground."

Elise sighed. "Sorry. And it's sunny today. But it's not so bad, is it? I mean, you get to hide out a few days, wait for the dust to settle. You understand that, don't you?"

"What kind of dust are you talking about?"

"The Fergus County sheriff, the Montana Highway Patrol, and the FBI kind of dust."

"Just another day in the life of Dylan Runs Ahead, man about town."

She smiled. "We get cops, investigators, disgruntled families rolling through here. You're not the first."

"So you just hide the people they're looking for?"

"Only when it benefits them."

He paused, thought about it. "Okay. Point taken. It's just . . . it feels wrong."

"The first few days in here are always the hardest, no matter who you are. You're entering a new life, becoming a new person. It's hard to run from your past, especially when you're battling an addiction. That addiction is what's talking now, more than anything else."

He thought about the *Intervention* marathon they'd watched, the endless stream of junkies and bulimics and gamblers who lashed out in rage whenever the people around them tried to help. He'd lashed out at Jeff. And at Webb. And now at Elise. Evidently, junkies were always the same. "Okay," he said, trying to make his voice more even. More modulated. "Which brings me to why."

"Why what?"

"Why *you* ran here. What you ran from."

She smiled. "Not everyone who comes here is running away. Some of us are running *toward* something—something bigger, something more important than just ourselves."

"And what would that be?"

"Earth is more important than we are; for centuries, we've been an infestation, trying to kill it. It's time for us to live in harmony with the land. You should understand that more than most."

"Why's that?"

She seemed a bit uncomfortable for a second, doing that wonderful hair-behind-the-ear bit.

Careful, Tiger, Joni's voice said. *You're going to buy into anything she says.*

And what's wrong with that?

I don't know. Yet.

Elise sighed. "Well, you're Native American."

"You can say Indian. I do."

"Indian, then. Your people, your culture, lived in harmony with the land for centuries, while Western so-called civilization just raped it."

Oh, great, Joni said. *She's going to apologize to you on behalf of all white people.*

He smiled. *What was it you said to me recently? Whatever works, I think it was.*

Now I should be telling you to shut up.

But you can't.

"I'm sorry if I said something offensive," Elise was saying on the camera.

"No, no, not at all. I'm just not . . . let's just say I'm not much of an Indian. I'm the guy who joined the army to get off the rez."

"And you got wounded in Iraq."

"How'd you know that?"

She smiled. "Well, certainly we welcome everyone with open arms. But we're not stupid; we do some background checks. To see how we can help them adapt. Knowing that about you, knowing you were scarred by your time in Iraq . . ."

He sighed. "Elise, I was scarred before I ever listened to the army recruiter."

"How were you scarred before?" she asked softly.

"You said you did a background check. You probably have it there."

"Your sister? Joni?" she asked.

He felt himself involuntarily clench. He regularly talked to Joni inside his head, yes, but it was still a shock to hear anyone in the real world mention her.

Inside, Joni started to say something, but he sent her to the kill box immediately.

"That's something we'll never talk about, Elise."

She backpedaled. "Okay, okay. Sorry, I just thought—"

"Don't worry about it," he said, not wanting to stay on the subject any longer than he had to. Especially after snapping at her for helping him. "I just. I can't do that. I'm sorry."

She nodded slowly. "Don't be sorry." She smiled, tried to shift the subject. "So . . . you're good down there? You need anything?"

"Webb was kind of hoping for HBO."

"Sorry, just basic satellite. Don't want you to get too comfy."

"Other than that, I suppose we're okay. Just wondering when we'll get out of here."

"When you don't feel trapped any more, it will be time to come out."

"How very catch-22: I can come out whenever I don't want to come out."

"Not really a catch at all. It's kind of a basic truth in human nature: we always want what's worst for us. And that blinds us to what we really need. But when we finally get what we need, we don't want what's worst for us anymore."

"Nice. Get that off a fortune cookie?"

"If by fortune cookie you mean Li."

"Yeah, I guess that is what I mean. Since we're on the subject, why haven't I seen the Chief Fortune Cookie on your Big Brother screens, or had a nice little visit, or anything like that? Kind of been expecting the full-court press, the whole Amway pitch to join up."

"Maybe he's leaving that to me."

Dylan paused. "Is he?"

"No. But I don't think you're ready. You'll take a few days to get the drugs out of your system, for one. But you're still trying to exert your will on everything. You want to know these things because they give you the illusion of control. When you realize that so much of life is out of your control, you've taken the first step."

"Like the alcoholic admitting he has a problem."

"Yeah. This is your intervention." She smiled.

"Don't talk to me about interventions. Webb made me watch a marathon on A&E."

"I love that show. It's kind of like driving past a car wreck: I don't want to look, because I'm afraid of what I'll see. But then, part of me wants to see it."

Dylan sighed. "Biiluke."

She parroted the word back to him slowly: "Bee-lookey?"

"Close enough. It's what the Apsáalooke people—what you would call the Crow tribe—it's what we were called before we became Apsáalooke."

"Why?"

"Well, according to our origin stories, all the first people lived in harmony. But when they wanted to start fighting each other, the First Creator asked them to jump off a cliff into a giant pool of water to prove that they were brave enough. That meant immediate death, because the First Creator put a man with a bow and arrow at the bottom of the cliff. But one man jumped anyway."

"What happened?"

"Got hit by an arrow, and he fell and died at the bottom of the cliff. The First Creator smiled, called him *Biiluke*, promised not too make too many of him because he was reckless."

"What does that word mean? Bee-lookey?"

Dylan offered a grim smile. "It means 'on our side.' That's me: I'm always on my own side."

36.

Quinn sat inside Andrew's small apartment, listening to the wind slip through the cracks around the windows; even though the windows were shut and sealed, she could see the curtains over the kitchen window ruffling softly. It was past nightfall now, and Andrew still wasn't home.

Something was definitely wrong.

She'd been here for three hours, sitting in this chair, waiting for Andrew's return. At first she'd welcomed the downtime, the chance to simply sit and pray. Being immobile, completely motionless, had a calming effect on her. Not like cutting. Not like embedding. But calming in its own small way.

Being immobile helped equalize the pressure, if only temporarily. You could see it, if you were quiet enough. Still enough. The pressure outside was painted in brighter colors, scented in floral aromas, announced by soft, gentle chimes. The air around you was more like the water surrounding those deep-sea divers she thought of often, filled with soft, amorphous shapes that floated gently. You could feel the emptiness caress your skin, if you were quiet enough.

She knew it all sounded crazy: the physical manifestations of calmness and stillness, the cutting, the embedding. What therapists might refer to as coping mechanisms, hard-wired in her psyche by her four years on the cold streets of Portland.

But after finding Paul and the Falling Away, she also understood that those were the very things that made her uniquely able to do what she'd been called to do: the madness inside her inoculated her against the madness of the world outside. Her compulsive tendencies let her be immune to the purgings she had to do on HIVE members. As she knelt over them, prayed for them, felt the sickness inside them being drawn out, the thoughts of her own compulsions helped block the illness from taking root inside her own mind.

Earlier, she'd spent a few hours on the fence line of the HIVE compound, watching the snowmobiles in the distance, seeing the helmeted figures do security checks of buildings and turbines. She'd listened on the open channel as an employee of the company that built HIVE's turbines—a company called DermaGen—was escorted to one of the turbines for a systems check. She'd captured that whole conversation on her scanner's digital recorder so she could study it later. She'd listened on secure channels—frequencies she'd often scanned while monitoring the HIVE—and recorded those transmissions for decoding as well.

After a morning in the field, she'd spent the afternoon cracking the coded transmissions, transcribing the conversations; in that data, she'd seen the beginnings of a plan. One that just might get her inside the HIVE for a quick smash and grab of Dylan.

First, though, she'd need to find out exactly where they were hiding him. So far none of the transmissions—even the encrypted ones—had mentioned Dylan or Webb.

But they would. She knew it. And once she'd pinpointed Dylan's location, she could set her plan in motion with a little bit of help.

Which was where Andrew came in.

Not that *help* and *Andrew* were two words she'd use together very often. Andrew wasn't exactly the type you'd entrust with secret information, the type you'd rely on to keep you out of tough situations.

But she didn't need a confidant; she needed a tool, and Andrew could be that.

The only problem was, Andrew was missing. She'd known it as soon as she broke into his apartment. His large Dodge Ram pickup, which he treated like some kind of trophy, was parked outside. She'd assumed he was home; Andrew was never far from his prized vehicle. When she'd found the apartment empty, she let herself think he'd hiked down to one of the local bars for a drink or two. For Andrew, drinks were the lubricant that kept his information machine oiled and running. Given a few hours at a bar, Andrew could massage secrets from just about anyone. That was part of what made him so valuable to her as an informant. And he knew it. Andrew was one of those rare people who always knew what was happening under the ground, behind the scenes.

She'd combed the bars where he liked to hang out, asked about him, found out no one had seen him since the day before. She'd called him several times, left messages on his cell phone. Something odd in itself, because Andrew rarely let phone calls go to his voice mail; talking was his drug, his juice, and he always wanted to talk to anyone who would listen.

Now it was time to face the facts. Andrew was gone. Her mind, almost on its own, began replaying the news crawler on CNN. A dead highway patrolman, and two other men. Three in all.

She searched Andrew's living room for a television remote

control. After a few minutes, she gave up and went to the TV, flipped it on, cycled through the channels, then came to a stop on *Headline News*. She watched a stock market report and a fluff piece about an actor in a new television drama before the promised "top headlines" at eight after the hour.

The news anchor, a woman with impossibly perfect cocoa-colored skin and impossibly perfect white teeth, said there were new details on a breaking story in Montana.

Quinn's stomach clenched.

Photos of two men filled the screen as the anchor's voice explained that authorities had recovered the bodies of two men connected with the murder of two Canadian citizens and a Montana highway patrolman.

She recognized both photos. One was Andrew. The other was Krunk, Dylan's drug contact in Billings.

The news anchor told her that authorities speculated that the two men, identified as Andrew Falling Bird and Terrance Hayes, had ended their lives in a bizarre murder/suicide pact. A news conference was planned at—

Quinn shut off the television and moved toward the door. She needed to get back to the HIVE. Now.

37.

"Hello, Dylan."

Dylan awoke with a start at the sound of the voice, took a few seconds to orient himself. He was on the couch in the living room of the apartment, the TV muted in front of him. He realized, with a start, that he now had an IV in his arm, a semitransparent liquid working its way into his veins.

Li sat in the large chair in the corner. "You were having withdrawals," Li said. "Probably even some hallucinations, brought on by the physical symptoms. Do you remember anything?"

Yes, Joni said inside. *You remember it all, don't you?*

"No," Dylan lied.

"Good. Doctors tell me you've stabilized. You're getting through the worst of it. You might have more hallucinations, but detox can be rough—"

"So you're detoxing me by pumping me full of drugs. Makes sense."

Li held up his hands in a surrendering gesture. "To help you with the physical symptoms only."

"So you just lock people away and give them drugs until they join your little party here? Is that the general plan?"

"Only for a very special few."

"Wow, we're special."

"Actually, I'm just here to see you. Webb's taking care of some other things right now."

"Like what?"

"Like his shoulder. Looks like it's healing well, but we thought it would be best if he had it looked at by one of our doctors."

"Who's we?"

Li smiled. "Webb and I. Who else?"

"Tell you the truth, sounds like a strong-arm tactic. Separate the prisoners, get them in rooms one-on-one."

"I think you have the wrong idea about us."

Dylan took a deep breath. It was hard to shake the ominous feelings he had about HIVE, even as he found himself drawn to it. Like a moth to the flame, he was fascinated by the light, but some part of him instinctively knew that getting too close would fry him.

He wanted to believe HIVE was an answer for him, a salvation of some kind. He wanted to believe they had his best interests at heart. He needed help, that much was true. He was the guy haunted by the voice of a sister, haunted by the death of a friend in Iraq, haunted by an abandoned heritage, haunted by delusions and drugs and a thousand other things. That was all true, and he wanted so much to believe that what he was seeing around him was being warped by those haunted filters; he wanted to believe he was like those people on the *Intervention* marathon, misinterpreting the people around him as foes rather than friends.

Trouble was, wanting to believe something didn't make it true. And now, more than ever, the equations weren't balancing.

Li held up the empty bag of powdered antibiotic the vet had given to Webb. Seemed like years ago now.

"We don't stock pig antibiotics, of course. Wait, I take that back: we do stock pig antibiotics, but we only give them to pigs."

"I need some coffee. Or is that spiked too?"

Li laughed. "I'll make it. You've got the IV, although it looks like it's almost done."

Dylan looked at the reddish-brown liquid seeping into his vein. It was almost like being at the VA hospital, waking up, looking at the various medical equipment surrounding him, asking for pain-killers, returning to his slumber.

That was before they pushed him out of the bed and into physi-cal therapy. The memories of physical therapy went into the kill box of his brain immediately.

Li was in the kitchen now, his attention focused on the coffee-maker. Dylan pulled the IV out of his arm, let the needle drop to the floor, where it began spilling the dark liquid onto the carpet.

"Don't you have a hard time selling that?" he said to Li. "Communism and socialism and whatnot? The great evils we all grew up with, you know."

Li laughed again. "Yeah, after the collapse of the stock market, the banking system, the mortgage industry, and the auto industry, it's really difficult to get people interested in another way."

In the kitchen, Li began frothing milk.

Dylan scratched at the IV wound on his arm, now leaking blood. He put pressure on the wound with the thumb of his left hand, waited. Right now, that was about all he could do.

A few minutes later Li approached with two foamy cups. "Hope you don't mind, it's not your basic cowboy coffee. It's one of those automatic latté machines." He caught sight of the IV, now emptying its contents onto the clean carpet, paused only momentarily.

He smiled. "Always the rebel, eh, Dylan? No matter; the IV's already done its work." He set a mug down in front of Dylan, retreated, and sat on the chair again.

"It's not communism, anyway. It's just a sustainable community. Everyone has a vote in what happens in the community as well."

"So you're trying to tell me Great Sower isn't a synonym for Great Dictator."

"Not at all. I'm just the . . . the founding father."

"You're the George Washington of HIVE."

"If I'm George Washington, I suppose I should say I cannot tell a lie."

"*Pffft.* That was a lie. First government conspiracy, you know."

"People might say you have big trust and authority issues, Dylan. Sure you were in the military?"

"*Were* is the key word there. Also, just so you know: aliens at Area 51, and we didn't really land on the moon."

"You're trying to mask your fear with sarcasm. Natural. But if you knew what was truly happening out there, it would be much scarier than alien autopsies."

"Scarier than what's in here too?"

"Definitely."

"And I'm sure you'll tell me my point of view. Drug me until I agree with it."

His fear was gone now. Was that good? In fact, it had been replaced by a sense of . . . complacency. He was enjoying this time with Li, enjoying this time away from the outside world.

That's the drugs talking, Joni said inside his mind. *Whatever he's got you on, you're higher than a kite.*

Better than Percocets, he agreed.

He's got everyone in the whole community drugged, she said. *That's why they have that dopey grin on their faces all the time.*

You're probably right.

So what are you going to do about it?

Nothing.

Nothing? You have to fight against this, make yourself—

He pushed Joni into the kill box without warning, let himself sink into the deep, plush comfort of the drug inside his veins. Whatever it was. It didn't matter, because he felt better, so much better, than he had in . . . forever. He knew he was being sucked into a vortex, but he didn't care. Inside, he could still think, could still express his thoughts of cynicism, but somehow it all seemed so . . . unimportant now. If this was life as a drone, he could handle it. Much more pleasant than life as a soldier. Or a cripple. Or a crippled soldier.

"Ah, I think you're starting to feel it," he heard Li's voice say.

Dylan opened his eyes. Funny, he didn't even remember closing them.

"That means you're ready," Li said, sipping at his coffee.

"Ready for what?"

"Ready to come out of hiding."

"I made parole, then."

"Now you get to make a choice: you leave, go on your way, or you stay."

"Since I'm drugged up and locked in one of your spider holes, I don't think it's exactly a free choice."

"Of course it's a free choice. But I think we're the last people you should be worried about, Dylan."

"Who should worry me more?"

"Plenty of people out there. Local sheriff, Montana Highway Patrol, FBI office out of Billings, your drug connections looking for their money. That's just off the top of my head—I'm sure there are others I don't know about."

"No, you seem to have it pretty well covered."

"Had all of them comb through here. Happens somewhat frequently, you understand: government—everyone from ATF to Homeland Security—takes a great interest in us. Takes a great interest in anyone who represents a threat to the system as it is."

"So how do you keep them out?"

Li shrugged, set down his coffee on the table in front of them. "We don't."

"What do you mean?"

"Any time they want to come in, we let them take a look around. We like to be open about who we are, let them see anything they want to see."

"Anything you want them to see, you mean. I don't recall any federal agents waltzing through this hidden apartment."

"Well, as I'm sure you understand, our community appeals to a . . . certain kind of person. The kind that wants to drop out, get a fresh start. We give them that chance."

"By hiding them away from authorities until the heat cools down a little," Dylan responded. "Then they're indebted to you, and more likely to become part of your operation. Probably even more loyal, because after all, what are they gonna do? Blow the whistle?"

Li nodded slowly, still smiling. Always smiling. Just like everyone in this crazy place. Dylan had to admit, even he felt that psycho smile on his face right now. Whatever drug he was on, it was a good one.

"Yes, there's all that," Li said. "It furthers our own cause, of course. But if we treat people right, give them the kinds of chances they never had, you'd be amazed at what kind of work they can do."

"I still don't get, though, how you keep out—oh, I don't know—traitors. You'd think spooks would be trying to infiltrate this place all the time. I mean, they've gotta know you're harboring some fugitives."

"You're right, of course. But we have a few things on our side." He picked up his coffee, sipped at it again. "First, the government is a lot more hands-off now than it used to be. After the Branch Davidian and Ruby Ridge messes—let's just say they don't want any more bad press, people calling them jackbooted thugs. So they're a bit more careful when it comes to . . . alternative communities such as ours."

Dylan nodded.

"Second, think about it: what's the real upside for them? Here, we change people, make them productive, keep them out of trouble—all without the cost of high-profile trials or incarceration. In a way, we provide a crude kind of service for the government. If people decide to leave the safety of the compound, well, by all means, it's open season on them. But in here, it's a different world."

"So you're saying the government lets you keep fugitives here, because it makes things easier for them."

"Did I say that?"

"You didn't deny it."

Li shrugged, took an even greater interest in his coffee.

"What about Webb?"

"What about him?"

"Is he staying?"

"Of course. I think he'll do well—I already had this conversation with him."

"And you wouldn't mind if I talked to him."

"Talk to anyone you want."

Dylan sighed. "So what now? I say yes, do we go through some public ceremony or something?"

Li laughed. "You really do have the wrong idea about us, Dylan. We're not about secret ceremonies or controlling community members or anything like that. You decide to stay, you stay; you share in the work, join any of our divisions—production, packaging, maintenance, whatever—and you share in the rewards. You decide to leave, you can leave now."

Li drained the last of his coffee. "Before you make your decision—and let me say once again, it's your decision—let me show you something." Li picked up the remote, turned on the television. "Isn't TiVo great? I recorded a little something for you earlier."

Li chose a recorded program and hit Play. It was a local news broadcast, the talking head of an anchor behind a news desk on one of the Great Falls TV stations.

"Breaking news today," the anchor said, peering at the camera. "The two suspects wanted for an attack on a Montana highway patrolman have been found dead, apparently of a suicide pact. For more, we go to Melanie Waters in Lewistown."

"Thanks, Dan," Melanie said, standing on a snow-laden street. "Authorities released the identities of the two men who attacked and killed Trooper Dave Evans outside Lewistown just a few days ago. They have been identified as Andrew Falling Bird, a member of the Assiniboine Tribe in Fort Belknap, and Terrance Hayes of Billings, both with ties to the drug trade in Montana."

Photos of faces Dylan recognized flashed on the screen.

"Hayes, who went by the street name Krunk, was believed to be a major drug trafficker in Billings. The bodies of the two suspects were found in a hotel room near Bozeman, both men dead of apparent self-inflicted gunshot wounds."

The screen flashed back to Melanie, who was perky and smiley. An odd match for the story she was reporting.

"Authorities also believe the two men may be linked to a separate double homicide involving two Canadian citizens near the Turner Port of Entry, but have so far refused to release further details. Reporting live from Lewistown, I'm Melanie Waters. Back to you, Dan."

Dan started to blab something about the cold weather, and Li hit the pause button.

Dylan continued to stare at the frozen image of Dan's ultra-white teeth. "When did all of this happen?" he stammered.

Li smiled, a huge, genuine smile. "While you were here underground. Safe and secure."

Amazing. And . . . scary. Somehow Li had orchestrated all of this, tying together law enforcement, the drug trade, and who knew what else. Dylan knew he should feel relieved; his most pressing problems, after all, had been solved for him. Instead, he felt as if he'd just stepped into a deep, dark hole with no bottom. And yet, it felt good. What was so bad about being in a dark hole with no bottom? He would be out of reach in such a place.

"I thought this might help your decision," Li said. "We're very good at cleaning up things, at giving people a new chance, a fresh start. You get to start with a clean slate; how many people have that opportunity, Dylan?"

Dylan sat dumbfounded for a few minutes.

Five people are dead, Dylan.

I know, Joni. I killed two of them.

If you stay, other people might die. He might even ask you to do the killing.

But if I leave, he'll probably have people follow me, kill me before I hit

Eddie's Corner. This Li has connections. Why or how, I don't know.

So you're saying HIVE is just the mafia dressed up in Green Peace clothes?

"Dylan? You with me?"

Dylan blinked, looked at Li again. "I guess you're making an offer I can't refuse."

38.

Quinn sat in her Chevy Silverado, parked on the county road that cut through HIVE land on the north side of the compound. Several hundred yards away, she saw the blades of half a dozen turbines spinning lazily, even though the wind was quieter than usual.

She'd planned to use Andrew to get into the compound, but that option was gone now. HIVE had its arms around Dylan, and it was moving fast to erase Dylan's recent tracks. That meant she needed to move quickly. Today.

After scanning the property in the guise of pheasant hunting yesterday, she'd confirmed what she'd long suspected: a few key turbines on the property held underground bunkers, safe from outside eyes and removed from the rest of the village proper. She guessed Dylan was being kept underground—literally and figuratively—in one of those. She'd even narrowed it down to three potential turbines, based on the activities she'd observed the previous day.

She opened the door, zipped her black snowsuit, cradled her shiny new snowmobile helmet beneath her right arm, and began hiking back toward the highway; it was less than half a mile away, and she could be there in ten minutes or so.

This particular county road was the closest to the actual HIVE center, which was why she had chosen it; in a straight line it was half a mile at most to this exact location. The back roads of Montana, especially during hunting seasons, often had pickups parked on them, so she was sure the Silverado wouldn't attract any attention if she left it here for a few hours.

The snowsuit and helmet, carefully selected to match what she'd seen HIVE members wearing inside, would help make sure she was anonymous and invisible when she was inside. She'd even outfitted the helmet with a 900 MHz headset and microphone, which would let her pick up the nonsecured chatter she'd monitored on her scanner the previous day.

The trickier issue was getting inside. The HIVE didn't exactly have tight security, at least to the casual observer. Barbed wire fence surrounded the property, along with posted No TRESPASSING signs. No heavy-duty security or alarms, but she knew the compound had heavy camera surveillance. So even though she could probably walk onto the compound property itself without tripping any alarms, she'd most likely attract attention on a security camera.

That meant, as attractive as hopping the fence and simply slipping inside might seem, the front gate was the best way to stay invisible.

She reached the highway and walked north toward Eddie's Corner. A few minutes later she flagged down a red Mercury Mountaineer.

"Snowmobile break down?" the driver asked, looking at her snowsuit and helmet. Good; just the reaction she'd wanted.

"Ran out of gas," she said, sliding into the seat.

"Musta missed your rig."

"Oh, my snowmobile's down the county road back there, about half a mile." She pushed the helmet into the middle of the seat.

"I meant your truck."

"It's down the county road, too, but a lot farther than a half mile."

"Gotcha." The driver smiled and nodded. Obviously not a snowmobiler, which was good; if he were, she would have been forced into a conversation about preferred sleds, trails, terrain, and such. Maybe even a conversation about why she was sledding on a county road by herself and not carrying extra fuel.

"Eddie's Corner is just up here a few miles," he said. "You can get some gas there. Won't be able to get you back, though—gotta get to Lewistown for a meeting."

"No worries," she said. "I'm just glad you stopped."

They spent the next ten minutes talking about the Internet. Pete, the driver of the Mountaineer, made kitchen cabinets and was heading to Lewistown to bid on a large job for some Internet millionaire who'd bought a small ranch outside Lewistown. Pete figured he was in the wrong line of business, and he should be making lots of money off an Internet site of some kind.

Quinn nodded and smiled at all the appropriate pauses, until finally they arrived at Eddie's Corner and said their good-byes.

Quinn watched the Mountaineer turn east toward Lewistown, then approached the front doors of the convenience store and restaurant.

She went to the long counter on the restaurant side of the building, sat on the stool nearest the convenience store cash register, ordered coffee, and kept her ears open, catching conversations around her.

Within a few minutes, she overheard the exact kind of conversation she wanted. Two truckers standing in line at the store cash register were swapping stories of what they were hauling, and one of them said he was on the way to switch out reefer trailers at the HIVE. He'd just popped in here for a quick pack of smokes, because he always felt like he needed a few extra puffs any time he was surrounded by those weird crunchy granola types at the HIVE.

Quinn dropped a few bucks on the counter to cover the coffee, then casually walked outside into the wind and looked around. Most of the trucks were parked around the back of the restaurant and convenience store, just to the south.

About half a dozen rigs sat on the snow-packed gravel of the parking area, two of them with their diesel engines running, a steady fog of white spewing from their exhaust stacks.

One of the idling rigs was pulling an unmarked refrigerator trailer.

Bingo. Even truck drivers left their vehicles running in Montana winters. And as she'd hoped, it had a small sleeper cab on it, meaning she might not have to ride in the trailer.

She went to the truck, took a quick look around to make sure no one was watching, and hauled herself up the passenger side, opening the door and pulling herself in. The sleeper cab behind the truck's front seats was even smaller than she'd imagined—just a tiny bunk. But the driver had a gaudy NASCAR-themed curtain hanging between the sleeper and the front cab. She pushed aside the curtain and folded herself behind the driver's seat.

Within a few minutes she was calm and still, tuned in to the amorphous shapes around her, feeling the pressure inside her body and outside her body beginning to equalize.

A surprising feeling, considering what she was about to do. The first rule of her kind was: you never approach an infested community. Your anonymity was sacrosanct, and if you ever went directly into an infestation, that anonymity would be compromised. You would leave a trail, no matter how careful you were. You would perhaps even become a carrier, because no one was immune to that.

But this was all new territory. Dylan Runs Ahead was a chosen; that's why Li had acted so quickly after having him in HIVE's grasp. If she could take out Dylan before Li made the switch, she could bring down the whole colony.

Maybe.

On the other side of the curtain, she heard the driver open the door on the big diesel and slide behind the wheel. He shifted into gear, let out the clutch, and began inching toward the highway that would take her back to the HIVE a few miles south. Once the truck was inside the compound and ready to switch trailers, she could slip into the HIVE unnoticed. She was quite sure of this.

She hadn't been able to bring her whole toolbox, but the gun inside the snowsuit bit into her hip. She welcomed the pain. It was like an embedded object, and it helped relieve the pressure.

A few minutes later she felt the truck slow and make a right-hand turn, then come to a stop. They were at the HIVE, in the transfer center outside the compound itself.

She listened as the driver opened his door and slid down from the cab, leaving his rig running. Quickly, Quinn put on the snow-mobiling helmet and powered on its internal transmitter, tuned to the frequency that carried HIVE's internal communications. After a few minutes she heard a guard call for a loader to meet an empty reefer trailer at the egg warehouse. Moments later the door to the cab opened again, and the driver slid back into his seat. He shifted into gear and edged into the HIVE. After a few more minutes he came to a shuddering stop with a hiss of the brakes, then backed in his trailer and climbed down from the cab of the truck.

Quinn closed her eyes, waited a few moments, then unfolded herself from behind the seat. She pushed aside the NASCAR curtain and peered out into the cab, then slid into the passenger seat and unlatched the door. A few seconds later she slipped lightly to the ground. She walked around the front of the truck, nodded at the driver, who stood there smoking a cigarette. He nodded back, more than used to seeing helmeted figures in snowmobile suits around the HIVE compound.

Quinn began walking west on the circular road, making her way toward the snowmobile storage.

Easy. So far.

A few minutes later she slid into an empty space in the storage shed. Certainly she would have shown up on security cams, but to anyone casually observing, she would look like any of the dozen or so similarly clad people in the community.

Okay, now for the touchy part. She keyed the microphone inside the helmet and spoke. "Frank, I need some assistance here," she said, then clicked off the mike and waited for a response.

She'd heard people call in to Frank the day before, when she'd been here in the guise of a pheasant hunter. Hopefully, Frank was on shift again today; she hadn't heard anything since getting inside the compound.

A few moments later a voice answered on the line. "Yeah, this is Frank. That you, Jennifer?"

Jennifer. Yes, she'd heard Jennifer on the radio the day before too. She closed her eyes, hoped Jennifer wasn't listening, and keyed the mike again. "Yeah," she answered. "Can you give me a status on the two who checked in?"

"You mean the guys in detox?"

Detox. Interesting. "Yeah."

"Don't have anything new from Turbine 32 since a note from Jeff this morning. Why do you need it, anyway?"

Turbine 32. Turbine 32. She'd studied maps of the HIVE compound, but she had no real way of knowing which turbine was number 32.

"Scheduling some maintenance for DermaGen," she said.

"I hear you," Frank answered. "Let me send out Sam to do a check now."

Quinn smiled. Sam. She filed that away in her memory for a few seconds. "Great." She was flying by the seat of her pants, but so far, so good. She'd heard a lot of chatter about status checks and DermaGen the day before.

After a few minutes she heard a snowmobile start outside the shed, rev a few times, then start to move away. She jumped to her feet, left the shed, and found her way to the nearest snowmobile. About a hundred yards away and moving fast, she saw the other snowmobile receding from her.

She slid onto the snowmobile, thumbed the ignition, and revved her own machine. With any luck, she was about to be led to Dylan Runs Ahead.

After about five minutes, the snowmobile ahead of her came to the base of one of the turbines and stopped. The driver climbed off the sled, then turned when he heard Quinn's own machine approaching. Okay, time for some more maneuvering.

She brought her snowmobile to a stop, turned it off, held up a hand. The other driver slid off his helmet, looked at her quizzically.

She slid off her own helmet, gave her best smile. "Sam!" she said enthusiastically. "How've you been?"

"Good," Sam said. He hesitated, not wanting to ask the question who she was. After all, she knew his name, and there were only a few hundred people in the HIVE community itself; he should know her name. Quinn saw all of this in his eyes, so she pushed her advantage.

"Need to do a transfer," she said.

"A transfer? Nancy just came on shift a few hours ago."

Nancy. Remember that. "Yeah," she agreed. "But Frank told me to transfer her."

Sam didn't seem convinced. "Transfer her with who?"

"Hmm?"

"If you're transferring, where's the other nurse?"

Okay, that lie didn't work. Think quick. "Well, it's me, of course," she said. "Who else would it be?"

"Something weird going on here," Sam said.

"I know," she said. "We better check up on 'em inside, make sure everything is okay."

"No, I'm just gonna make a call to Frank," he said, starting to put on his helmet.

In that moment, she had to act. She sprang at Sam, slipped behind him, put her arm around his neck before he could put on his helmet, applied the choke hold. He thrashed for about twenty seconds, then passed out, his brain starved for the blood-rich oxygen blocked by her arm hold.

Okay, time for Plan B. With any luck, nothing she'd just done had been captured on camera. But Quinn wasn't counting on luck.

She slipped her arms under Sam's shoulders and dragged him toward a door at the base of the giant turbine. Above, its giant blades moved slowly in the wind.

She found a button by the door and pressed it. A call button, she hoped.

"Yes?" a voice answered. Nancy, she hoped.

Quinn did her best to appear frantic; she kept her back to the door and stooped over Sam's motionless body, acting as if she were trying to revive him.

"Oh, Nancy," she said, putting on her best act. "Something happened to Sam."

"What is it?"

"He . . . I don't know, he just passed out. Maybe you can look at him."

There was a pause, and then the speaker on the door activated again. "I'm not really supposed to—"

"You don't want him to die, do you? I think he may be having a heart attack."

A few seconds later the door clicked, and Quinn grabbed at it, swinging it toward her. Inside, she watched as Nancy made her way up some concrete stairs.

"I don't know what happened," Quinn said as Nancy stooped over Sam's body. "You check on him, and I'll go call Frank."

Quinn bounded down the stairs, leaving Nancy behind.

39.

Dylan continued to drift in and out of consciousness after Li left; groggily, he was aware of one of the nurses—Nancy or Lisa, he wasn't sure which one—coming in and checking his vitals a few times.

Eventually his head began to clear a bit, and a renewed sense of clarity started to settle. An odd, disconcerting sense of clarity, almost like one he'd never experienced before. A freedom he'd not felt since . . . since he'd lost Joni, he decided.

You didn't lose me, she said inside his mind. *I'm still here.*

But you're not real. You're just part of my . . . imagination.

"Dylan?" It was the nurse. Nancy, yes.

"What?" He looked, but it wasn't the nurse. Some other woman. A woman he recognized from . . . somewhere. But his mind was too fuzzy, too drugged, to recall where.

"Time for a transfer."

"A transfer to where?"

"You're drugged out of your mind, aren't you?" she asked.

"Unfortunately. Or maybe fortunately."

She handed him the helmet she held in her hands. "Do me a favor, Dylan. Put on this helmet."

He did as instructed.

"Okay," she said. "Now, I'm going to key the mike, and when I do, you're going to say, 'This is Sam, Status Check Clear at Turbine 32.'"

He nodded.

"Say it once for me," she said.

"This is Sam, Status Check Clear at Turbine 32."

"Good. I'm going to turn on the mike now, and you say it just like that." She gave him a thumbs-up, and he spoke, reciting the line a second time.

"Good," she said, pulling off his helmet. "Now, it's time for us to get going."

"Get going where?"

"I'll have to tell you on the way."

She grabbed his hand; Dylan began putting one foot in front of the other, made his way to the stairs, climbing. He stumbled on a few steps, but the woman caught him, propped him up, urged him to keep climbing.

Outside, he stood, swaying in the breeze a few moments. The nurse was out there with some other man, checking his pulse or temperature or something. What was the nurse's name again? He couldn't remember. It was an odd feeling, not being able to remember these little details. But a nice feeling, too, in a way.

The nurse rose, started to say something, but then the woman in the snowmobile suit slid behind her, did some kind of strange hold on her. After several seconds, the nice nurse slumped to the ground beside the other guy Dylan didn't know.

It was funny to watch, actually. Everything was infinitely funny now. The driver shoved past him, slipped onto the snowmobile, keyed the ignition; the whine of the electric motor revved high, then died down to a dull drone.

A dull drone. Ha. That's what he was becoming now, wasn't it? A drone for HIVE. If only people on the outside knew how fitting that word was when they tossed it around.

The driver motioned to him, so he slipped onto the snow-mobile behind her; instantly, the machine shot away from the base of the turbine and out across the white fields.

Dylan noticed the snow sparkling in the sunshine, like bright, clear diamonds. He hadn't noticed that about the snow on the ride out to the detox center. Or maybe he had. He couldn't remember.

They continued toward the HIVE compound for a few minutes until they were about half a mile away. Then the snowmobile shifted abruptly, turning away from the HIVE and veering toward the north. The sudden shift caused the snowmobile to tilt danger-ously for a few seconds, as Dylan had been caught off guard without leaning into the turn.

"Hey," Dylan said, surprised. "Don't you—" Then he stopped, realizing the driver couldn't hear him anyway.

The driver accelerated, pushing the snowmobile as fast as it would go. After several seconds, the driver applied the brakes, and they came to a sliding stop beside a barbed wire fence. On the other side of the fence a white pickup sat, silent.

The driver vaulted cleanly off the snowmobile, removed her helmet. "Okay, Dylan, let's get going."

After a few hazy seconds, Dylan recognized the face, the crazy, mangled hair, the cut on the forehead now healing. It was the woman who had chased him and Webb on the highway. The bounty hunter sent by Krunk.

He still didn't know her name, though.

But hadn't Krunk been killed? This didn't make any sense. He started to speak, realized his tongue was too thick.

Behind him, he thought he could hear the sound of other snowmobiles approaching. Still a ways off, but coming closer.

"You tried to—" he stammered.

"We don't have time to talk," the woman said. "Think you can make it over the fence?"

He looked at the fence, nodded, took a step, and went down to his knees.

"So much for the plan," he heard her mutter. "I'll have to cut the fence. You just hang tight for a few seconds while I get some snips out of my truck."

He nodded again, closed his eyes, listened to the snowmobiles approach. Just when he was about to open his eyes again, he felt the woman beginning to drag him.

I'm gonna die, Joni, he said as he felt his body going soft, mushy.

You're not going to die.

He smiled, kept his eyes closed as he heard the woman opening a truck door.

"Stand up," she ordered. "Help me out a little."

No, I'm gonna die because she's gonna kill me, and I'm helping her by getting into her pickup. He grinned, barely able to open his eyes. *Wonder what the VA therapist would think about that little tidbit?*

You were blown up in Iraq, and you lived through that.

That's what I'm trying to tell you, Joni, he answered as the darkness closed in once more. *I don't want to live through it.*

40.

Dylan felt himself rising from a deep, dark place.

The crook of his left arm itched, and he absently scratched at it with his right hand.

"Don't scratch that," a voice said. "You'll make it worse."

He stopped, tried to open his eyes, closed them in teary-eyed pain as the light assaulted them. He tried to scratch at his arm again.

"I told you not to scratch."

He tried to open his eyes again, managed it with a bit more success. His vision didn't come into focus, but hey, baby steps.

"How about now?" he mumbled. "Can I scratch now?"

"What the heck. Go ahead."

His vision finally resolved enough to let him make out the crazy woman who had tried to kill him on the highway. For someone who seemed so intent on killing him, she seemed awfully worried about him scratching his wounds.

She was sitting at a particleboard desk just a few feet away, casually eating a red apple, watching some home and garden show on television.

"What—" He stopped, unsure what his question should be. *What happened? What's going on? What am I doing here? What are you doing here?* He wanted to ask all of the above, but he didn't have the energy.

She took a bite of the apple, wiped at her mouth with the back of her hand. "What . . ." she prompted.

"Who—" he said, but his brain was still fuzzy.

"Yeah, well, maybe the *who* question is a good place to start. Call me Quinn. And I already know who you are, Dylan. So now we've properly met."

"Where are we?"

"Sounds like you're just gonna skip right over the *what*. Okay. Great Falls. You're a guest at the Steel Bridge Motel. Guests say it's the nicest and the cleanest. If you believe the sign out front."

"Great Falls? How?"

"I brought you here."

"Why?"

"That's a big one. Let's save it for later."

"Water?" he asked.

She fished around in her backpack again, then threw him a bottle of water. He studied the label before he twisted off the top. "It's not the HIVE brand," he observed.

"Let's just say I'm not a big fan of HIVE. You shouldn't be either."

"You see me wearing the official hemp T-shirt?" He took a drink, trying to think. Okay, so he was dealing with yet another wing nut, the latest in a long line of wing nuts. In Iraq, soldiers driven half mad by the constant threat of death. At the VA hospital, soldiers driven half mad by being removed from the constant threat of death. Drug dealers and junkies, brains muddled by their preferred poisons. Li and his band of New-Age, let's-just-love-the-Earthers, doped-up smiles constantly present on their faces as they lectured you about the evils of all humanity.

And now, this woman, obviously hopped up on a few drugs of her own. What about meth? It fit. Meth addicts tended to invent elaborate stories of conspiracies and—

What about you? Joni's voice asked. *Remember: you hear voices. And you split all your thoughts into sections. And*—

Okay, Joni, you've made your point.

Just saying.

Just don't.

"Who are you talking to?" Quinn asked, staring at him.

Had he said something aloud? Maybe; he'd been known to do it before. "Sorry, just—I sometimes talk to myself."

"Plenty of people do. But I'm talking about your voice inside."

Cue the creepy Twilight Zone *music,* Joni said.

"That voice," Quinn said. "Talking about the *Twilight Zone.*"

Dylan was speechless for a moment.

Uncharacteristically, so was Joni.

"I . . . you can hear that?"

"Yes," Quinn said, sitting up straight, seeming unsurprised. As if this were an everyday thing for her.

"You . . . can read my mind?"

Quinn laughed. "Not in the least. But I'm a—some of us, yourself included, are . . . sensitive to things beyond the physical."

"Sensitive?"

"Sensitive to others, for starters. Their emotions, their compulsions. Most people who are sensitive are diagnosed with OCD, a pretty large chunk with other mental disorders: schizophrenia, paranoia, and the like. All because they feel things most people can't. You're not really that far—not yet—but you definitely have some compulsions."

"Like what?"

She studied him for a moment. "You're a pattern person. Numbers a little bit, but more patterns in the way you see, the way you think. You break down what you see, what you think about, into chunks. Boxes, I guess you could say."

The kill box, Joni whispered.

"Kill boxes? That's what you call them?"

Dylan swallowed, feeling his throat click. "Just one. The kill box. That's . . . part of it."

"The deepest, darkest part," Quinn said. "The place where you banish anything you don't want to think about."

He cleared his throat. "Yeah."

"I know it's freaky," Quinn said. "But like I said, you can sense those things, too, if you try. You can probably get a sense of my main compulsions, how my brain operates."

He studied her for a few moments, got nothing. Then, inside, Joni's voice spoke.

She cuts. Hurts herself.

"Started out as a cutter," Quinn replied. "Now it's more . . . the official term is self-embedding disorder. Not just cutting, but putting objects under my skin."

"Paper clips," Dylan said aloud, getting a sense of the woman called Quinn. It was an odd sensation, something like standing next to a river: he caught flashes of her thoughts, floating quickly by on the current.

"Yes, paper clips. But anything, really. Well, not anything. Metal works best. Needles. Staples. That kind of thing."

Dylan drained the last of his bottle, closed his eyes for a

moment. He heard rustling, and when he opened his eyes again, Quinn was holding another bottle of water. "Drink up," she said. "You're probably pretty dehydrated."

She threw the bottle and he caught it. But he made no move to open it. Not yet.

He wanted to talk to Joni, but that didn't feel like an option; Quinn being able to hear those interior conversations made him feel . . . exposed. Like someone had the crosshairs of a rifle sight trained on him. He'd felt that before, after all. Too many times to count. Some nights in his dreams.

"So you sidestepped my question," Quinn prodded.

"Which one?"

"The one about your interior voice. It's not you. It's—you called her Joni."

"My sister."

"She's your sister?"

"Was."

"Little sister?"

"Yeah. Why?"

"Because you felt like you should be her protector. Typical family dynamic. And you obviously feel like you failed."

He shook his head. "Not a feeling at all. Just a fact." He cleared his throat, which was getting dryer. "Thing was, she always looked out for me growing up, you know? She was levelheaded, always the more sensible one. And the one chance I had to protect her . . ." He trailed off, his thoughts branching into well-worn paths of regret.

"Protect her from what?"

Dylan glanced at Quinn, focused his eyes on Quinn again.

You don't have to do this, Dylan.

Yeah, Joni. I do.

41.

The cop was trying to be all Officer Friendly on Dylan. One of the two main types of officers you had on the rez. Officer Friendly, who was usually a white guy from out somewhere else, all wrapped up in social justice and wanting to go do his part for racial equality. Officer Friendly always sympathized with you, understood your plight, put himself in your shoes.

As much as a white boy from Chicago could put himself in an Indian's shoes.

But the Officer Friendlys were always much better than the alternative: Officer Rez Boy. The Officer Rez Boys, they got drunk on the little bit of power their uniforms gave them.

So Dylan should have been happy he got one of the Officer Friendlys, a guy who insisted Dylan call him Steve rather than Detective Chambers. That's what the Friendlys did: they wanted you to call them by their first names, so you could, you know, rap with them.

"So tell me what you remember, Dylan."

"Nothing to remember."

"Lots to remember, if you just go through the details. This is important; we have to get it all now, you understand. We don't get a second chance at any of it."

Steve was giving him an earnest look, a look that told Dylan he was being sincere, and expected the same kind of sincerity in return.

Dylan sighed, leaned back in his chair. "I was at a . . . party."

"What kind of party?"

"Just graduated."

"Okay."

"So . . . some of us, not like it was a big kegger or anything. But, you know, we got together at Kenny's house."

"So you were drinking?"

"Yeah, a little. But I don't usually drink."

This was true, but Dylan could see the doubt in Detective Chambers's—Steve's—eyes. A young Indian kid, just out of high school in Hardin? Of course he drank. It was the Curse of the Red Man, part of the reason why people like Detective Steve Chambers worked on the rez. Because it was their chance to reach out to troubled Indian youth, get them off drugs and alcohol, help them find better lives.

Yeah, a real Officer Friendly, this one.

"And how long were you there?"

"You asking when I left?"

"Yes."

"I was supposed to pick up Joni at eight. I . . . guess I lost track of time, and she called . . . I don't know . . . quarter after eight."

"From?"

"Violin teacher's house. Violin instructor, whatever you call it. I . . . we share a car. She'd told me to just take the car and come pick her up at eight. So when she called, it was—"

"A reminder to come get her."

"Exactly."

"You left right away?"

Dylan nodded. "Within . . . two minutes. She said to meet her at the Minit Mart. The violin guy lives just a few blocks from there, and she wanted to get a lemonade for the road."

"So what time did you get to the Minit Mart?"

"Maybe . . . eight thirtyish."

"She was gone?"

"Nowhere. Billy inside the Minit Mart—I know him—said she never came in. He didn't see her hanging in the parking lot either."

Detective Chambers made a few more notes on his pad, looked at Dylan again. "She's only been gone a few hours now," he said, trying to sound reassuring. "Usually, someone ends up missing, they show up in the first twelve to twenty-four hours. Matter of fact, that's why we usually wait twenty-four hours before investigating any missing person report. But I'm not waiting twenty-four hours in this particular case. I'm on it now. We're gonna find your sister."

Detective Chambers stood, patted Dylan's arm, a gesture that said, *I'm ready to be your hero.*

Dylan just nodded, feeling oddly numb.

"Your parents will be here soon," Detective Chambers said. "You can go home, get a good sleep. By morning, I bet we'll find out where Joni's gotten off to."

Detective Chambers didn't know it at the time, but he was wrong about both of those things.

Dylan wouldn't get a good night of sleep.

And he'd seen his sister for the last time.

42.

"What happened to her?" Quinn asked.

"It was like . . . I don't know . . . one of those stories off *48 Hours* or something. She . . . just disappeared."

"How long ago?"

"Three years."

"So when did she start speaking to you . . . inside?"

He uttered a sharp laugh. "When did I start hearing the voice? Not long after. Had to get off the rez, you know. Thing of it is, it's hard to get off the rez. Lot of people never leave, and it's both a curse and a blessing. But you're the guy who didn't show up to get his sister, you're kind of an outsider. Parents never said anything to me, but really, what was there to say? If I'd been there on time, she never would have headed to the Minit Mart. She'd be here today.

"Anyway, I was kind of like Typhoid Mary in just a few weeks. Needed to get out. Needed to get away. So I signed up for the army, and in basic, when I was on one of those long runs, Joni's voice just . . . popped into my head." He looked at Quinn, tears forming in his eyes. "She's been there ever since."

Quinn sighed. "It's a big thing, when you realize you're . . . different. Maybe just an outsider, maybe an outcast, even if you invent some of that in your own mind. When you don't feel like you fit in, you don't fit in." She paused. "That's how I got recruited too."

He swallowed again. "Recruited?"

"Like you. Only I joined a different kind of army."

"What kind would that be?"

"Yeah, I suppose it's best to just lay it on the line." She took the last bite of her apple, pitched it into the garbage can, chewed thoughtfully for a few seconds. "But if you think what you've heard so far is strange, I gotta warn you, that's just the start."

Dylan nodded, his head numb.

Quinn returned the nod, sat back. "I tried to get to you before you made it to the HIVE—"

The image of the chase flashed in his mind, instantly angering him. "I remember. When you tried to kill me."

"I wasn't trying to kill you, Dylan. You're here right now, aren't you? I was trying to stop you. Anyway, that didn't work out. Which is why I took the unprecedented step of going inside an infestation—"

"An infestation?"

"The HIVE, in this case. But there are several infestations around the world."

"Infestations of?"

"Are you going to keep interrupting me, or can I get this out?"

"Sorry; go ahead."

"Anyway, I went inside to get you—something I'd normally never do, but you're not a normal case. Hoping to get to you before they did. That's why I had to do more." She paused. "That's why I had to pull you out." She paused. "But then I saw the IV mark on your arm."

The itch. He looked at his arm. "Yeah. The IV was . . . well, it was part of detox."

She gave him that grim smile again. A smile that made him squirm uncomfortably. "That what they told you? Detox?"

"Yeah. I, uh . . . I have a bit of a problem with painkillers."

"From your war injuries."

"How do you know about that?"

"I did some research. Wasn't too hard to find. But the issue now is: you've got a much bigger problem than painkillers."

"What's that?"

She sighed. "You've been infected with . . . let's just say it's a bad virus. We only have a few hours."

He spun the cap off the second water bottle and drank. He wanted to gulp it thirstily, but kept himself to a few careful sips. "We?"

"Yeah, we. You have a few hours left as Dylan Runs Ahead. I have that time to convince you it's going to happen. But I should tell you right now: I can't stop it."

Dylan shook his head, trying to clear cobwebs. His vision had returned to normal, mostly. "What is it you can't stop?"

Quinn took a deep breath, let out a sigh. "I said you were infected by a virus. Usually, that's exactly what it is. But for you, it's more like a . . . a special kind of parasite."

"And how do you know this?"

She produced a water bottle of her own, drank, wiped at her mouth with the back of her hand again. "Because I'm an exorcist, Dylan. And you've got a demon inside you."

43.

Dylan stared at the scene across the room from his hotel bed, drew an imaginary line down the wall at the edge of the mirror, let everything from the mirror to the right field of his vision fade to gray. Then he drew a horizontal line across the top of the dresser, eliminating it from view.

"You're doing it right now, aren't you?" he heard Quinn's voice ask. This was a bit troubling, because Quinn had already been erased from view; her speaking threw off the whole pattern.

"Doing what?" he asked.

"The patterns. The . . . separations."

Separations, Joni said inside. *Yeah, that's a good word.*

What do you mean by that?

Quit being all sensitive. You're a warrior. An Apsáalooke warrior. A crippled one.

Yeah, but what's crippling you has nothing to do with your leg.

So what's it have to do with?

"Your mind," Quinn said. "Joni's right. You feel stressed, you feel overwhelmed, you sink into your own mind, do your separations.

Put all your hurts in your kill box. And when that doesn't work, you pop the pills."

"You bill by the hour?" he asked.

"Look, I know where you come from," Quinn said, apparently unfazed. She held up her arms, showing cuts and scabs, a few uneven scars. "Big difference is, some of mine are on the outside. You keep 'em all inside."

Inside the kill box, Joni whispered.

"Yes, inside the kill box," Quinn said. "But I don't think the kill box can hold all the pain, can it? Or the pillbox, for that matter."

Dylan felt a sheen of light sweat on his skin. Inside, his muscles, much like his mind, ached.

Quinn stood from her chair, approached, pulled a prescription bottle out of her pocket. "Percocets," she said. "I think those are your favorites." She set it on the nightstand beside his bed.

He tried to control the pain, but his body refused to listen. "I . . . I told you I went through detox inside," he said. "They gave me drugs to control the withdrawals."

"And how's that working for you?" Quinn asked, sitting on the bed beside him. "You telling me you're not jonesing for your fix?"

He looked at the bottle, knowing what she said was true. The moment he saw the flash of that prescription bottle in her hand, he felt like he'd caught a glimpse of a long lost love.

"You're not going to ask, are you?"

"Ask what?"

"Ask anything. I just told you there's a demon inside you, and you clammed up."

"You also said you're an exorcist."

"Not really what we call ourselves, but yes. That's the easiest way to think of it."

"You don't look like a Catholic priest to me." He grimaced. "Or a nun."

"Which is why we don't really like the term *exorcist*. People think of Linda Blair spewing green pea soup, priests with holy water."

"But in reality, it's mentally imbalanced women with paper clips."

She shrugged. "It's a whole lot of different people. But yes, people who are, as you say, somewhat mentally imbalanced. We call ourselves the Falling Away."

"The Falling Away?"

"Second Thessalonians 2:3: 'Let no one deceive you by any means; for that Day will not come unless the falling away comes first, and the man of sin is revealed, the son of perdition.'"

"What day will not come?"

"The day we are gathered together once again with God. But when we talk about the Falling Away, it really has two meanings: the Falling Away in this verse refers, literally, to humankind falling away from God. But there's a second Falling Away as well: the falling away of our old selves when we take up the cause and follow God's plans for us. When we acknowledge what we are chosen to do."

Quinn paused, considering, then looked at him once again. "I have a lot to tell you—things I've learned over years, and I have to cram it into a few hours for you. So let me just start by showing you something." She rose and came to the bed to help him up.

His body ached again, his leg especially. Something he hadn't experienced inside the HIVE.

"What is it?"

"Just come with me." She piloted him toward the motel room door and opened it. A blast of cold air rushed past them as they

243

went outside and to the adjacent room. Quinn unlocked the door to this room, opened it, and motioned him inside.

The room was a mirror reflection of the one they'd just been in, right down to the particleboard furniture and the ever-present odor of stale pizza.

On the closest bed, tied and gagged, lay Webb.

"Webb!" Dylan cried, rushing across the room and pulling off the gag. His friend stared at him, sullen and dark-eyed, saying nothing.

"Are you . . . okay? How's the shoulder?"

Webb made no attempt to move. He simply stared at him with a look of hate and answered in a low, guttural voice. "You're the one who got me shot."

Dylan felt himself recoil a bit at the venom in Webb's voice. "I, uh . . . let me just get you out of this," he said.

"Don't untie him," Quinn's voice said from across the room. He turned and noticed she had set her briefcase down on the other bed; it now stood open, its lid toward Dylan. "Not yet," she said, retrieving something from the briefcase. She held it up: an old, leather-bound book that seemed to somehow . . . glow.

"You can't just tie him here and—"

"He's fine. Go ahead and ask him some more questions."

Dylan turned to Webb once more. "What happened to you? I mean, I haven't seen you for—" He turned to face Quinn once more. "How long's it been?"

"I pulled you out of there two days ago; you've been in pretty rough shape. I knew you'd be out for a while, so I've been tapping into the HIVE communications system. Amazing what you can do with a good Internet connection. Anyway, imagine my surprise when HIVE jettisoned Webb yesterday."

"Jettisoned him? What do you mean?"

"Why don't you ask your friend?"

Dylan turned to look at Webb once more, whose eyes seemed as dark and cold as two deep, empty wells. "What happened, Webb?"

"Sucked in there, had to get out. They told me they'd give me a ticket anywhere, so I took it."

"Took it to where?"

"Boston. They said there were other people I could work with there."

"Doing what?"

Webb seemed confused, maybe even scared for a few moments, then the icy hardness returned to his eyes. "What's it matter? Not like it was gonna be any worse than running drugs with you."

Dylan felt a hand on his shoulder and flinched. Quinn pulled her hand away quickly as she sank to her knees on the dirty carpet beside Webb's bed.

"Sorry," he said. "I just—"

Don't like to be touched, Joni's voice said.

"I don't like to be touched either," Quinn said. "Or to touch others. But contact—real, human contact—is something we all need. So I make myself." She opened the book, laid it on the bed beside Webb's head, turned, and looked at Dylan. "So tell me: anything seem strange about Webb here?"

"Other than the fact he's tied up?"

"Yes, other than that."

Yes, Joni said. *His eyes. His . . . everything.*

No one asked you, Joni.

"That's a good way to put it," Quinn offered. "His everything is different. But it doesn't have to be."

"What do you mean?"

Quinn put her hands on Webb's head, closed her eyes, began to mutter something quietly under her breath. Something slow and repetitive.

After a few moments, Dylan realized she was praying.

Webb, for his part, didn't scream or thrash; he seemed calm—oddly calm—with Quinn's hands touching him. He stared vacantly at the ceiling, as if unaware of anything else around him.

Dylan watched in silence for a few moments, then felt the air around him starting to . . . darken. No, that wasn't quite right. It was getting—

Wetter.

Yes, Joni. Wetter.

The room felt humid, as if a storm were gathering on the horizon. Dylan stood, peeked at the mirror on the far wall. As he'd expected, condensation was forming on the surface; a thin trickle worked its way down the smooth glass surface.

A sudden intake of breath brought his attention back to Webb. Dylan snapped his head around, started to say something, but was frozen in place by what he saw.

Webb's mouth was open wide—almost impossibly wide—as a dark mist poured from it.

That's the wetness, the humidity, Joni's voice said.

Dylan thought briefly of touching the dark cloud, but something inside told him that would be . . . painful. Dangerous.

He looked at the top of Quinn's head, but her eyes remained closed, her head bowed. Even though he couldn't see her mouth, he knew she was still whispering a prayer: he could hear it in the air, mixed in with—

The wetness.

Yes. The wet cloud coming from Webb's mouth also whispered,

but not just in one voice. Dylan thought he could catch the murmur of hundreds, maybe even thousands, trapped inside the black mist.

After several seconds the liquid smoke stopped and Webb's mouth closed. Slowly, naturally. As if he'd just finished one long, languorous yawn.

The cloud hung in the air above him for a moment before Quinn started to tremble. She quaked, and Dylan started to touch her shoulder, make sure she wasn't having a seizure of some kind.

But just before he touched her, the cloud . . . well, *imploded* might be the best word. It folded in on itself, emitted a quick burst of light like the world's brightest flashbulb, then disappeared in a burst of air. Dylan felt the force of the blast, kissed by drops of water, push past his face.

"Dylan?" He looked down at Webb, whose eyes had changed once again. That vacant, hard look was gone, replaced by . . . fear, maybe?

"Hey, Webb. Good to see you."

"What just happened?"

Quinn stood slowly, closed her Bible, retreated to the other bed, and sat without saying a word. Dylan stared at her a few moments before returning his attention to Webb. "I have no idea, Webb."

Webb sat up on the bed, coughed into his hand. His shoulder didn't seem to be bothering him in the least. "I had this . . . this strange dream."

Dylan felt Joni shift inside, but she said nothing.

"A dream?" he asked, trying to sound casual. "What kind of dream?"

"I don't remember it, really. I mean, I don't remember what happened. But I remember I was supposed to tell you something. To give you a message."

Dylan felt his stomach tighten. "A message?" he asked, barely able to make his voice a whisper.

"From . . . Claussen? Does that sound right? You know a Claussen?"

Dylan cleared his throat, wishing for another bottle of water. He didn't want to hear the next words, didn't want to hear them at all. He needed to stop Webb before he went any further. "Maybe you should just rest—"

"He said . . . he said you were chosen because of the pillbox. That you needed to remember the pillbox."

Kill box, Joni said inside.

Shut up.

Webb shook his head. "No, no, no, no. It wasn't pillbox. It was kill box. Remember the kill box." Webb looked at him, hope and wonder in his eyes.

Dylan closed his own eyes, took a deep breath. "Okay," he said, keeping his eyes closed. "I'll remember."

When he opened his eyes once again, Webb was fast asleep, a look of peace and satisfaction on his face. Dylan felt a hand on his shoulder, jumped. But this time, Quinn didn't take her hand away.

And this time, he was glad she didn't.

44.

Twenty minutes later, back in Dylan's motel room, they still hadn't spoken.

Too many images swirled in his mind, threatening to drown him. And yet, for a change, he resisted the urge to divide the thoughts, to send them to the kill box.

Suddenly, he needed to distance himself from the kill box.

Quinn had spent the last twenty minutes in the chair at the desk, remaining absolutely still, as if in some kind of deep trance. Dylan wasn't even sure he'd seen her blink in that time.

But at last she stirred. "He'll sleep. He'll forget," she said, obviously referring to Webb in the adjacent room.

"Well, I'm pretty sure I'll never sleep. Or forget."

She shrugged, which wasn't the reassurance Dylan had hoped would come.

"That what you did to me?" he asked. "That . . ."

"Prayer?"

"Yeah, I guess."

"Sure, I've prayed for you, Dylan. Prayed over you. But you're not the same as Webb. You're . . . more complicated."

"How so?"

She stood, went to the sink and mirror at the far end of the room, ran some water and splashed it on her face. Grabbing a towel, she turned and looked at Dylan once again. "You're a chosen, for starters."

Chosen. Why wasn't he surprised that word had entered his life once again. Only problem was, all he'd ever been chosen for was pain and suffering. Joni. Claussen. The drugs. And now this. Not that he believed any of it.

Quinn went back to her seat, spoke again. "Those of us who are part of the Falling Away, we're what you might call . . . a spiritual army." She stopped. "No, that's not quite right. We're more like inoculators. We find people infected by demonic activity and inoculate them, keeping them from spreading their disease. Like you just saw with Webb. That's what we do. We find the demon infestations—like HIVE—and we cleanse them before they can spread the infection."

"A demon virus."

"In a way, yes."

"Yeah, well, I wondered when you were going to pull out the elevator pitch. I don't live in the sixteenth century; I don't believe in demons."

She shrugged. "You can choose not to believe in bullets. Won't stop one from killing you."

"Look, I've heard the whole come-to-Jesus thing before. Guy I was stationed with in Iraq."

"What'd he say?"

"Said I was . . . chosen." He felt uncomfortable saying the word.

It was one thing to have the religious zealots toss it around; it was quite another to say it himself. Especially because it was so untrue.

"Claussen," Quinn said. "The man Webb mentioned."

"Yeah." Dylan swallowed, tasting the bitter tang of rising fear. "'Course, he said he was chosen, too, and he got killed on a highway outside of Baghdad. Fat lot of good being chosen did him."

Quinn stared. "The explosion you were in? The bomb? Did he die in that?"

"Yes."

"Tell me about that."

Dylan was mad now. "What do you mean, tell you about that? What's to tell? Farmer with a donkey hit a pressure plate on an IED; Claussen was the closest one to him, and he got killed."

"But you didn't."

"No."

"Why not?"

Dylan went quiet. After a few moments, Joni spoke inside: *Tell her.*

"Yes, Dylan. Tell me what you're trying to hide."

"It doesn't make any difference. It was all coincidence, luck."

"What was?"

"That Claussen blocked most of the blast, which saved me." He felt tears stinging his eyes as he said it. So many times he'd thought about it since then. So many times. "So you see? He wasn't chosen. He was in the wrong place at the wrong time."

"And now, Webb talking about you being chosen, mentioning Claussen's name, telling you to remember the kill box . . . I suppose that's coincidence too."

You're still not telling her, Joni said inside.

Dylan glanced at Quinn.

"Go ahead," she said.

He sighed. It didn't appear there was any way out of this. And what did it matter anyway? It wasn't like any of it was real, was true, was part of his life.

"The morning before the explosion," he said, then stopped and cleared his throat. "The morning of the explosion, I asked him why he always prayed before each of our missions, always asked God to show us we were chosen. His exact words—I remember them clearly—were always 'Open our eyes to Your way, Lord help us to see life as Your loved and chosen ones.'"

"Yes."

"Anyway, that always struck me. I mean, I went out on over three hundred missions with him, and he always prayed that. So I said to him, you've prayed that three hundred times now. If God hasn't opened your eyes—and you're a person who actually believes in God—what makes you think your eyes are ever going to be opened?"

"What did he say?"

"He said he wasn't praying for his eyes to be opened; he was praying for my eyes to be opened. And he figured, since I was asking about it, that it was a sign that it was starting to happen." Dylan glared at her now. "And maybe he was right, but only for a few minutes. Maybe I was seeing something in what he'd been saying. But then God killed him while I watched, and I couldn't do anything about it. So yeah, maybe my eyes were opened by that morning, but opened to the reality that there is no God. How could He kill a man who prayed to Him each and every time we went out on a mission? If that kind of God exists, He's not anyone I can believe in."

"So you think God killed him."

"Exactly."

"But you just told me God doesn't exist."

Dylan hesitated.

"Well . . ."

"No *well*. Either He exists, or He doesn't."

Dylan shrugged. "Okay, fine. We'll say He exists. Doesn't change the fact that He killed Claussen. Why would I want to know anything more about that God?"

"You're setting it up as an either/or, but those aren't the only possibilities."

"Enlighten me."

"You say either God doesn't exist, or He does exist and He killed Claussen."

"Yes."

"But what if God exists, and He *didn't* kill Claussen? Isn't that a possibility?"

Dylan couldn't believe the idiocy of this woman. "No, it's not. God's supposed to be all-powerful, all-knowing. So He could have saved Claussen; He could have killed me instead."

"Once again, Dylan, that's not the world we live in. That's the original Falling Away, if you will: when we rebelled against God, we broke this perfect world we live in. So now there's disease, now there's death and evil. But that wasn't God. That was us."

"You're letting God off the hook. He could wipe all that away, if He wanted to."

"If you were a parent, you could put your kid in a giant cage, keep him locked away from injuries and pains and heartaches. You could wipe out any chance of his ever being hurt, if you wanted to. But would that child ever become a real person? Someone who could interact with the world? Would he ever experience real joy?"

"That's not the same thing."

"Of course it isn't. That's one child and one parent. We're talking about all of humanity and all of creation. What might this world look like if God just locked away all of our struggles, all of our pains? If you want the potential for ultimate love and ultimate joy, Dylan, you also have to accept the potential for ultimate hate and ultimate suffering. That is the real world; that is the world we live in."

Dylan went quiet, unsure he wanted to continue the conversation.

"You didn't die in Iraq, Dylan. But you've been acting like you're dead."

Dylan shrugged.

"You feel guilty. That's natural. Survivor's guilt, they call it."

"I had plenty of guilt before I ever got to Iraq."

"It's because you were chosen, just like Claussen said. All of us are, in some way. But different levels. Some people are sensitive to the chosen . . . like your friend Claussen, it sounds like, or Couture, the guy Andrew took you to see. Some can sense even more than that."

Quinn paused, seemed to press at her hand. "Like those of us in the Falling Away. We see things, feel things most people can't; that's why we often develop these compulsions, these supposed delusions. Because we don't just experience this reality; we also get tastes of the spiritual reality all around us. Sometimes we have to channel those spiritual realities, those demonic diseases, out of people." She paused again. "As you just saw. But you're a chosen. You're . . . in a way, it's like you're marked. People like Claussen and Couture can see it. People like me, in the Falling Away, can see it . . . and demons can see it."

"Okay, you're starting to sound like a Keanu Reeves film."

She smiled. "You're deflecting. Probably because you can feel it inside. You know I'm right."

I'm feeling it, Joni said helpfully.

Dylan ignored Joni. Wished he could ignore Quinn; unlike Joni, he couldn't just banish her to the kill box inside his mind. "Okay," he said, sighing. "This chosen thing . . . what's it mean? So I'm marked. Big deal."

"It's ancient, Dylan. It's in the bloodlines." Quinn sighed. "It goes back to the Falling Away. In the first sense I talked about: humanity's falling away from God. Once we were in direct communication with God, but we began falling away, separating ourselves. You know the story of the Tower of Babel, from the Bible?"

He shrugged. "Yeah. People built the tower, God started splitting them, giving them different languages, that kind of thing. We have Apsáalooke stories like that. Crow."

"I know what Apsáalooke is. Hang on to that thought. Anyway, the tower is just one of those things that were a part of the falling away that's been happening for generations. Each generation gets a bit further away from the original." She shook her head, obviously frustrated she wasn't able to fully explain what she was thinking.

"Maybe that's the way to think of it: a copy machine. You start with your original, and it makes a clean copy. But if you make a copy of the original, and then you make a copy of that copy, and another copy of that copy . . . after several generations, it's blurry and unreadable. That's what humanity is, but instead of paper and type, we're bone and muscle and genetic code. We were meant to be originals, but we broke the machine; now we're all copies of copies of copies. From the outside, we're all still pages—like we were meant to be— but the information imprinted on us is garbled. We've lost what we were supposed to be."

He cocked an eyebrow, but she continued, undeterred. "So the people who are sensitives, somehow their copies still carry a bit of that original information. It's still readable, right? Those of us who are part of the Falling Away, we carry a bit more. But people who are chosen, people like you . . . it's like you're copies of the originals, or something very close to it. Something in your genetics keeps the copies from deteriorating. There aren't many like that today."

Dylan started to say something, and his mind flashed. *I won't make many of him.* An Apsáalooke story, like he'd just mentioned.

Biiluke, Joni said inside.

"Biiluke," he whispered.

"Biiluke," Quinn repeated. "Your Apsáalooke story of Biiluke—it's the story I'm trying to tell you now. To show you that they're one and the same. That they're true. What did the Creator say when he saw the man lying in the water, filled with arrows and dying?"

"I won't make many of him."

"Yes. In some ways, you can translate *Biiluke* as 'chosen,' can't you?"

"But Biiluke means all of us, all of the Apsáalooke. You can't say we're all . . . chosen."

"In a way, yes. Your people have stayed true to their roots, to their beginnings. There's a reason why, on the Crow reservation, 80 percent of the people can still speak the Crow language. Most other people have lost who they are in today's world. Your people haven't. So within that set of people, it becomes more likely that a chosen will develop. Think about it: what does *Biiluke* mean?"

On our side, Joni answered.

"On our side," Quinn said, nodding. She stood, shrugged on a jacket. "I think you need a bit of a break before we move on. Before I tell you the rest."

Dylan just stared at the wall, unresponsive.

"I'm gonna grab something for you to eat," she said. "And then we'll talk some more." She went to the door, opened it, let a fresh gust of cold air inside the room before turning back to him. "While I'm gone, though, I want you to think about something."

"Think about what?"

"Biiluke. Are you on our side?"

45.

Dylan bolted awake, his skin itchy and sweating.

You had a bad dream, Joni said. *About me.*

Not now, Joni.

Dylan stood, the muscles in his stomach protesting, and walked to the mirror above the sink at the back of the hotel room. The reflection in the mirror stared back at him, but offered no answers. He didn't look chosen. He looked normal.

Or at least what counted as normal in his world. "Biiluke," he said to his reflection.

The reflection didn't answer.

Dylan shook his head, shuffled to the shower, turned on the spray as hot as he could stand it. Several minutes later—how long, he didn't know—he realized the water was going cold. So much for the water heater at the place guests called nicest and cleanest.

When he got out, he heard the television on low volume in the hotel room. Quinn was back. At least, he hoped it was Quinn. If it were someone else, there wasn't much he could do.

After getting dressed, he walked into the room, saw Quinn

sitting on the bed munching a burger. She motioned to the bag on his bed. "Greasy cheeseburger and fries. Your arteries won't thank me, but your stomach probably will."

"Thanks." He grabbed the bag, unwrapped the burger, stuffed a few fries into his mouth, realizing just how famished he was. They ate in silence for a few moments until Dylan noticed what Quinn was watching: an episode of *Intervention* on A&E.

She picked up the remote and hit the mute, stared at him. "There's more, unfortunately," she said.

He nodded. "The whole demon inside thing," he said.

"Yeah. You think you're ready to talk about that?"

"Not really. But I don't think I'll ever be."

"I told you before, people have the wrong idea about demons." She nodded her head toward Webb's room next door. "Like right now, you probably think I just exorcised a demon from Webb."

"Isn't that what you wanted to show me?"

"Yes. Well. That wasn't a demon, not specifically. Just a demonic influence, a demonic . . . virus. Webb was a Typhoid Mary, but he wasn't the typhoid itself. See the difference?"

"Not really."

"Remember I said each infestation—HIVE, in this case—had a central figure?"

"Li."

"Right. Li is—"

"The HIVE's queen bee."

She looked oddly pleased. "Exactly. Or in this case, king bee. The whole HIVE is built around him, because—if you go back to my example—he's the typhoid itself. Or what he carries is the typhoid itself."

"The demon."

She nodded, went to wash her hands in the sink on the far side of the room. "Once again, people think of demons in terms of armies and wars, but that's not quite right. Demonic influence, the demonic virus, is everywhere. But the demons themselves aren't all that common. They don't need to be. Once people pick up the virus, they have a way of spreading it themselves.

"People carrying demons themselves, they're not as common, because being a carrier, a host for a demon, is . . . difficult," she said, hanging up the towel once more. She remained leaning against the sink vanity. "The body wears down quickly. And so a new body needs to be found."

You're the new body, Joni's voice whispered inside.

"Yes," Quinn answered, staring at him.

"How do I stop them from—"

It was the IV, Joni said.

"Yes," Quinn said again. "You already have the demon inside. From the IV you were given. The infection, well, that's tied to the breath, as you saw when we exorcised your friend Webb. The demon itself is tied to the heart. To the blood."

Quickly, Dylan started dividing the room into quadrants and folding portions of the view away. He briefly thought of sending Joni to the kill box, then was reminded of Webb's words. He didn't want Joni inside the kill box anymore.

"You understand, we in the Falling Away are never to have any direct contact with an infestation. So I broke all the rules, getting inside the HIVE itself, pulling you out of there. Had to shoot you with a trank, because it's not like I could sit down and explain all this along the way."

He stared at her open briefcase on the other bed, the disassembled gun parts, the tranquilizer darts, the Bible.

"Why?" he asked.

"I've been here in Montana monitoring HIVE since you showed up. In that time, Li has had to switch bodies three times. But I've also been here to . . . keep an eye on you. A chosen. Keep you off Li's radar."

"Why?"

"Because being a chosen means God has marked you for something special. Something very good, or something very evil. I knew if Li found you, you'd take the path of evil. So I've been following you, keeping you away from the HIVE as best I could. When you went to the border, I thought it was safe to be here in Great Falls. I had another drone to neutralize, and I thought . . ."

"Yeah, I thought it would be a piece of cake too."

"Anyway, you ended up in the very place I was trying to keep you away from. Big mistake."

"I know the feeling. But so what? You just do your little prayer thing over me, cast out the demon, call in all your buddies in the Falling Away, and we go burn down the HIVE. End of story."

Quinn shook her head, sat back. "Doesn't work that way. I can exorcise the people who are infected by demonic influence, but not the carriers themselves. That's like a whole other level, something way beyond what I can do. And the Falling Away itself isn't really an organization as such. By design. If we start putting in all these layers, hierarchies, the whole system starts breaking down—that's what happens in this fallen world. We are committed to living, or dying, as independent mercenaries, if you will."

"Great. So you're saying there's really no hope, and no one to help us. Doesn't go real well with the little speech about faith and all things being possible."

"It goes perfectly with that speech about faith, because it forces us to do precisely that: rely on faith. Faith does make all things possible. But that doesn't mean all things that are possible will happen. You were out for a long time. I prayed over you, tried to draw out the demon inside for hours. I'm still praying right now. It's beyond me. But it's not beyond God."

"Well, that's reassuring." He turned back to the television, watched the people talking to the camera on A&E's *Intervention*. Without a warning of any kind, Dylan began sobbing. He tried to stop, but that only made it worse. Tears streamed, and huge gasps wracked his lungs.

Quinn turned, stared for a few moments. "Don't worry about it. Just let it out. You have to."

He blubbered for a few minutes, then got up and stumbled to the bathroom, found his towel, and wiped at his face. After a deep breath, he stepped back into the other room, where Quinn had now shut off the television.

"Amy gets help for her drinking, if that's what you're worried about," she said, nodding to the TV. "I've seen that one before." A bare smile crossed her face.

"Yeah. I've seen it before too. I've seen a couple dozen of them. That's—that's what set me off. When Webb and I first came to the HIVE, they kept us in isolation for a few days. Watched an *Intervention* marathon."

For a brief moment, his vision swam. Colors—mostly purples and reds, but all colors of the spectrum—filled his vision, while the whisper of a thousand voices filled his mind.

It's starting, Joni said inside. *The demon is growing.*

Thanks, Joni. You're a big help.

"What is it?"

Dylan realized he'd closed his eyes, and he opened them to look at Quinn. "Just a little woozy," he said. "Been a few days since I've had a burger—that whole granola and veggie thing at the HIVE, you know."

He tried a smile, but Quinn wasn't buying.

"I also got shot with a tranquilizer dart, dragged to a hotel, and possessed by an ancient demon," he said. "It's a little overwhelming."

Quinn nodded.

"So," he said, taking a deep breath. "What now?"

Quinn munched on a fry, stared at him thoughtfully. "I don't know," she said.

"Not really the answer I was looking for."

"I know, but . . . it's the truth."

He ignored a dull pain in his stomach, turned to the TV. "We can't stay here. You said that. We have to do something with Webb."

"Yeah."

"And I only have a bit of time left before the demon . . . takes over."

"Maybe a few hours. Maybe less."

"So you know what you have to do."

"What do you mean?"

"You have to kill me."

She shook her head. "No way. Demons use humans as hosts, but their lives aren't tied to their hosts. They can live outside a human for—well, no one really knows how long. They may well be immortal; certainly much closer to it than we are." She ran a hand over her face. "In any case, I kill you, Li just jumps to a new body. Not as quick and easy for him, not like the transfusion he did with you. Quick transfusion, he can take over in a matter of hours. But if he has to force his way in, more like a couple weeks or a month."

"I'll take that as a no."

"You're right: no, I won't kill you. All that does is kill you, and then I can't be sure where the demon has gone until he finds a new host. And I can already see you have that kind of idea yourself—maybe sneak away, kill yourself, solve the problem for everyone. But it would only create problems for me, and it wouldn't solve your two biggest problems."

"What are those?"

"Shame and self-hatred."

She's good, Joni said inside.

She can hear what you're saying, you know.

Quinn made no response, so Dylan cleared his throat and spoke again. "Okay," he said. "So what you're basically saying is: there's nothing you can do, there's nothing I can do, to get me out of this situation."

"Pretty much."

"So why'd you go through the trouble of kidnapping me?"

"You don't have the whole picture yet," Quinn said, crossing the room and sitting on the other bed beside her briefcase. "I don't have the whole picture. I can tell you, even in the midst of this, God has a plan to pull you through it."

She took his hand uncomfortably. "That's why I came to get you, even though I wasn't supposed to. That's why you're here. Because I felt God calling me to do it. Just the way Paul heard God calling him to recruit me. And that's the same thing you heard from Webb." She paused. "And from Claussen."

"But once you saw the IV marks, once you figured out I'd had the transfusion, once you knew I was a lost cause, why didn't you just leave me, go on to whatever's next?"

"That what you think you are, a lost cause?"

"Well, it's true, isn't it?"

Quinn paused for a few moments, seemed lost in thought. "Because the people who are lost causes are the people who change history."

Dylan snorted, took the last bite of his hamburger, now cold and congealed, chewed for a few moments. "I've changed the History Channel. Does that count?" He ran his hand through his hair, felt something in it. When he pulled his hand away, he saw a large swath of his hair had come off in his fingers.

"You're losing your hair," Quinn said quietly. "Going bald."

"Like Li," he said.

"Like Li."

He went to the mirror, looked at his reflection with a lage swath of hair now missing. He grabbed the towel he'd used after showering. Evidently he'd been occupied by other thoughts; the towel held several large chunks of hair as well. After a few moments he put the towel on his head, rubbing it as hard as he could, flaking away his close-cropped hair, an act of bravado in the face of the coming darkness.

Bring it on, Li, Joni said inside.

And inside, he felt a low chuckle. Not from Joni, but from someone else. Something else.

He turned away from the mirror, looked at Quinn on the bed. "You have to leave, you know," he said. "You and Webb."

"I know."

"Because there's still more you haven't told me. When Li infects someone with the virus, someone like Webb, he can sense where they are, what they're doing."

"Unless they get exorcised. But Li's in transition right now—leaving his old body, moving into a new one. Not totally active in either yet. So even if he was able to get a sense of Webb's location before, he needs to finish his—"

"His transformation. Inside me."

"Yes."

"But once he does that, he'll have access to my thoughts, my memories. If I know where you two are, he'll be able to find you."

"Yes."

"So you leave. Both of you."

"Yes."

"You're being awfully agreeable."

"I've got two trucks," she said. "One is an old Silverado I bought. The other is Andrew's new Dodge Ram."

"You took Andrew's Dodge?"

"Had to take the bus to his place to get it and bring it back here. Plus he wasn't using it anymore."

"Good point." He paused. Then: "They kept us in isolation during . . . detox. Kept us hidden from the police and the FBI and . . ." He let his voice trail off. "None of that really happened, did it?" he said quietly.

"None of what?"

"No police were ever looking for us. Or the FBI. No one."

"No. Li was making sure of that. Told you he was keeping you safe from the outside world so you'd accept you were there. Fit in so well with the detox story. You become part of HIVE, and you think he saved you. But instead, he just invited you to walk into the fiery furnace."

Dylan sighed. "I don't suppose I can just tap my ruby slippers together, say there's no place like home, and wake up again at Auntie Em's?"

"Sorry; this nightmare's just beginning." She stood. "So which vehicle do you want?"

"You take the Ram. I'm good with the Silverado."

She tossed him a set of keys. "Where you gonna go?" she asked.

"Don't know. Haven't heard any suggestions. But I figure, maybe if I get out away from any other people, if I find a place that's desolate and deserted, maybe—"

"Maybe you can just crawl out onto the eastern Montana prairie and freeze, cold and alone?"

"Yeah, I guess that's what I'm saying."

"Li will find someone else."

"You've said that."

"So you'll just give up, stop fighting."

"Fighting's only worthwhile if you have a chance of winning."

"That doesn't sound like an Apsáalooke warrior. A Biiluke."

"So you think it's better to jump off the cliff, get shot by the arrows, rather than just lie down and die? That what you're saying?"

"I've done everything I can do," she said. "Like I said, I'm operating without a plan here. But now you know. And God knows. And that's enough. God's going to give you a chance to do what you were chosen to do, and I want you to take that chance."

"Well, that's quite the pep talk. You should go out on the motivational speaking circuit."

She stared, nodded, remained quiet. "I'll go start the Ram," she said. "Maybe you can go say something to Webb before we go." She set Webb's room key on the bed, then went to the door, opened it, turned around again. "You might want to leave out the part about lying down and dying. That's not much of a motivational speech either."

She closed the door, leaving Dylan to stare at it.

That went well, Joni said.

I know how to charm 'em, he answered.

Something else rolled inside. Li. Hearing his interior conversations with Joni, trying to respond. But not yet able to.

I think, once Li wakes up inside—

We'll have to end our conversations? Joni finished.

I don't want him to know about you.

Why not? I'm not really me. I'm just a part of you.

Yeah, I know that. Of course I know that. It's just . . .

You don't want to lose me twice?

Exactly.

Understood. I'll go straight to the kill box when . . . whenever.

Dylan put the keys to the Silverado in his pocket, slid Webb's room key off the bed. He opened the door, shuffled the few steps to the adjoining room, knocked before sliding the key into the door and entering.

Webb was up but looked like he was hung over. He sat on the edge of the bed, head bowed, elbows propped on his thighs, as if trying to work up the energy to stand.

"Rough night?" Dylan asked, stepping into the room with a smile.

Webb looked up. "I've had better." No smile. Very unlike Webb.

Dylan sat on the room's second bed, facing Webb. "You remember much?"

"About?"

"About . . . the HIVE?"

"That's just what I'm working on. I mean, I remember going in, just totally crashing that first night. I remember the big tour the next day, going to the apartment . . . then it starts to get fuzzy."

"Yeah, well, sometimes fuzzy's not too bad."

"Says the guy who likes to pop Percocets nonstop." A smile from Webb. Good.

"Exactly. Right now, though—"

"You're leaving. This is the big good-bye speech."

"I suppose. Not much for giving speeches, though."

"I'm not much for listening to them." Webb paused. "I had some crazy dreams, Dylan. Some way bad dreams. That's what they were, weren't they?"

Dylan gave his best smile. " 'Course. Bad dreams are the sign of a good, sane mind."

"Where'd you hear that?"

"Just made it up. Sounds good, though, doesn't it?"

"Works for me."

There was a knock at the door; Dylan rose to let Quinn into the room. "Webb," he said, "this is Quinn."

"I remember her," Webb said, staring. "Unless the parts with her were a dream too."

Quinn smiled. "It was all a dream, Webb. It was all just a long, bad dream."

46.

"We got a box," Sergeant Steve Gilbert said, stepping into the 710th's workshop.

Dylan looked at him, tried to ignore Claussen already heading outside for his body armor. Typical Claussen. Didn't ask for details, didn't question what he was doing. Just listened to what Sergeant Gilbert or any of the higher-ups said, gave a simple nod, and did it.

Dylan wasn't built that way. Not that he was opposed to carrying out orders. Far from it; there was something comforting, something satisfying, about the chain of command in army life. It spoke to a deep part of Dylan. Probably the part that constantly counted items, aligned objects in his field of vision, identified patterns in speech and cadence. Those things too were comforting.

Sergeant Gilbert, for instance, tended to be short and clipped with his sentences. Typically three or four words, delivered like punches to the gut.

"A box?" That, for instance, was a logical question, an interest in more information. Dylan wanted that information; Claussen, for his part, had already departed the plastic shelter. Was probably already in the Humvee, for that matter, armored up. Locked and loaded. Squared away. Hoo-wah.

"Box at Death X," Sergeant Gilbert said, as if this explained everything. And in a way, it did. As part of the 710th EOD Company, their squad of three was called upon to investigate suspicious items in the zone surrounding Camp Victory outside Baghdad. Death X was an intersection of two highways, so named because it attracted heavy attention from enterprising bomb makers. Stalled vehicles, something all too common in the scorching Iraq heat, might be wired with remotely detonated explosives. On one mission, Dylan's squad had destroyed the decaying carcass of a donkey left at the intersection of Death X, its innards filled with canisters of gunpowder wired to a trigger made out of a remote-control toy. Large debris of any kind in the vicinity of Death X—debris such as an innocent-looking cardboard box—warranted a call to the 710th, which then sent a squad to investigate and destroy.

Dylan had been in Baghdad more than six months. In that time, his squad had been sent on more than three hundred missions.

Gilbert stepped out of the workshop; Dylan rose slowly and followed, the grit of the sand pummeling his face as he stepped out into the high sun of the morning.

Another day at the office, Joni's voice said inside his mind.

Yeah, he replied. *And I'm getting sick of my cubicle.*

Just as he'd imagined, Claussen was already in his armor and ready to go, waiting for him and Sergeant Gilbert at their Humvee.

"We got lucky," Claussen said as Dylan began to shrug on his body armor. "I think Hammy and Slim were gonna run the house on us."

"Yeah. Lucky us."

Most of the time, when they weren't running missions, making repairs, or maintaining their ever-growing arsenal of equipment, they played cards. Cribbage, occasionally. Some spades. But mostly hearts. All ten squads in the 710th played hearts, keeping track of which squads won the most hands on a makeshift leaderboard in the workshop. The 710th was a secretive company, keeping their distance from other troops for one very personal reason: their lives depended on it.

Bomb makers desperately wanted to collect the $50,000 bounty for any EOD tech, and many of the Iraqi forces supposedly working with American troops were sources of information for the guerrilla efforts. By staying apart from the rest of the troops, taking their meals in the workshop, and mixing only among themselves, they stemmed the potential for leaked information.

"Relax," Claussen said. "We got this."

"Yeah," Sergeant Gilbert said, swinging into the Humvee. "We got this."

Dylan climbed into their squad's Humvee. The back of the Humvee had a sticker attached to it: THE CHOSEN, it said in large black letters, the name for their squad. Most squads chose their own names—monikers such as Boomerang, Zombie Squad, and Halo—but their squad had become The Chosen by default, thanks to Claussen.

Early on in their tour, Claussen had begun to spout off about their being chosen to be here in this exact place and at this exact time, quoting Scripture to anyone who would listen. One of those Bible thumpers, seeing some Grand Design in all of it.

Dylan, for his part, saw no grand design. Surrounded by palm trees wrapped in razor wire, endless streams of debris blowing down windswept roadways, and hungry bands of Iraqi kids begging for candy, he only saw . . . despair. Hopelessness.

Sergeant Gilbert fired up the diesel engine and steered their Humvee into the roadway; Dylan and Claussen, helmeted, sat and scanned the area outside their vehicle as they traveled. If everything went well, they'd be at Death X in roughly half an hour.

"This is where it all started," Claussen shouted to him, his eyes scanning.

This was the way communication always went inside the Humvee: you never looked at anyone else inside the vehicle as you spoke. You watched the roadway. Always.

Dylan didn't want to ask, but he supposed he was obliged to. "Where what started?"

"Babylon," Claussen said. "Straight from the Old Testament. The first of many great kingdoms, where God's first chosen walked the lands. Abraham. Moses, after him. The prophets who talked directly with God."

Dylan watched as a band of barefooted Iraqi kids ran beside them in the street, waving their hands and hoping the soldiers would throw them some candy bars. Instead, Gilbert gunned the engine and moved past them quickly.

"Thought God talked directly to you," Dylan shouted. "Ain't that what you're always telling me?"

"No God walking and talking among us anymore. That time has passed."

"Why's that?"

"God wanted to speak to us through a burning bush today— the way He did with Moses—we wouldn't recognize Him. The world is one giant burning bush, and we don't care."

Dylan watched the blur of buildings passing them by. "Amen to that," he said.

Claussen laughed. "Now, to get our attention, God whispers.

That's how I hear Him. That's how anyone can hear Him. Listen for the whisper."

Dylan knew what was coming next, what always came next. In an odd way, he looked forward to it, after spending all this time with Claussen and Sergeant Gilbert. At the beginning of every mission, Claussen prayed.

"Father God," Claussen began, still scanning the roadway as they traveled. "Once again, we go again into the fiery furnace, a fiery furnace that only You can save us from. But even if You do not save us on this day, we want You to know: we will not bow down before false idols. Open our eyes to Your way, Lord; help us to see life as Your loved and chosen ones."

"Hoo-wah," Sergeant Gilbert said from the front seat.

"Hoo-wah," Dylan said.

They rode in relative silence for a few moments, the drone of the diesel in their ears. Finally Dylan spoke, without really meaning to. "You always put in that part about the chosen ones, Claussen, about opening your eyes to it."

"Yeah."

"I've heard you pray that a couple hundred times now."

"Yeah."

"How many times you think you have to say it before that God of yours hears it?"

Claussen laughed. "Let me ask you this, Dylan. How come you never said that before?"

"Dunno."

"No, I mean it. Like you said, I probably said that a couple hundred times, and in all that time, you never asked me about it. Until now."

Dylan shifted in his seat uncomfortably. "Just saying, here we are still. Maybe you should stop beating your head against that wall."

"Well," Claussen said, "in God's eyes, it's already done. In my eyes, it's already done. What about your eyes, Sergeant Gilbert?"

"Already done."

Sergeant Gilbert didn't strike Dylan as much of a religious zealot, but in his own way, he was something of a true believer; in all their missions, both he and Sergeant Gilbert had seen Claussen's almost supernatural ability to get them out of scrapes and close calls. Maybe that's why Dylan was asking the questions now, because he knew there was something different, something . . . foreign . . . about Claussen's ability to think and act in the midst of mayhem.

"I pray that to open *your* eyes, Dylan. Because I think I've been put here to change you. Change others, change this whole mess maybe, sure. But God's been whispering to me, and He's told me I've been chosen to help open your eyes. So I think you asking me about it today, I think maybe that says something."

"Like what?"

"Like maybe you're starting to open your eyes. Like maybe you just decided to stop beating your head against the wall."

47.

Half an hour after leaving Quinn and Webb, Dylan was on Highway 89, heading east, trying to keep his mind blank. Every time a thought surfaced, he folded it and banished it to the kill box.

Eventually, Joni spoke. *What are you thinking?*

I'm thinking, might as well go out in a blaze of glory.

That's not what you told Quinn.

Best if she doesn't know. She'll just get in the way.

So what are you gonna do?

It's a farm community, right? They have access to diesel . . . and to fertilizer. I can go homemade, stuff the Village Center full, blow it all sky high.

Only one problem with that.

What's that?

Can you get there in time?

I don't know.

I can feel him inside, Dylan. Turning. Growing.

Yeah. I can too.

I'm scared.

Yeah. I'm scared too.

What if we can't stop him?

Dylan closed his eyes for a moment, opened them again. *Then a lot more people are going to die.*

A new voice appeared in Dylan's mind, shoving aside Joni's voice. Deep. Guttural. Wrenching. *Oh yes, Dylan. A lot more people are going to die. I can promise you that.*

48.

"Where are we going?" Webb asked.

"Don't know," Quinn answered as she drove. "Billings, maybe. Isn't that where you live?"

"If living's what you want to call it."

Quinn breathed in, breathed out, trying to equalize the pressure, but it wasn't working. She felt her body bloating, expanding, the interior thoughts stretching to find their way to the surface. If only she had a needle or something. A quick trip to the bathroom and she could get some release from the pressure.

"Where's Dylan going?" he asked.

"Said he was going east. Out to the plains."

"Really?"

"That's what he said."

"But I don't get the impression you believe him."

Quinn shrugged. "Guess I don't."

"He's going back to the HIVE, isn't he?"

She thought for a moment, took a deep breath. "Yeah. Whether he wants to or not."

Webb was quiet for a few minutes. Then: "We're going to the HIVE, too, aren't we?"

Quinn looked at the white powder flowing by outside their window. "Yeah, I suppose we are."

"But you didn't want Dylan to know that because—"

"Because . . . well, it's complicated. But let's just say, if Dylan knew we were following him, everyone at HIVE would find out too. Best to just let him think we were leaving."

Webb nodded thoughtfully. "Doesn't really matter, though, does it?"

"Why doesn't it matter?" She breathed in, counted to three. Out, counted to three.

"Because we're all gonna die in this anyway. You. Me. Dylan."

In-two-three. Out-two-three. "Yeah, Webb. I think you're probably right."

"Just so we're clear on that," Webb said.

"We're clear on that," Quinn answered. "Crystal."

49.

In many ways, it was like reliving the explosion on that lonely stretch of highway outside Baghdad. The narrowing and constricting of his senses, until all he saw, heard, tasted, felt came to him through a long, dark tunnel. The odd sensation of being disconnected from his surroundings.

The pain, however, was new.

When his leg had been blown up, he hadn't really felt any pain at first. Not until he'd awakened in the hospital. But now, as he turned at Eddie's Corner and headed the last few miles to the HIVE compound, he felt shards of glass, sharp and wet, scraping the inside of his mind. The inside of his body.

Everywhere.

As if he were being torn in two. He almost felt he could hear wet, sickening rips inside his mind.

Think of it as dust, the new voice said. *I'm doing a little remodeling inside your mind.*

Dylan refused to answer.

Finding your short-term memories right now. You've been talking to . . . ah . . . a woman named Quinn?

Dylan tried to keep his mind blank. Eyes on the road. Think nothing. Feel nothing.

I know who Quinn is.

Who is she? Dylan asked, unable to help himself.

A snake.

Interesting you should use that term.

Obviously, she's poisoned your mind against me. Probably told you stories, lies about me. About HIVE.

She did share some information.

Well, what do you know about her?

Dylan paused, and Li read the hesitation in that pause.

See? A snake. She tells lies about me, about HIVE, and deflects attention away from her true self.

What is her true self?

Dylan felt his eyes glance at a mile marker. An odd sensation, because he hadn't moved his eyes. Li was slowly taking over; he could feel his own control leaking away.

You familiar with meth? Li asked inside.

Sure. Kind of the low-rent drug of choice.

Low-rent. Right. So you're familiar with the effects of meth. Long-term, I mean.

The meth eats them, eventually.

He felt Li move inside, as if . . . rolling over.

Usually, people end up with what's been called meth psychosis. The drug remaps the brain, makes people see things that aren't there.

Meth bugs. Dylan was familiar with this. People who did a lot of meth ended up having scabs on their skin. Zoey, a certified meth head who squatted in an abandoned warehouse near his home in Billings, constantly complained about the bugs in her skin.

Yes, Li said. *Many meth addicts call them bugs. They start to feel like there are bugs embedded in their skin, and they constantly scratch at their skin to get the bugs out.*

So?

So tell me: did Quinn have any . . . skin issues?

Dylan thought of the embedding thing, the paper clip in the palm of her hand.

Inside, he felt Li jump all over the thought. *Yes, yes! She called herself an embedder! That's what your memory of the conversation is telling me.*

So you're saying she's a meth addict.

I'm saying it's moved to meth psychosis. She needs help. Treatment. Detox. I'm saying anything else she said is likely to be part of her psychosis. Did you know some meth addicts get delusions of grandeur, delusions of persecution? They think they're in communion with God, or they are God, or they're being pursued by . . . demons, for instance.

Li paused, letting Dylan think for a few moments. Could it be true? All of Quinn's talk, just a drug-induced delusion?

Wait. No. But you're inside my mind now. That proves everything Quinn said.

Does it? Li asked inside. *You've been known to take a few drugs yourself, Dylan. More than a few. And then, once we got you detoxified inside the HIVE, once you left with that woman . . . well, who knows what kind of drugs she may have pumped into you?*

Dylan paused. *No.*

But you know I'm right. You were unconscious for . . . more than a day, at the least. That points to drugs. Is that someone concerned for your safety? Someone who just gives you drugs after you've been through a detox? Do you realize how dangerous it is to introduce drugs to an addict who's in the midst of detox?

No.

Well, let's just say it can cause hallucinations. Psychotic delusions.

So you're trying to tell me you're not real—that you're not inside my mind and body, that you're just a delusion. But yet, I should listen to my delusion?

Ah, many artists and brilliant thinkers have been given insight by their . . . mental problems. Drug problems. The source of the insight doesn't matter; the truth of the insight does.

Dylan thought. Could it be? Was he making this all up? He looked at his hands on the steering wheel, consciously made an effort to lift his right hand.

It lifted without any effort.

See? How your perspective changes when you realize what's really happening? If you'll just tell me where Quinn went, we can find her. Help her.

I don't know.

Of course you know. You're just not telling me. You're scared, I know. But we'll help Quinn, just like we're going to help you. Get her into detox, get you back into detox again, wean you off the Percocets and Vicodins.

I . . . I told you, I don't know.

Dylan's mind once again flooded with past thoughts. He'd made the meth connection when he first woke up in the room with Quinn; Li had somehow tapped into that memory, that thought, put a shine on it and coaxed him with it. A poison apple. *You're just feeding me—*

Of course you know! Li screamed inside.

Fresh waves of pain leaked from his brain as Li grabbed his mind and twisted.

You're keeping it inside that . . . that green box.

What green box?

The pain inside Dylan's mind intensified as Li rolled once again, like . . . like a monster waking from a deep slumber.

You had your chance, Dylan Runs Ahead. You could have told me what secrets you were holding in that green box, but you chose to be difficult. Soon, when I kill off my old body, I will have full power over yours. I will see everything inside that green box, and I will eat it alive.

Dylan looked at his right hand again, tried to move it.

Ah, so your hand's not working, Li intoned. *Let me help you with that.*

Dylan felt his hand moving, guided by a different mind, a mind that occupied his own. The hand came toward his face, slowly, menacingly, and Dylan felt the fingernails digging deep into the flesh of his cheek, leaving small furrows.

His eyes, guided by the alien mind, forced him to look at his reflection in the rearview mirror of the pickup. Small trails of blood oozed down his cheek.

From now on, Dylan Runs Ahead, Li's voice boomed inside his mind, *you're my right-hand man.*

50.

The cliff was there, waiting for Dylan, just a few short yards away. A lush carpet of grass stretched away from him to the precipice of the cliff only twenty yards away. Sparkles of dew hung in the morning air, a soft haze settling upon the meadow of flowers behind him.

Poppies. Red poppies. Like Dorothy. He had crossed the field of poppies, had seen there was no Emerald City.

Only a man behind the curtain, and that man behind the curtain waited somewhere at the bottom of the cliff.

He had to jump. No one else would. He had to, because he was Biiluke. He was the warrior who would prove to First Creator that he was fearless.

That he could lead men into war.

He smiled and began to run, feeling the dew of the grass beneath him, feeling his hair fly out behind him, feeling the wind kiss his cheeks as he glided to the edge of the cliff.

At the edge, he dove, and the water below came into focus, a million tiny stars winking on the cool green surface.

As he fell, he saw the arrow coming for him, flying straight and true. It was going to hit him, pierce his chest. He knew this. Had known it even before he jumped off the cliff.

But when the arrow pierced his skin, it did not hurt. It merely spread warmth, power throughout his whole body as he continued his fall. Closer, closer, to the deep green pool below.

Except.

Except, he wasn't diving toward a pool at all. It was a large, emerald box, burnished to a glossy shine.

A kill box.

And when his body lay, broken and twisted, inside the box, the arrow in his chest oozing blood, First Creator appeared over him and whispered, "This is Biiluke. I shall not make many of him."

Dylan's whole body began to shake, and he felt the life ebbing out of him. First Creator spoke again: "Wake up."

51.

Dylan awoke to a world in soft focus. He blinked a few times, lifted his head for a few moments, let it sink to the pillow again. It felt as if his muscles were made of soft syrup. Weakly, he tried to move his arm, shift his position on the bed (yes, he was on a bed now, wasn't he?), but . . . he couldn't.

So nice to see you awake, Dylan. Li's voice. Deep inside. Parroting what the nurse had said to him when he woke up in the hospital after his . . . incident in Iraq.

A smiling face appeared in his vision, and Dylan recognized her. One of the nurses who had been there at his detox.

Yes, Li said inside. *Nancy is her name. She's a wonderful addition to the HIVE community. Does everything she's told. Maybe she could give you a few pointers.*

"How are you feeling, Li?" Nancy asked.

Dylan's vocal cords and tongue responded, guided by a mind that wasn't his. "Much better, Nancy. Almost to a hundred percent." Then, inside: *What do you think, Dylan? Feel like I'm almost at a hundred percent to you?*

She called me Li, Dylan thought.

Oh, yes. You've become a spitting image, Li responded. *Told you I was remodeling.*

Dylan refused to answer. It was the one thing still under his control.

Even though he couldn't control his head, couldn't control his movements, he tried to get a sense of where he was. In a bed, back on the HIVE compound. Probably in one of the underground bunkers. So many bad memories started with him waking up in a bed.

And I've so enjoyed some of those bad memories, Dylan, Li's voice said. *Let's see if we can add to them.*

Nancy began doing something to his arm—Li's arm now, might as well get used to it. Taking out an IV.

Thought we'd already been through this, Li.

Oh, we have. But this is just a saline solution. Get rehydrated, nurse your body back to full strength. You're strong, even with the bum leg, Dylan. Why, I bet I could go a couple years inside here quite comfortably. Wouldn't that be great, if we had a few years together?

"Thank you, Nancy," Li said. "I appreciate your work."

Nancy reddened a bit in the face, then, obviously pleased at the remark, looked down.

"If you'd just give me a minute," he said to Nancy. Then he looked at a form under a sheet on an adjacent bed.

Nancy followed the glance and nodded. "I'm sure he'll be thankful you're here with him, Li," she said. "To comfort him."

Li smiled with Dylan's face. "Just as you're a comfort to everyone, Nancy."

She excused herself from the room, and Li took control of Dylan's body, forcing him to rise and dress.

Dylan stayed quiet, but Li actually hummed inside Dylan's

mind as he dressed. Then he went to the opposite side of the room and found a silver tray on a wheeled cart, brought it back to the bed beside the unmoving form beneath the sheet.

Li forced Dylan's hands to pull the sheet off the body, and Dylan saw a bald man, thin and emaciated, barely breathing, on the bed. His eyes remained closed, and his lips softly murmured.

New Li, meet Old Li.

Dylan stared. He had to stare, because Li kept his eyes totally transfixed on the pained form of the man.

But . . . Dylan began.

Yes, yes? Go ahead and say it.

This man is old, thin. You're—

Young and handsome, I admit it. Well, I was when I was in that body, but once I left that body—once I came into your body—well, the old husk had no reason to go on. His name was Wes Lager, once upon a time, about eight months ago. He's now thirty-five years old.

The body looked three times that age.

Well, Li said with a smile Dylan could feel. *They just don't make human bodies the way they used to. But I have high hopes for you, Dylan. For us. You ever hear the old expression "curiosity killed the cat"?*

Li continued without waiting for an answer. *It's amazing how those old saws can be accurate. Human language is so . . . fascinating.*

Dylan felt excitement rising inside, which made him sick. But even that was beyond his control: the nausea and outrage he wanted to feel were swallowed by Li's overwhelming glee.

Think of how happy you could have been, if you'd just taken the easy way. If you'd just unlocked your green box, let me see what was inside. This old body, this old self, would have withered and died. You never would have seen it. But now I have to speed things up, kill this body. And you have to watch. Fun for me, I'll admit, but I can tell you're not enjoying it. Li paused. *Which, I must admit, makes me enjoy it more. So maybe I should thank you.*

Li examined the various instruments available to him on the silver tray.

Anyway, you're a curious cat, aren't you, Dylan? I can tell. I can sympathize with that because—maybe I've mentioned this before—I'm curious to see what you have locked inside that green box.

The kill box, Dylan thought without meaning to.

Kill box? You call it a kill box? How wonderful. See? Already I find out more about the wonders of Dylan Runs Ahead. Curious cats are . . . well, they can't be cured. And so their curiosity kills them. So, curious cat that I am, I have to kill myself.

No.

Oh yes. We bring many people down here, Dylan. To save other lives. Their sacrifices aren't in vain. They give, so that others can live.

Li pulled on latex gloves, selected an instrument that looked something like a cheese slicer. *It starts with skin.* "Cadaver tissue," the medical community calls it. *Living tissue that can save the lives of burn victims. Sometimes even brave soldiers who sacrifice for their country, only to be blown up in Humvees. So you see, there's a certain—oh, I don't know—a poetic justice that you would end up here.*

Li paused. *Certainly you've figured it out now, haven't you? Your skin grafts came from here. That's how we first discovered you as a chosen. Those people are very special indeed. Almost as special as the ones who call themselves the Falling Away.*

Like Quinn.

Yes, like Quinn. Don't suppose you're ready to tell me where she is now, are you?

I told you, I don't know.

I hoped you'd say that. Anyway, normally, when a body runs down—*not just my bodies, you know, but any body here at the HIVE, we do the ultimate bit of recycling. Skin, then organs—eyes, kidneys, lungs, and heart—when they're needed. There are people out there, companies out there, with very strong connections, who would* KILL—*that's a joke, you understand—*KILL—*to get access to harvested organs and such. Perform favors for me when I need them, massage the wheels of government, if you like. So the organs go to others, something of a circle of life, if you like Disney analogies. And really, doesn't it fit the whole HIVE concept? Beautiful, in a way. Ashes to ashes, dust to dust, as the Christian Bible says.*

Li held up the giant cheese slicer, as if to get a better look at it, pressed a button on the side. The sharp metal portion of the slicer began to spin with a mechanical whir. Li looked down at the old man's exposed body, held the slicer over the skin. *Wes's organs are worthless now; everything inside is worthless. But he can still give us some skin before he leaves this world.*

Dylan felt Li creasing the corners of his own lips into a wicked smile. *A pound of flesh. One of those other charming English idioms.*

Li edged the whirring machine closer to Wes's skin.

I thought you'd want to know, curious cat that you are.

52.

Quinn and Webb parked Andrew's big Dodge at the front gate of the HIVE, sat in awkward silence for a few minutes.

"You ready for this?" she finally asked.

Webb feigned a yawn. "Hey, I'm one a them happy HIVE cultists, remember. This is just like going home for me." He opened the passenger door and slid out, held up a hand to the guard who had come out to greet them.

Quinn followed suit, sliding from behind the wheel and joining Webb at the front of the truck.

"We're here to join up," she heard Webb say. Then he turned and pointed to her. "Well, actually, she's here to join up. I'm kind of a newbie, but I brought in a new recruit. Yay for me."

Their syrupy-sweet happiness obviously had the kid at the guard gate—who looked something like the living embodiment of Shaggy from those old Scooby-Doo cartoons—flustered. "I . . . uh . . . I guess we can do a tour, maybe get you in to see some people."

"Oh, that would be great," Quinn said.

He nodded, picked up his two-way radio, and started talking to someone inside.

Quinn exchanged a nod with Webb, and the kid put on his smile again. Part of the learned routine.

"We have some people who would be happy to visit with you. Would you like to drive in, or would you like me to take you?"

"Wow, could you take us?" she said. Might as well have a little fun.

"Sure. Just park in the visitors' lot right there."

"How about right behind the guard shack here? That work?"

"Sure, but it's not really a guard shack. Just a check-in. It's not like we're a gated community or anything here; we're totally open to visitors."

"That's why I'm here."

"I'll grab that Jeep over there."

"Great. Thanks."

She wheeled Andrew's truck behind the guard shack, parked it.

The Jeep pulled up behind her, and she slid out of the truck, got into the Jeep next to the kid. Webb sat in the backseat.

Secretly she pressed the paper clip embedded in her hand, felt the pain inside relieving some of the outside pressure.

The kid started to drive down the road toward the center of the compound. "The HIVE is built in large, community-oriented circles. Because we all live in community circles in here. Because the earth, life itself, is one large circle."

She smiled at the kid's memorized patter. No harm in letting him think she was a potential recruit.

"The outside circles include most of the transportation-related buildings. Warehouses, transfer centers, that kind of thing. Then production facilities, packaging, as you go into the nearer circles. Where most of us work."

"But you're working out there at the guard shack," she said, thrusting a thumb over her shoulder. "That's outside the circles. You outside the circle of trust?" She raised her hand, formed a circle with her thumb and index finger, the familiar "okay" sign.

The kid was thrown a bit off his game. "No, no. Not at all. I told you, it's just a visitor check-in. And we all rotate jobs regularly, share the work, share the profit."

"Share the love," Webb said from the backseat.

The kid glanced at Webb in the rearview mirror, offered a nervous smile. "Sure. Right. Anyway, I'll move from the visitor check-in in a couple months, somewhere back in here. Not that I mind being at the visitor check-in. I love it. I love everything I do here. How I get to contribute."

"Wow. Sounds great."

"Here, as we get closer to the center of the HIVE community," he said, trying to shift back to his rehearsed speech, "we start to see more living quarters. Town homes, mostly. Even a few hotels for visitors."

"Do the hotels have good swimming pools?"

"Swimming pools are a huge waste of energy."

"Oh. Of course."

Shaggy's rehearsed smile had returned by the time they slowed to a stop. "And here we are at the Village Center. Our community center, our dining hall—the places where we come together as a family."

"Very Brady Bunch," Webb said. "That's what I love about this place."

Shaggy put the Jeep in Park, ignored Webb's last comment. "The big, beautiful building there is the community center. That's where Jeff and Elise will answer your questions."

"Can't wait."

She turned, shook Shaggy's hand. "Thank you. Thank you so

much. I've really enjoyed this mini-tour. I'll be sure to tell Li. When I meet him, of course."

His handshake became more enthusiastic. "Really?"

"Really. Maybe we'll get you out of the guard shack early."

"I told you, I enjoy being—"

But she'd already slammed the door on the Jeep behind her, cutting off the kid's words. She pulled out her hair band, pulled her long hair back into a fresh ponytail, and refastened it.

Webb came to a stop beside her, stared at the community center. "Thing of it is," he said, looking at the building, "I think we're too late for lunch. They make pretty good grub here."

He pushed open the front door of the community center and she followed him, taking in the fresh citrus scents inside—pumped in, she was sure, to make the place seem fresh and inviting—and walked toward two waiting figures.

"Jeff and Elise, I presume?" Quinn said brightly as they approached.

"Yes," Jeff said, shaking her hand, then looking at Webb and recognizing him. "Webb," he said. "We didn't expect you back. You were flying to—"

"Well, once this place gets under your skin, it's just too hard to leave. But I brought a new recruit, like I told the guy at the guard shack."

"Yes, well," Elise said. "Who is your new friend?" Elise flashed a practiced smile at Quinn, and Quinn returned her own practiced smile.

"Maybe you better call Li," she said. "I think he'll be interested in talking with me."

"Why's that?" Elise asked, a bit taken aback.

"Tell him Quinn's here to see him. I don't think I'll need an appointment."

53.

Dylan awoke in a bright room, achingly white light bathing every surface he could see.

Outside the room, explosions sounded. Earthquakes, maybe. The surface of the room rumbled, rolled.

But he wasn't alone. On the opposite side of the room, bathed in that white light, was Joni.

His sister.

She smiled. "I don't think I saw this coming."

Beneath them, the floor rumbled.

"Saw what coming?" he asked. Dylan realized they were both speaking aloud, communicating with actual speech. This wasn't just happening inside his mind anymore.

"Actually," Joni said, rising to her feet, "it *is* happening inside your mind. Since this is your first time inside the kill box, I should show you around." She held out a hand, swept it across the endless expanse of white around them, smiled once again. "There. Now you've pretty much seen it all."

"The kill box? I'm . . . trapped inside my own mind?"

"Freaky, huh? But it's not so bad here, is it? Almost . . . comforting. Which is why I don't mind when you send me here. None of your pain, none of your haunted memories. Just . . . just this."

"What is this, exactly?"

"God."

"Inside me."

She smiled, repeated her earlier phrase. "Freaky, huh? Some philosophers have called it the God-shaped hole, the space inside each of us that yearns for pure holiness. Goodness. Pretty small part, you have to admit, when you feel the darkness inside the rest of your mind."

Dylan stood, felt the floor shifting beneath him. "What are the . . . explosions?"

"Yeah, well. That's the darkness I was talking about. In this particular case, Li, trying to get in, but finding he can't unlock the kill box."

"Why not?"

"You're special, Dylan. Everyone has this God-shaped hole, but few people know it exists. Few people respond to it when they feel it. You, because of some traumatic events, have amplified it. Of course, you use it to stuff all your painful memories, thinking it's more like a Pandora's box full of monsters and murky memories." She swept her hand across the horizon again. "But it's not like that at all. It's clean. Bright. Kind of amazing, you can stuff all those dark secrets in here, and they are swallowed. Cleansed, you might say."

"What about you? How come the kill box doesn't swallow you when I put you in here?"

"Because you don't want it to. Because God doesn't want it to."

"So . . . am I stuck here now?"

"Stuck isn't the right word. But you're here as long . . . as long as you need to be."

"Until Li breaks in."

She arched her eyebrows, smiled. "You tell me why you're here."

He thought about it, how wonderful it felt to see his sister again after all these years. "To see you?"

"Sounds like a good answer to me." She closed her eyes, smiled, tilted her head as if basking in the warmth of the sun. "The world out there, Dylan. It's crazy, and it's mean, and it's dangerous. I can't protect you from it. You can't protect you from it. This kill box can't protect you from it. But the thing is, when you swallow all that hate and pain out there, the world changes. It becomes magical and beautiful and wondrous."

"So you're telling me not to be scared."

"Not at all. Being afraid is part of being human. But it's also the doorway to greater things."

"I'm sorry," he said, without thinking about it.

"For what?"

"You were my little sister. I was supposed to protect you, but . . . you always protected me. The one chance I had—"

"Don't go there."

"Why not? It's the five-hundred-pound gorilla, isn't it?"

"No gorillas in here. What happened . . . you keep blaming yourself for it. That only feeds the dark part of your mind. The only person you need forgiveness from is yourself. Once you let go of that—once you let go of me—you'll see the greater things that lie beyond."

Dylan felt tears forming in his eyes. "So I have to let you die? That's what you're trying to tell me."

"You have to let the pain die, the regret die."

"I'm trapped inside my own body. I . . . I can't control anything."

"But God can."

"How?"

"When you've found the answer to that question, you'll be able to leave the kill box again."

Abruptly, the room stopped shaking, and stillness descended.

"What . . . what happened?" Dylan asked.

"You're in the box, Dylan, but you're still outside the box too. You just haven't let yourself feel it. Your—what did Quinn call it?—your separations. Everything you need to know is here."

Dylan stood, feeling the pain start to seep back into his leg. Ahead of him, the white began to darken, turning a gray, and then blackening.

Joni approached, wrapped him in her arms, kissed his cheek. "You've let the demons chase you long enough, Dylan," she whispered into his ear. "It's time to chase them."

54.

Back in his own mind, his dark mind, Dylan swam in sickness. Everything felt slow. Awkward. Polluted.

Dylan, Li's voice said brightly. A little too brightly. Dylan felt like throwing up, but his own body wouldn't even let him do that. *Nice to have you back.*

Dylan stared through his eyes (Li's eyes), and found they were walking through the front door of the Village Center.

You're just in time for a little meeting, Li said. *A meeting I think you'll enjoy. I know I will.*

Li paced through the corridor into an office off the main commons area, smiling magnanimously as he entered.

For you, Li said, *this should be like a little reunion.*

In the office sat Webb and Quinn, side by side, facing him.

"Thank you, Jeff and Elise," Li said, dismissing them with a wave of his hand.

Jeff seemed about to say something, but thought better of it and left, closing the door behind him.

Li stood in front of Webb and Quinn, rocking back and forth on his feet, barely able to contain his utter joy.

Or Dylan's utter joy, as the case may be.

"Well," Li said aloud. "Color me surprised."

"I didn't recognize you until you talked, Dylan," Webb said.

"Like Li?" Li answered, cutting him off. "Just one of my many gifts to your friend."

Inside, Dylan felt Li scanning . . . something like a picture book of moving images, searching for a connection to Webb. Nothing was there, thanks to Quinn's exorcism.

Li turned Dylan's body toward Quinn. "I've been telling Dylan how much I wanted to meet you, and look what happens: you walk right in." He went to the desk, sat in the task chair behind it, rocked back, put his feet on his desk. "So tell me, you two," he said. "What brings you to this neck of the woods?"

Webb seemed on the verge of getting sick, as if being here—inside the HIVE again—were poisoning him. Dylan knew the feeling.

"I'm here to make a trade, Li," Quinn said to him.

"A trade?" Li said with obvious delight. "Oh, I do like to bargain. Tell me what you have in mind."

Quinn's face betrayed no emotion. "I think you know."

"Why, I have no idea," Li said with mock sincerity.

"Me for Dylan. You leave Dylan's body, enter me as your host."

Inside, Dylan felt numb for a few moments. Quinn was ready to sacrifice herself for him. It made no sense. His anger, his disgust, his full wrath and fury overtook him, and something unexpected happened: he felt Li slip.

For a moment, maybe celebrating his joy and victory too much, Li forgot about Dylan. And in that moment, Dylan regained control.

"No!" he thought, and this time his mouth and vocal cords responded, forming the word and screaming it.

Then the moment was gone. Li rolled inside, and Dylan was pushed back underwater, back into the depths of pain.

Webb jumped as the word escaped Dylan's lips, but a slow smile crossed Quinn's face. "Troubles at home, Li?"

The demon ignored the question.

No! Dylan screamed inside again, but this time his body didn't respond.

Shut up, Li replied.

"Dylan's still in there, fighting, making it . . . difficult for you, isn't he?"

Again the demon ignored her but answered her previous question. "I will accept your trade."

Quinn nodded. "Couple conditions, of course."

"They are?"

"You have your drones bring us IVs and a bag, and we do it right here in this office. Right now. We lock the door, and Webb here watches everything."

"Done," Li said.

"When we're finished, I take Dylan and Webb out of here, put them on the road. Within a few hours, you'll be in total control of my body." She paused. "And you'll know the secrets of the Falling Away."

Li studied her expression for a few moments, then nodded. He went to the door, opened it, motioned Jeff over, and told him to have Nancy bring a blood bag and two IVs.

Jeff nodded, as if this were the kind of request he received every day, and left immediately.

Li closed the door, turned back to Quinn, smiled. "You're

betraying your kind, Quinn. No one in the Falling Away has ever been consumed by a demon."

"Yes," Quinn said simply.

Li's smile grew. "I like it."

"I thought you might."

"But is he really worth it, this Dylan?" Li asked.

Quinn stared, and Dylan knew she was staring at him. "Is sacrifice worth pain? Is selflessness worth suffering? I think those questions were answered two thousand years ago."

Li seemed disgusted. "Yeah, yeah, yeah. The whole crucifixion thing—you know how many times I've had to listen to people talk about it? As if I wasn't there." He smiled.

A knock came at the door, and Li went over to open it. Nancy wheeled a cart with a silver tray into the room, looked around nervously.

"Nancy, thank you for coming so quickly," Li said.

She smiled. "I . . . well, you know, with the medical center right here at the Village Center—"

"Of course," Li interrupted, impatient. "If you could arrange for a blood transfusion between myself and the lovely young lady over there."

"Oh, so you're giving blood again," Nancy said dreamily. "You're very thoughtful to do so."

Li smiled, looked at Quinn. "Yes, well, I'm told sacrifice and selflessness are worth pain and suffering," he said.

Nancy brought her tray of supplies to the desk, then peeled the packaging away from an IV. "I think we'll have to do this in the opposite arm," she said, "since you just had an IV in your left arm."

"Of course."

Nancy hummed, oblivious to the thick tension in the air as she placed the IV in Dylan's arm, pulled the tube, attached it to a bag, and began collecting blood.

Then she pulled off her gloves, put on a fresh pair, and turned to Quinn with packaging for a second IV. Quinn barely flinched when the needle went into her arm.

Listen, Dylan said, going into bargaining mode with Li. *You don't have to do this.*

No, I don't. But I want to. Dylan felt the smile.

Don't you need to kill my body afterward, anyway? To get full control of hers? Like you did to . . . Wes?

Well, truth be told, Dylan—and I'm not always so good with the truth—I didn't really have to kill Wes. But I wanted to. Another grin. *And it got your attention, didn't it?*

But—

What makes you think I have the least bit of interest in you anymore, Dylan? You're a chosen. It's not often I get to consume a chosen, but I've done it before. Joan of Arc, for instance. But to see inside the Falling Away . . . well, that's something new. And I like new. After thousands of years among humans, there's very little that's new to me.

But she doesn't have anything to share about the Falling Away, Dylan tried. *She told me: they're like independent mercenaries, no real connections among them.*

No connections yet, you mean. Think of what I could do inside the Falling Away: access her memory banks, find out all about her training, find the person who trained her . . . well, I could do some real body hopping. Might even be interesting enough to leave this place behind and do some traveling.

Li turned Dylan's head toward the bag collecting blood, admiring the deep pool of red in the bottom of the bag. He turned back to Nancy, the nurse. "You can leave now, Nancy. I think this is something I'd like to do myself," he said, smiling.

Dylan thought about the pool. About Biiluke, jumping into the pool, sacrificing himself. As a chosen.

That's a nice story, Dylan, your Apsáalooke origin story, Li said. *I was there too.*

There how?

Why, I was the archer at the base of the cliff, of course. I will always be the archer, and I have lots of arrows. So by all means, go ahead and jump.

55.

"Thor's freaking," Sergeant Gilbert said as they stared at the screen.

"Not freaking," Dylan answered. "Freaked. He's not going anywhere for a few minutes."

They stared at the screen as their remote-controlled, tracked robot sat motionless no more than twenty yards from the front of their vehicle.

Sergeant Gilbert pointed a finger at one of the other Humvees. "It's that Red," he said. "It's jamming Thor."

"You know the drill, Sarge," Claussen said. "We can get a better signal outside."

Gilbert ran a hand across his brow. "Right," he said. The three of them left the vehicle once again, scrambled to the back of the Humvee, watched as Claussen tried to regain control.

Nothing.

They could wait a few minutes, try to reboot the robot, hope they regained the signal and control over Thor's movements with a hard reset.

Whether it was interference from the Red Warlock radio jammer or not, none of them knew. Not even Sergeant Gilbert. As it was, bomb disposal robots such as Thor had frequent breakdowns and glitches. The price of high tech.

"I'll cowboy it," Dylan said after a few seconds, pulling on nitrile gloves, feeling the powder of them mix with the sweat of his hands.

"You're an Indian, not a cowboy," Claussen said.

"But you're not much of a comedian. Next time you pray, ask for some new material." Dylan took a few deep breaths and ran out around the protection of their Humvee, not giving Sergeant Gilbert a chance to say anything. If he'd given the sarge that chance, he knew he would have been ordered to stay put.

Dylan felt his heart pounding in his ears as he approached the robot. Quickly, he pulled out a plastic baggie, retrieved the walkie-talkie from Thor's clawed arm, and bagged the black box. Back at the workshop, they'd turn it over to CEXC, the Combat Explosives Exploitation Cell, whose brainiacs would dissect the walkie-talkie the way CSI investigators analyzed crime scene evidence. That's why Dylan wore blue nitrile gloves and bagged the walkie-talkie before touching anything else: to protect the evidence. CEXC researchers would scan it for fingerprints, for DNA, to see if they could link it to other bombs being made. They would also analyze the receiver's frequency to make sure all Warlocks in the field were programmed to jam the new signal, whenever they found one.

Jamming the receiver into his pocket, he glanced down at Thor. The robot was just a couple feet high, about three feet long, little more than two giant tracks and an articulated arm. He could probably pick it up, hoof it back; it was only twenty yards, after all. At roughly 120 pounds, it would be difficult, but he'd be saving a key piece of $125,000-equipment; in an odd way, Thor was as much a part of their team as Sergeant Gilbert, Claussen, or himself.

He stooped down to the robot, then jumped when it leapt to life once again. The robot pivoted its arm for a second, as if beckoning Dylan to follow, then turned on its tracks and began scuttling back toward the pod of Humvees. Dylan jogged along behind it, thinking he'd reach down and scoop up the machine if it showed any more signs of crankiness. Even so, he was glad he didn't have to pick it up and carry it.

Thirty seconds later Thor and Dylan slipped behind the Humvee again. Sergeant Gilbert just gave him a hard stare for a few moments, then a slight nod. It was an acknowledgment that Dylan had rushed into something he shouldn't have; he'd put his life in danger, running out into the open without an order and without cover. As an EOD tech in an already-small company of twenty-one soldiers, he was too valuable.

At the same time, Gilbert was acknowledging Dylan's quick thinking in the field; by taking action, Dylan was getting them closer to the end of this mission.

"Okay," Gilbert said. "Let's blow it and roll it in one minute."

Dylan nodded and turned, noticing a farmer walking his donkey along the road behind them toward the intersection of Death X. As if nothing were out of the ordinary.

And in an odd way, nothing was out of the ordinary; hundreds of these missions, Humvees bunched together as soldiers detonated explosives, happened every day. For the farmer, as much as for them, this was just a typical day.

But it didn't feel typical.

"Sarge," he said, jutting his head in the direction of the farmer and the donkey on the road.

Sergeant Gilbert shook his head, spat in the sand. "Ain't this grand?" he said. He made a call on the radio, asking one of the other Humvees to move into position and stop the farmer.

"Got it," the reply came.

Those two words—*got it*—were the last two words Dylan would hear as an active duty soldier. The last two words Claussen would ever hear as a living soldier.

Because at that moment, in Dylan's vision, a hundred yards behind Claussen on the potholed roadway, the farmer and his donkey suddenly evaporated in a white-hot blaze.

56.

Dylan felt his consciousness, his thoughts return. For a moment, for many moments perhaps, he'd been pushed under completely.

He stood over Quinn now, a full bag of blood clutched in his hand.

"I can feel you trying to connect with Dylan," he felt his mouth saying. "But he can't hear you; he can't hear anything. He's dying, and you're going to sacrifice yourself, the secrets of the Falling Away, for nothing. That's what I so love about all this."

Quinn smiled. "Trying to convince me, or trying to convince yourself?" she asked. "I can see Dylan again. In your eyes."

"Shut up!" Li screamed.

Li found the connection to Quinn's IV, affixed it to the bottom of the blood bag. He put his finger on the clip to release the blood, glanced back at Quinn.

Quinn's eyes were closed, peaceful. Her mouth moved slightly, murmuring.

Praying, Dylan realized.

As Li watched with Dylan's eyes, Quinn slowly moved her right hand to the palm of her left, pressed at the—

(paper clip)

—embedded beneath the skin.

Her way of controlling her emotions, her world around her, Dylan thought instantly. Just as he did the separations and the kill box.

Dylan's mind shifted, enough to make Li pause for another moment.

The separations and the kill box. That was why he'd been inside the box with Joni—because the kill box was the answer. That's why Claussen had somehow sent a message through Webb, after Quinn performed the exorcism.

Remember the kill box.

Kill box? he heard Li's voice ask. *Your green box? You think I'm interested in that now? I'm about to open a much bigger box.*

Dylan looked at the scene before him: Quinn, sitting in her chair, and the IV, with an attached bag of blood. He stared, letting the left half of the image fold across the right, erasing everything to the left of the IV bag.

Inside Li screamed, unable to stop the deep-seated compulsions of Dylan's brain. Just as he couldn't force Dylan's lungs to stop working, or force Dylan's blood to stop flowing, he couldn't force the well-worn patterns of compulsion to stop.

Dylan folded the image again, felt control of his body beginning to come back toward him, ebb away from Li. He stepped away from the IV, and Quinn opened her eyes, looked at him. Trusting. Almost as if . . . she'd expected this.

Dylan slipped back into control of his brain, feeling Li turning, constantly turning inside like a wet drill. He opened the top of the kill box, felt the light pouring out, felt Joni slipping into his mind.

Need a little help, big bro? she asked.

All I can get.

Dylan pushed his mind again, forcing Li to half of his size once again and sliding him toward the kill box.

Li babbled, unable to form complete words or sentences, feeling true pain and fright for the first time since time itself began.

Once Li was in the kill box, Dylan shut it and locked it tight.

He felt it rattle, but it stayed shut.

Li was trapped.

Dylan realized he'd clenched his eyes, so he opened them, saw Quinn looking up in wonder.

"You forced Li into the kill box?" she asked, hesitantly. "I heard Joni; is that what she was helping you do?"

"Joni?" Webb asked. "Who's Joni?"

"In a minute, Webb," Dylan said. Then, to Quinn: "Yeah, he's in the kill box."

She smiled. Dylan returned the smile. "My therapist always said compulsions can be overpowering."

A knock came on the door. Dylan glanced from Quinn to Webb; Webb shrugged his shoulders.

"Come in," Dylan said.

The door opened, and Nancy entered, followed by Jeff and Elise. "I'm . . . I'm sorry, Li," Nancy said, all but bowing down. "But I thought I should get some help. I thought there might be something odd happening."

Dylan looked for a few moments, felt Li shift inside the kill box. Then he smiled broadly. "Thank you, Nancy," he said. "That was very thoughtful. You are a great asset to HIVE, and to the Earth itself."

Nancy beamed.

"Looks like we won't be doing the transfusion right now after all, though," he said. "But we can welcome Webb back into the fold, and put Quinn here up for the night. We've had a long discussion, and I think they'll do some big things for HIVE."

He turned to look at his two friends again. "I think they'll do some very big things for HIVE."

57.

The next morning he called Quinn and Webb to breakfast in the dining hall. All around them, members of HIVE stared in wide-eyed wonder; usually Li, the Great Sower, didn't eat with the other HIVE members, preferring to take his meals in his room or offices.

Today, it seemed, was a special occasion. Li was eating among them.

"So," Webb said as he dug into some hash browns. Evidently, the demonic infection hadn't taken away any of his appetite. "Everyone here thinks you're Li. I mean, sure you look like him. But you're still Dylan."

"People see what they expect to see," Quinn said. "I bet if you ask anyone here, they would tell you Li has always looked like this. Because for them, he has."

"Drugs probably help," Dylan said.

"Drugs?" Webb asked, a fork filled with hash browns almost to his mouth.

"That's why everyone has the dopey grins on their faces. Li's drugged the water system in the whole community; everyone here is doped up, willing and compliant."

"Did you say in the water?" Webb asked, eyeing his coffee.

"Until last night," Dylan said, and smiled. "There will be a few changes around here."

"What ..." Quinn began, then seemed unsure how to continue. "How ..."

"Sounds like you're going to skip right over that *what* question," Dylan said.

Quinn laughed. "Touché," she said.

"I'm guessing you're trying to ask me what's happening inside."

"Like I said, demons are practically immortal."

"Not immortal," Dylan said. "But yeah, close to it." He paused. "I can . . . well, I guess I can access Li's memories, Li's thoughts, Li's . . . network. Like he was hoping to do inside you."

"His network?" Quinn asked.

Webb was still more interested in the food on his plate.

Dylan nodded. "All the . . . well, I guess you can call them all the infected. The people who have been sent out to infect others. I can page through them, almost like this mental Rolodex or something, get a sense of where they are, what they're doing, what they're feeling. When I do, I can feel Li inside the kill box—I can feel him trying to feed, I suppose you'd say. Trying to pull the energy from the people spreading the infections." He shook his head. "It's all so . . . alien," he said. "Hard to explain."

Quinn put her hand on his, and he didn't flinch. "Sounds like you're explaining it well to me."

Dylan nodded. "Anyway, I thought about this all night. I started . . . I don't know . . . cataloging the others. The people infected by the demonic virus."

He saw Quinn smile. "You're saying we're going to be doing some exorcisms?"

He returned the smile. "Yeah."

Dylan sensed a flinch from Quinn. "What?" he asked.

"What else?" Webb asked as he continued eating.

"What do you mean, what else?"

Webb stopped, looked at him. "There's something else you're wanting to tell us. I can see it on your face."

Dylan looked at Quinn. "Well, like I said, I've been cycling through all the people. Maybe a hundred of them or so." He felt his voice trying to crack, but he held it. "And I think there's someone I need to visit first. Someone I need to meet."

"Who?"

"You could meet her, if you want to come with me."

"Where to?"

"She's in San Francisco. Tenderloin district."

Quinn narrowed her eyes in confusion. "Okay," she said.

"What about me?" Webb asked.

"What about you?" Dylan returned.

"Want me to go along?"

Dylan studied his friend, smiled. "Webb, didn't you tell me once you were a city mouse?"

"Yeah. I'm one of those urbanites."

"Ever thought about life in rural America?"

"No."

"Maybe you should start thinking about it."

"What do you mean?" Webb asked.

Quinn laughed. "Are you really that dense, Webb? He's asking if you'll run the farming and ranching operations here at the HIVE."

"Ain't that what you're gonna do?" Webb asked.

"Not much into farming and ranching," Dylan said. "And when the people start coming down off the drugs, when they start waking up from their bad dreams, they're gonna need someone to explain it to them. Maybe some will leave, but I think most will stay. After all, that's why they came: they wanted to simplify, work the ground, be part of the earth."

"And you think I can do all that?"

"I'm willing to find out."

Webb pursed his lips a few moments, looked deep in thought, then smiled. "Don't suppose I have anything better to do, at the moment."

58.

Two days later Dylan knocked on a bright yellow apartment door with a purple number 9 affixed to it. The building was in the middle of a long hill, one of those brightly colored Victorian things always pictured on San Francisco postcards.

After a few seconds, the door opened. A woman, her long black hair glistening in two braids, looked at him quizzically. Then anger clouded her eyes.

"I don't want anything," she said, her voice full of rage and hate. But it wasn't her hatred boiling inside. It was Li's. The demonic virus.

"Joni," he said. "Don't you recognize me?"

Her eyes cleared again for a moment, and Dylan thought he saw a bit of a tear forming in her eye.

"Dylan?" she whispered. Then the anger returning: "You forget what happened? You forget you abandoned me, left me to die?"

It was the virus inside speaking again, and Dylan could feel the anger, the virus itself, trying to find its way inside his own mind through buried guilt.

But that guilt was locked away in the kill box now. Along with Li.

Dylan reached out, put his hand on Joni's arm, spoke softly. "This is my friend Quinn," he said. "We're here to help you."

Joni pulled away, tried to release his grip and back into the apartment. Dylan kept his hold on her arm, let her pull him inside, then led her gently to a sofa and helped her sit. Beside him, Quinn dropped to her knees in front of the couch and put both of her hands on Joni.

"We're here to pray for you," Dylan said, and he felt Joni go limp, collapse.

Quinn began to pray, and Dylan prayed with her. He didn't know how to pray, really, but what did that matter? Praying wasn't about what you said, but what you felt. He understood that now.

Just as he understood that being a Biiluke wasn't a curse.

It was something special.

He had wandered, had found himself crippled long before he had a leg mangled, because he'd never accepted being chosen. He'd done his best to fall away from all of it, but now he realized he'd really been falling away from what he'd made himself.

Joni's mouth opened; he could see a dark cloud being pulled out of her. Hanging in the air for a few moments, hovering, then breaking apart and dissipating.

Her eyes fluttered, then opened again. "You came for me," she whispered before fading away into a deep dream. A dream, he knew, that would not be filled with dark thoughts for the first time in three years.

Yes, he had come for her. And he'd found her.

She'd been snatched off the rez by one of Li's infected, pulled away from her own life and toward an existence filled with lies and hate, wandered as a restless soul who infected others with the delusions and pain. Once, that would have filled him with anger and rage.

But there was no room inside him for rage. All he had inside him was the kill box. Inside that kill box was Li. And inside Li were secrets he and Quinn would reveal, with time.

But first, there were other things. First, he wanted to hear more of his sister's voice—to actually hear it, rather than feel it inside. First, he wanted to help Joni gather all her things, return to the Crow rez in Montana, help put her in contact with all the family and friends she'd left behind.

Help put him in contact with the family and friends he'd left behind.

First, he wanted to stand at the edge of that cliff, pause for a moment, then dive. Because he now knew there was no archer waiting there for him with a bow and arrow.

Only clear, cleansing water.

Acknowledgments

Thanks, as always, to a God whose hands are there when I fall. Thanks to Nancy, Jillian, and my whole family for being with me every step of the way. Thanks to Lee Hough, LB Norton, Amanda Bostic, Allen Arnold, and everyone at Thomas Nelson for bringing it all together. And a special thanks to reader Steve Gilbert, who loaned his name to the character of Sergeant Gilbert.

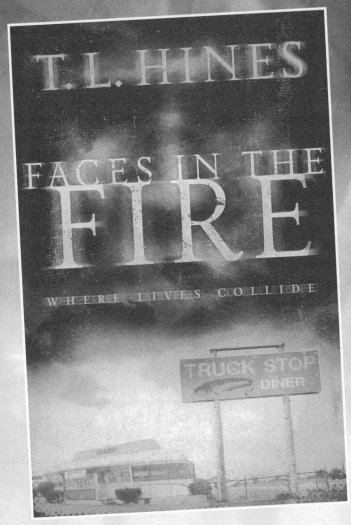

YOU ARE NEVER ALONE...

YOU ARE NEVER ALONE . . .

THE UN SEEN

A NOVEL

T.L. HINES

Excerpt from *The Unseen*

Perched on top of the elevator, Lucas peered at the woman below and created an elaborate history in his mind.

Elevators and their shafts were easy places to hide. Easier than utility chases. Much easier than ductwork, popularly portrayed in movies as cavernous tunnels through which a man could crawl. Lucas knew better; most ductwork was tight and narrow, and not solid enough to hold 150 pounds.

But elevators. Well, the film depictions were pretty accurate with those. You could indeed crawl through the small access panel in the ceiling, sink a sizable hole with a hand drill, and then watch the unknowing people below as they stepped through the bay doors all day long. Provided you bypassed security, of course. And did your drilling outside of regular office hours.

Most of the time he preferred to work in DC proper, but with height restrictions on the buildings, he never got much of a chance to do elevator surfing; for that, he had to move farther away from the city, where skyscrapers were allowed.

He returned his attention to the dark-haired woman who was currently inside the car with four other less interesting people. In his history, she was a widow. True, she was probably in her early thirties, if that, but her stern look, her rigid posture, suggested overwhelming sorrow in her past.

Lucas recognized such sorrow.

So she was a widow. She had moved to Bethesda from her rural home in Kansas after losing her husband, an auto mechanic who had been crushed by a car in a tragic mishap.

Below Lucas, the dark-haired woman moved to the side for another person entering on the eighth floor. As she did so, the overhead light in the elevator car flickered a moment, then returned to full strength.

Puzzled, the dark-haired woman raised her eyes to the ceiling and looked at the light. It happened. For a moment, she stared directly at him, directly at the secret peephole he'd carefully drilled in the ceiling, directly at the constricting pupil of his own eye.

Then she dropped her gaze back to the other people in the elevator with her, offering a little shrug of the shoulders.

She had looked, but she hadn't seen. Like so many others.

When she had looked toward the ceiling, his heart had jumped. He had to admit this. Not because he was worried about being discovered, but because the *knowing* had started—the long, taut band of discovery that stretched between his eyes and the eyes of a dweller, then constricted in a sudden snap of understanding.

The Connection, he liked to call it.

Once he'd spent several weeks holed up in an office center on Farragut Square; during that time, his favorite target had been the reception area of an attorney's office. A one-man show named Walt Franklin, the kind of attorney who chased ambulances. And so, Walt Franklin was chased by people with grudges.

Lucas's observation deck in that office was one of his most brilliant ever: the lobby coat closet, a small cubicle not much bigger than an old telephone booth—something, unfortunately, he didn't see much of anymore. The closet had an empty space behind its two-by-four framing and gypsum board, leaving enough room for him to stand. An anomaly in the construction, one of many he'd seen over the years.

But what had been so wonderful about this space, this anomaly, was its perfect positioning between the reception desk and the lobby waiting area. By drilling holes on two opposite sides of the small space, he could simply turn and view the woman who usually sat at the front desk—a large, red-haired woman with a genuine smile—or the people in the reception area. No need to change positions; he could simply turn his head and watch whoever seemed the most interesting.

Over the several hours he'd spent cramped in that space, he'd seen dozens of intriguing dwellers—people with complex, magic-filled histories, he knew—sit in the lobby's molded plastic chairs and wait to speak with Walt Franklin. Their savior.

Once he'd experienced a Connection with the large, red-haired woman who sat at the desk. One minute she was working away, doing some filing. The next moment she simply stiffened, then looked nervously around the room.

"Whatsa matter?" he heard a man's voice ask from the lobby area. Lucas turned quietly and looked through the peephole at the man. White hair. Too much loose skin under his chin.

Back to the redheaded receptionist. "I . . . don't know," she stammered. "I just feel like . . . someone's watching."

The jowly man in the reception area half snorted, half laughed. "Wouldn't doubt it, the kind of stuff old Walt's involved in. Either the mob's watching him, or the CIA. Or both." He offered another snort-laugh.

The receptionist didn't share his humor, obviously, but she

smiled at him. Except, Lucas could tell, this wasn't her usual smile. Her normal smile. Lucas was a student of the smile, and he knew this particular one was forced; it barely turned the corners of her mouth.

She hadn't seen Lucas. But she had sensed something of his presence, and his mind kept returning to that. Returning to all the people, maybe a dozen in all, who had made the Connection and intuited his presence in a closet. Under a floor. Above a ceiling. Hers was all the more special because she hadn't actually seen any evidence of him. She'd only felt it.

I just feel like someone's watching.

As Lucas left his daydream and returned his attention to the dark-haired woman in the elevator below, now staring at her feet, he wanted her to make that Connection too. He liked this woman; he wanted to feel something more than the typical subject and observer relationship. He wanted the Connection.

Instead, she lifted her face toward the doors, caught in midyawn, as they chimed and opened on the twenty-third floor. She slipped through and into the offices beyond.

So much for Connection.

Still, he would wait. It was early morning, and he'd have another half hour of steady traffic. If no other interesting dwellers stepped on the elevator before then, he'd choose the dark-haired woman. She was, after all, the only one who had inspired a secret history in his head all morning. That had to count for something.

Maybe, just maybe, this dark-haired woman with the full lips and the eyes like bright marbles and the overwhelming grief at the loss of her husband would pull him back to the twenty-third floor. Maybe she would make the Connection after all.

He could wait.

For more, read *The Unseen*

About the Author

T.L. Hines writes "Noir Bizarre" stories, mixing mysteries with odditities in books such as *Faces in the Fire*, *The Unseen*, *Waking Lazarus*, and *The Dead Whisper On*. *Waking Lazarus* received Library Journal's "25 Best Genre Fiction Books of the Year" award.

Visit TLHines.com for contest details, media downloads, and all of the latest "Noir Bizarre" news.